POINT OF
NO RETURN

by

Ethan Ross

Shield   Crest

© Copyright 2018 Ethan Ross

All rights reserved

ISBN: 978-1-912505-09-8

MMXVIII

A CIP catalogue record for this book is available from the British Library

Published by
ShieldCrest Publishing Ltd.,
Aylesbury, Buckinghamshire,
HP22 5RR England
Tel: +44 (0) 333 8000 890
www.shieldcrest.co.uk

This book is dedicated to my son

Simon

without whose inspiration, love and
unequivocal enthusiasm this book would not
have been completed.

A true leader has the confidence to stand alone, the courage to make tough decisions, and the compassion to listen to the needs of others. He does not set out to be a leader, but becomes one by the equality of his actions and the integrity of his intent.

US General, Douglas MacArthur

Nairobi

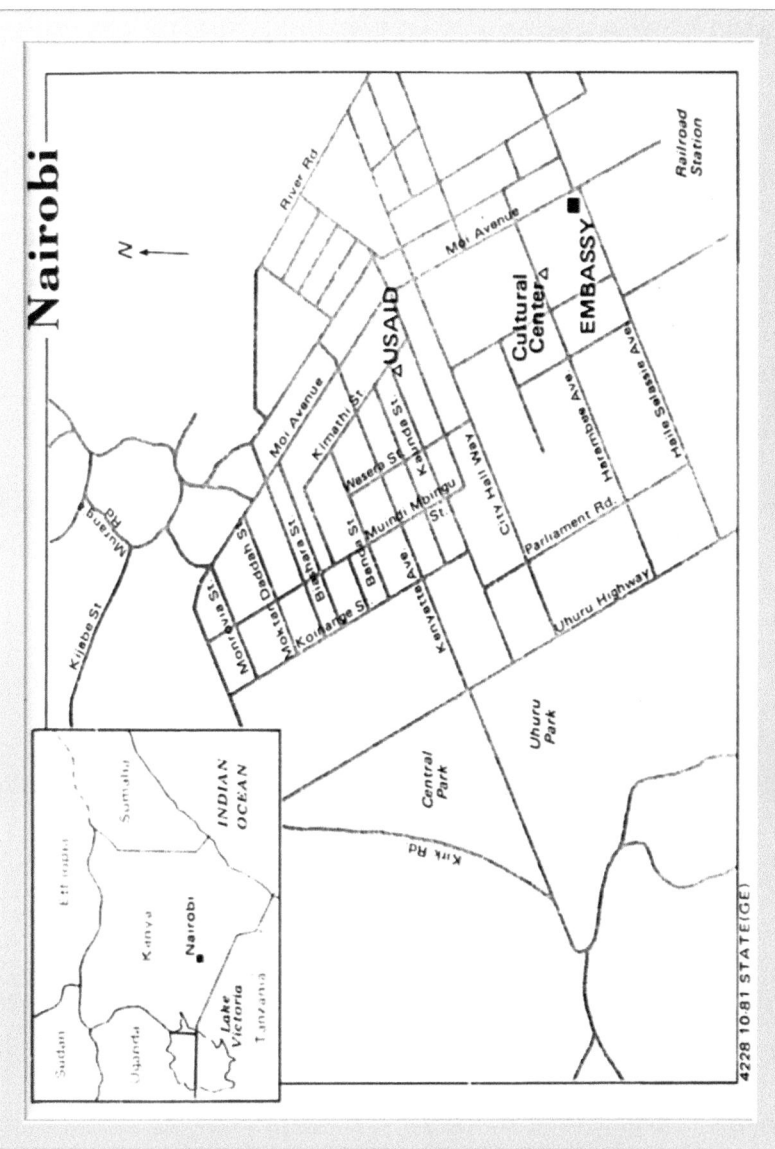

Dar es Salaam

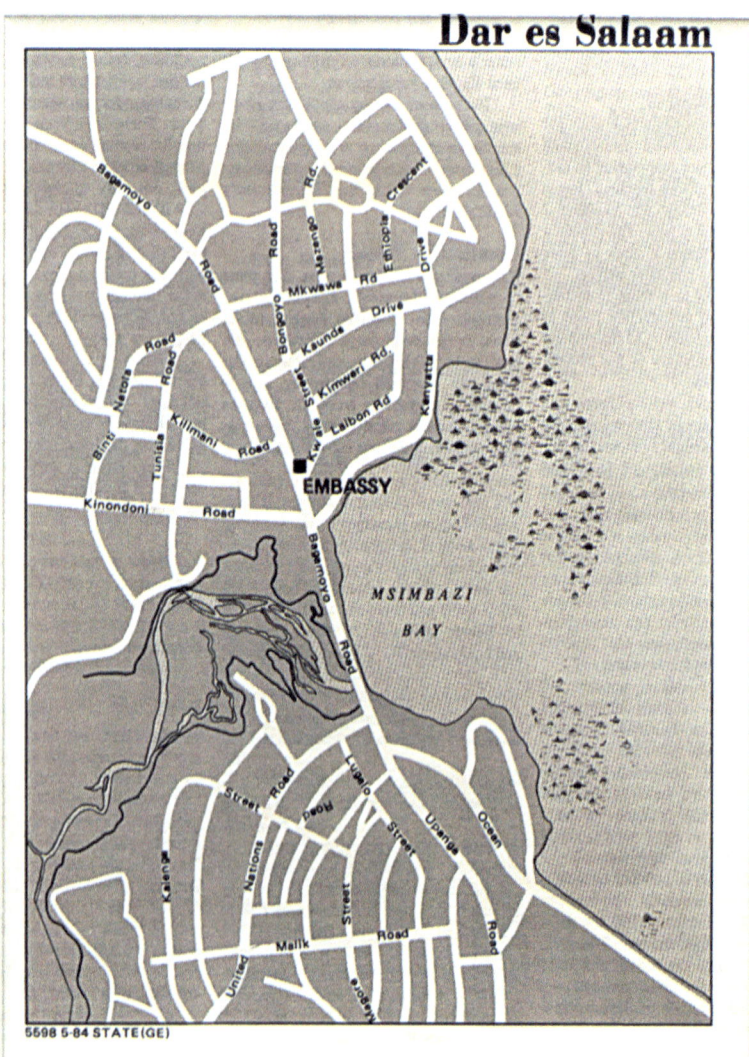

Bagamoyo Road

Road

Rd.

Mkwawa Road

Mazengo Rd

Ethiopia

Crescent

Drive

Bongoyo

Kaunde Drive

Natora Road

Kwale Street

Kilwerl Rd

Laibon Rd

Kenyatta

Bini

Tunisia Road

Kilimani

Road

Kinondoni Road

■ EMBASSY

Bagamoyo Road

MSIMBAZI

BAY

Street

Road

Lugalo

Street

Upanga

Ocean

Nations

Kilenge

Street

Malik

Road

Road

United Street

Mazengo

5598 5-84 STATE(GE)

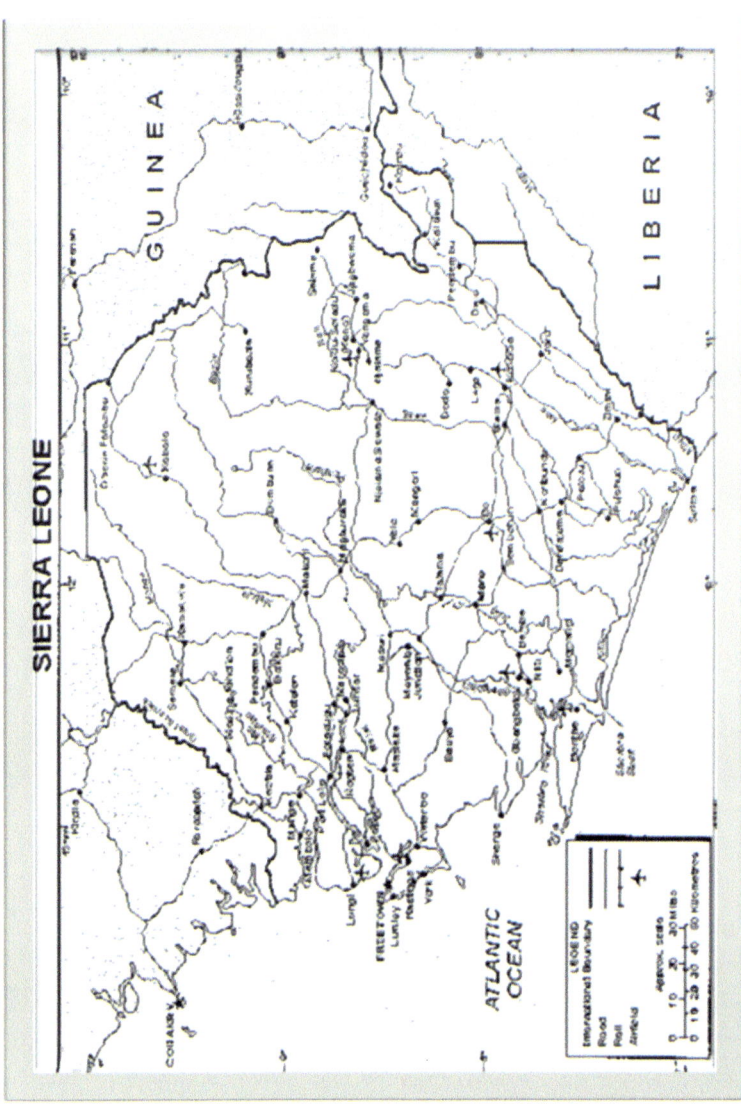

SIERRA LEONE

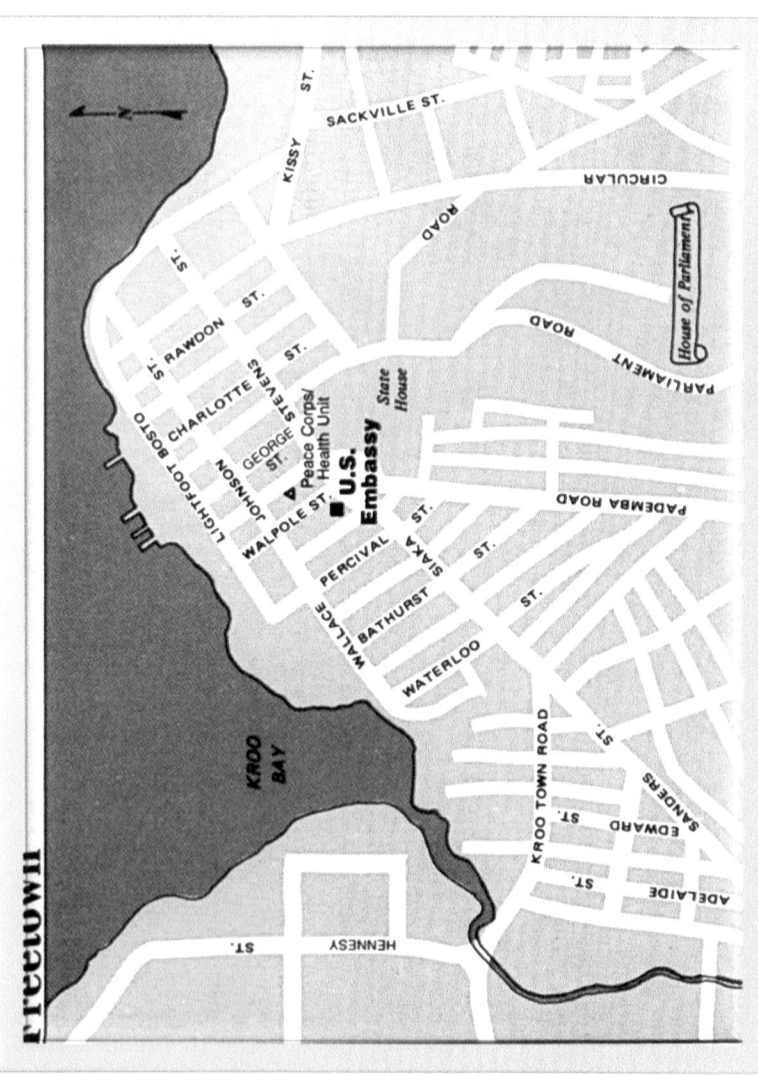

Freetown

Abbreviations

AFB	Air Force Base
AFSOC	Air Force Special Operations Command
AGM	Air to Ground Missile
ALCM	Air Launched Cruise Missile
ANVIS	Aviators Night Vision Imaging System
ASAP	As soon as possible
CAG	Chief Air Group
CET	Central Eastern Time
CIA	Central Intelligence Agency
CINCLANT	Commander in Chief Atlantic Fleet
CNN	Cable News Network
CRRC	Combat Rubber Raiding Craft
DC	District of Columbia
DME	Direct Measuring Equipment
DoD	Department of Defence
DoI	Directorate of Intelligence
DZ	Drop zone
ETA	Estimated time of arrival
FM	Frequency Modulation
FMC	Flight Management Computer
FOV	Field of View
Helo	Helicopter
Herc	Hercules
HF	High Frequency
HK	Heckler & Koch
HLS	Helicopter Landing Site
IMINT	Image Intelligence

INTEL	Intelligence
LAM	Laser Aiming Module
LANTFLT	Atlantic Fleet
MAYDAY	International distress code
MILSAT	Military satellite
NASA	National Aeronautical Space Agency
NSA	National Security Advisor
NTM	Notice to move
NVG	Night Vision Goggles
OHWS	Offensive Handgun Weapons System
Recce/Recon	Reconnaissance
REPLEN	Replenishment of stores/ equipment
RPG	Rocket Propelled Grenade
RUF	Revolutionary United Front
RV	Rendezvous
SATCOM	Satellite Communications
SEAL	Sea, Air and Land
SET	Standard Eastern Time
SLFF	Sierra Leone Freedom Fighters
SLR	Self-loading rifle
SOCOMM	Special Operations Command
TWaID	Tactical Weapons & Intelligence Division
UHF	Ultra High Frequency
VHF	Very High Frequency
XO	Executive Officer

PROLOGUE

Nairobi, Kenya

Six weeks prior to Fri, Aug 7th, 1998

Mohammed Abdul Naseer knew that to travel through the day would be suicide at the worst, but he had a delivery deadline and he intended to keep to it at all costs. He pushed the guides and animals to the limit of exhaustion. To go beyond that limit would only lead to a long trek on foot. Whatever his timetable, and whatever his personal feelings with respect to human life, he needed those around him.

The heat was torrid and it showed no sign of letting up. Touching fifty-two degrees Celsius throughout the day, *'It has to be the worst season on record'*, he thought to himself. He was thirty-five years of age, born and raised in Saudi Arabia, and had studied at the University of Cairo where he majored in Chemistry and graduated with high second class honours. His childhood was spent mostly in the desert following his father as they shepherded goats through and around settlements, scraping together as much money as they could before returning back to their humble Bedouin tent on the outskirts of the large metropolis that was Riyadh. His father had taught him everything that he knew and, to Mohammed, the desert had never been a friendly place. It always seemed inhospitable and unforgiving with its dry shimmering heat, and distorted wind-sculptured dunes as far as the eye could see. He learned a lot during his childhood years and certainly knew that those who admired this natural landscape saw it as an idyllic picture of beauty, serenity and tranquillity, but hidden beneath its calm exterior, this vast inimical landscape held no mercy for those who ventured unprepared into its iron grip. Mohammed was confident, but he also knew his limits.

He looked up at the sky, which was the most amazing azure colour that he had seen in a long time. It was clear, not a blemish or cloud to be seen for miles, even hundreds of miles. Vapour trails from jet liners created roads in the sky as they crossed over, adding an artistic touch to an otherwise bland canvas. Guided by Sudanese Bedouins, he knew their journey would cover nearly four thousand kilometres crossing through Egypt, Sudan, and finally into Kenya. As they headed south from Cairo, the sun, having risen from the east, was directly overhead making the temperature blisteringly hot, and progress painfully slow. He squinted against the sun's powerful rays, which reflected off the sand and exacerbated the brightness, almost to the point of blindness.

The train of twelve bull dromedaries, known in Arabic as 'Jamals' was ideal, but the heavy wooden boxes carried by four of them were bulky and awkward, and seemed to hinder more than anything else. The heat and the excessive weight caused the loss of three of the Jamals, which were left behind as rich pickings for the vultures that circled overhead, waiting for just such a meal. The exchange of a few hundred US dollars with the Customs Officials at the border controls of Wadi Halfi and Lockichogio on the Kenyan border made the crossings that much easier. Not an eyelid was batted, nor a conversation engaged in as the strangers meandered through unchallenged. Dressed in his traditional brown 'Gandoura' robe and a 'Kofya' headscarf, Mohammed sat astride the second camel. His face was hidden by the scarf, which showed only the menacing look in his eyes. A black 'Egal' rope formed a circle on top of his head, holding the 'Kofya' in place. He barked his instructions to the lead guide, gesticulating where necessary to augment the urgency in his voice. In response, the guides shouted, *'Asriaa, Asriaa!'* Go, Go! and then struck the camels with improvised whips as if they were champion jockeys on the homeward stretch. The camels looked clumsy as their great bulks trotted for a short distance, walked a little, then trotted again.

Some four weeks later, exhausted and relieved, they arrived on the outskirts of Nairobi.

*   *   *

Private Airfield at Jizan, Yemen – Two weeks earlier, 0900 hrs

A white unmarked Beech King Air 350 aircraft taxied to the departing runway. Its flight plan was filed as a Humanitarian flight, with essential medical supplies for the warring factions in the south. Six wooden crates with the markings 'Handle With Care' emblazoned on the two longest sides had arrived the previous evening aboard a freighter from Canada, been warehoused on the dock overnight and guarded by Sudanese Government Intelligence Officers. All six boxes were now in the hold of the '350.

Two and a half hours later it was on the tarmac at Embu in Kenya, some sixty miles north of Nairobi.

*   *   *

It had taken nearly three hours to meet the aircraft at Embu, transfer the cargo to a white Toyota pick-up, and return to the house in Nairobi. The two-storey house on the outskirts of the city looked incomplete with iron rods still protruding from the support columns, the dank grey cement rendering covered the outer walls, and plastic sheeting filling the gaps in place of windows. In addition to Mohammed, the house was occupied by an Iraqi, a Moroccan, and another Arab from Mohammed's homeland. In the weeks that followed, Mohammed regularly made the ten to twelve hour bus ride to Dar-es-Salaam in Tanzania, buying his ticket at the Arusha Xpress office on Accru Road at a cost of eighteen US dollars.

He carried with him a large plain black canvas grip bag, which was taut and looked heavy on the way out, but returning with the same bag, its appearance was sallow and somewhat deflated.

In his absence, the remaining Arabs prepared the contents of the boxes that had been delivered, and had hired a further two vehicles: a Mercedes and a second Toyota pick-up. They travelled the streets at various times of the day, and shopped the least amount of times as possible, buying only goods that were necessary. As the days went by their confidence was high and they knew everything was ready.

*　　*　　*

Friday, Aug 7th 1998 – 1030am Local (0330 EST)

Their patience had paid off and the morning they had been waiting for had arrived. They loaded one of the pick-up trucks with half of the contents collected from Embu. Mohammed had moved the remainder during his frequent trips to Tanzania. It was time to exchange their attire for Levi jeans and tee shirts, and then one last read of the Koran before setting off. There would be no more communication between any of them. Mohammed, driving the Mercedes, travelled behind the Moroccan and the Saudi Arabian in one of the Toyotas, with the Iraqi in the hired second Toyota leading the way.

It was market day, as it was most days, and the streets were coming to life as people sought the early morning bargains. They drove cautiously through the town with good spacing so as not to provoke any suspicion. Turning onto the dual carriageway of Haile Selassie Avenue, the two Toyotas stopped alongside the Co-operative House, a short distance down from a four-storey building identifiable by its flag flying proudly at the top of the pole and rippled by a light zephyr.

Mohammed continued past them, through the traffic lights, and turned right at the roundabout onto Moi Avenue. He stopped his vehicle after a short distance, stepped out of the car, turned and stood beside it. He looked in the direction of the two Toyotas, casually glancing at his watch as he did so. Satisfied that everything was in place, he smiled, climbed back into his car and drove away.

"This is only the beginning," he murmured to himself, as he took one final glance through his rear view mirror, before joining and disappearing into the morning traffic.

CHAPTER ONE

Oval Office at the White House, Washington DC

Friday, August 7ᵗʰ 1998

"*A pair of powerful explosions, said to have been car bombs, targeted US embassies, rocking the capitals of Kenya and Tanzania within ten minutes of each other, early this morning. At least eight Americans are among the sixty-five bodies so far recovered from the embassy here in Nairobi. We have also received reports that two of the terrorists were killed in a gun battle with the embassy Marines. It has been reported initially that no Americans were killed in neighbouring Tanzania, where five others are known to have died, but the embassy building in Dar-es-Salaam was badly damaged. These attacks conjure up images of Beirut in 1983, when a bombing at the US embassy killed sixty-three people. A subsequent attack on the US Marine Barracks that same year killed two hundred and forty one people. Embassy security has been hotly debated in Washington in recent years, yet nothing tangible seems to have been put in place. As further news develops, updates will be given throughout the night. This is Elisabeth Young for CNN, Nairobi.*"

"Jesus H Christ!" blasphemed a stunned President, as he stared at the large TV screen in his office displaying the CNN logo. He turned to his

Chief of Staff, James Walker. "Get all the facts you know on this James and have the Communications Chief prepare a speech for the press in one hour."

Press Briefing Room at the White House – One Hour Later

The President began. "These attacks against US embassies in Kenya and Tanzania are Abhorrent and Inhuman, and all efforts will be made to catch the perpetrators. The explosions have all the hallmarks of terrorist attacks, but as yet no one has come forward and claimed responsibility. The FBI and a team of US Marines are flying to the region to bolster the security, and to begin the investigation. All flags at all US government buildings will be flown at half-mast as a mark of respect to the victims. My deepest sympathy of course goes to those who have lost loved ones in these appalling attacks. With two hundred and eighty-eight US diplomatic facilities around the world, it is extremely difficult to sanitise each and every one of them, and with the best will and intelligence in the world, we do our utmost to ensure that our facilities and the people who work for the United States are able to go about their daily lives without fear or in trepidation, but security can never be one hundred per cent guaranteed."

Six months later

Egypt Air Boeing 757 flight number EA985 from Cairo to New York's JFK International Airport touched down thirty-five minutes late. For one Arab passenger, Mohammed Abdul Naseer, the delay was thirty-five minutes too long. He hated flying. He didn't like the idea of crossing the ocean on a twin-engine airliner. Four was the right number, he thought, since losing one meant losing twenty five per cent of the aircrafts available power, whereas on this flight, it meant losing half.

Having left the aircraft, he walked along the telescopic arm that connected the aircraft to the terminal building, and into the concourse, following other passengers and the signs for Customs and baggage reclamation. He'd never been to the US before and was starting to feel a little intimidated by the size of the airport. This was The Big Apple, after all.

Most of the flight seemed to have been American passengers. He followed the signs for 'Non US Citizens' and handed over his passport to the waiting immigration official who sat behind a desk, protected by a glass screen.

"Have you been to the States before, Mister Naseer?" enquired the official, as he flicked through the pages, then looked at the Arabs eyes for a response.

"First time," he replied without flinching.

"What's the nature of your visit?"

"Business."

"What kind of business?"

"Telecommunications."

"Are you travelling alone?"

"Yes."

"Where are you staying during your visit?"

"I'll be travelling most of the time from state to state."

As the official continued to ask questions, Mohammed knew that his details were being put into the computer under the desktop. He knew that he was also being photographed.

"Okay, Sir, enjoy your stay in the US. Have a nice day," concluded the official, as he stamped the passport and handed it back to Mohammed.

He could sense the official look towards him as he walked towards baggage reclamation. He had to be normal, so as not to arouse any suspicion. He checked his flight number against the screen that showed him which carousel would have his luggage. As the carousel began to move, he soon found his luggage: three large suitcases, and a black canvas holdall. Placing them on a trolley, he cleared Customs, and headed towards the exit where an abundance of black and yellow cabs were lined up as if they'd just been delivered from the car plant.

"I need to get to Arlington in Virginia," Mohammed said as he approached the vehicle. The driver nodded, jumped out of the vehicle and began to load the cases into the trunk, whilst his passenger climbed into the back.

"Is this your first visit to the States?" enquired the cabbie as he climbed back behind the wheel a few moments later.

"Yep."

"Welcome to New York! Where in Arlington d'you wanna go, buddy?" enquired the cabby.

Mohammed pulled out a single sheet of paper from the inside pocket of his jacket. "One three two five Wilson Boulevard. It's the Hyatt Hotel."

"No problem," the driver confirmed, tripping the meter.

The taxi sped away, and he sat back and enjoyed the scenery as it slipped by. One tall building after the next seemed to disappear into the blue sky, and one crowded street after the next effortlessly joined another no matter which way you turned. He was in no rush. He knew what he had to do and it could take days or even months, but he didn't care.

CHAPTER TWO

Somewhere in Southern United States

March 1999

The MC130H Hercules gunship made its final approach first, closely followed by a C5 Galaxy. The pilot busied himself with his routine, as he extended the flaps and lowered the landing gear.

"Three greens," the co-pilot announced.

"Three minutes to landing, Colonel," the pilot advised over the intercom to his passenger on the flight deck, Colonel Jack Copeland, US Army. The pilot turned to Copeland: "Sir, I'm gonna have to make a tactical landing on this one," he warned with a wry smile.

Copeland knew what that meant. In short, he would bang the Herc down with such force that it would bounce back up again and fly on a bit before settling down a second time, so the aircraft could land in a shorter distance than normal, but it also meant no runway markers or glide scope lights to follow.

Colonel Jack Copeland had been with the Tactical Weapons and Intelligence Division of SOCOMM at Fort Bragg for six years. He was forty-five years of age and divorced from his long-suffering wife, who just couldn't understand the nature of his job. At twenty-six he had joined the British Special Forces of 22 SAS at Hereford and one operation after the next earned him promotion to Captain. By the age of thirty-eight he had been head-hunted by TWaID, resigned his Commission in the British Army, and took up the offered post almost a year later. He was happy with his new life.

Back in the cargo hold, the Air loadmaster had already warned his passengers that a rough and heavy landing was minutes away. Copeland visualised his men grabbing the cargo nets to stop them from flying through the air as the Herc hit the deck.

Moments later, the aircraft banked at four thousand feet on a twenty degree angle with two miles to go to touchdown. The aircraft was reconfigured and the change in engine noise was felt throughout the airframe as the pilot eased back on the throttle, reducing the power to the four Allison T56-A-15 Turbo Props.

As if choreographed, both pilots lowered the night vision goggles that were clipped to their helmets transforming night into day. Designed by NASA at their research facility in California, they were far superior to the standard military NVG, which gave a horizontal field of view of one hundred degrees, as opposed to the standard forty degrees. Image intensity too, was sharper as it boosted the ambient light thousands of times over the earlier models.

Without warning, the pilot pushed forward on the yoke causing the aircraft to pitch down in a nosedive at a descent rate of two thousand five hundred feet per minute. It took Copeland by surprise. He hadn't registered any audible tones that often precede a problem, but his heart missed a beat, and he gripped his seat edge tightly until his knuckles turned white. He disliked not being able to see where he was going and would've preferred control over his vehicle!

To his relief the pilot levelled off, but then dropped the aircraft like a stone hitting the runway with a hefty bang before bouncing back into the air, and then down onto the tarmac. He was glad commercial pilots didn't adopt the same landing method.

Once on the ground, the Air loadmaster moved to the back of the aircraft, pushing the button that split the tailgate in two. He stood on the ramp and plugged his headphones into the intercom, speaking with the pilot as the plane began to reverse.

As it moved backwards, the warm evening air rushed into the cargo area, as did the distinctive roar of the reverse thrusters on the C5 Galaxy. Once the Herc came to a standstill on the apron, Copeland removed his headset.

"That was one hell of a ride, boys. You sure know how to fire me up," he said before continuing, "I'll never get used to it but I'll never give it up either. See you on the return trip."

"Our pleasure, Colonel. Have a good op."

Copeland left the flight deck and climbed down the short ladder into the cargo area. He stepped between the scattered bodies and equipment to reach the tail ramp.

"Okay, heads up people. Once the C5 has closed down it'll take about an hour to get the birds up and running. Major Bell will run through some of the finer points of the op before we move out."

He looked at every man in turn. All were dressed in black complete with balaclavas and looked like ninja warriors. The only things showing were the whites of their eyes. He knew they were ready. Confidence was high and adrenalin was starting to surge. Copeland had trained with each and every one of them, commanded covert and infiltration missions with them, and was proud that he had brought every man back alive. Copeland hadn't found it difficult to make the transition from the Army to this unit, and quickly earned the confidence and respect of his fellow officers and men alike. He would not settle for second best. Failure was not an option.

He stepped off the tailgate and onto the tarmac. He glanced across to his right to see the huge shape of the C5 silhouetted by a full moon. The internal lights lit the inside of this beast of an aircraft. He activated his stopwatch. Timing was critical and he always liked to beat the manual times set by cautious managers and engineers.

As the cargo of four collapsed MH-60 Blackhawk helicopters rolled out one by one, he looked at them as he would a beautiful woman. He admired their silhouette: the contours, the curves, the smooth profile, and the strength and practicality of the weapons platform. What an exceptional work horse they were.

A few years earlier he'd been responsible for some major upgrades, having convinced the Pentagon that the change was necessary in order to keep his unit at the cutting edge. He needed air-to-air refuelling, and an improved navigation system that had a multi-mode radar to improve pinpoint navigation in all environments. Comms were crucial and he got the lot: FM, UHF, VHF, HF, Saber, and satellite comms all secure capable. He needed a combat helicopter that could stand up to most things so he opted for the M134 7.62mm mini-gun in a six-barrel link-fed Gatling gun with a range of one thousand metres. He also requested an M261 19 tube rocket launcher firing 2.75-inch special purpose warheads, as well as an M230 30mm chain gun rapid-fire cannon with an effective range of 1500 metres. For Missiles, he got the AGM-114 laser guided ones using M272 launchers with an effective range from five to eight kilometres. No one was more surprised than Copeland when he got back his requisition order with the authoritative word 'APPROVED' stamped across the middle.

The Blackhawks were assigned to the 160th Special Operations Aviation Regiment (Airborne) under the control of SOCOMM –Special Operations Command. Their focus on night operations had earned them the nickname Night Stalkers.

The unloading of the C5 was gathering pace and Copeland sensed that they might be on the way to breaking another record. He could hear behind him the distinctive tones of Major Bell going through the last minute brief, filling in the gaps left by the one they'd already had prior to leaving Fort Bragg.

Major Mark 'Dinger' Bell was forty-three and had been a soldier since he was eighteen. He, like Copeland, had been married, but although divorced, he had no regrets. He joined TWaID a year before his Commander and saw the Army as his life. Jack Copeland was the only family he had.

As Copeland turned, he saw the eight-man SEAL unit checking their equipment: comms, weapons, and other survival gear, including the Rubber Raiding Boat. At fifteen feet long and weighing in at two hundred and sixty five pounds, it was ideal for just this kind of infiltration op.

Copeland approached the senior ground crew mechanic, John Grovehurst. "How much longer, John?"

"Three minutes, boss, tops. Only a couple more bolts to attach then they're all yours."

He looked at his stopwatch. It read fifty-four minutes and thirty two seconds.

"This could indeed be a new record tonight."

He walked back to the Herc, and then turned towards the C5 in time for the mechanic to give him the thumbs up. The Blackhawks were complete. It had taken fifty-seven minutes and forty four seconds. That *was* a new record.

Smiling, he headed for the SEAL unit. "Ian, are you all set?" asked Copeland, as he spoke with the unit commander, Sgt Ian Pritchard.

"Yes Sir, just put the last coordinates on the map."

"Okay, get your kit and men loaded on board Helo three, and take off ASAP. Radio through to me when the situation is secure."

Copeland watched as Pritchard loaded the Combat Rubber Raiding Craft on to the helicopter, followed by his team. The pilot began the start-up procedure, and once the blades were in full rotation, Helo three took off and headed towards their objective. With the navigational co-ordinates already loaded in to the Flight Management Computer, they wouldn't be seen again until extraction. All that the rest could do now was wait until Pritchard relayed the message, "*Perimeter Secure – GO GO GO.*"

CHAPTER THREE

Helo three was inbound at sixty feet above the ground and at a speed of eighty knots. ETA at the Drop Zone (DZ) was fifteen minutes. The pilot had put on his NVG prior to departure, and decided to hedge hop to eliminate as much noise as possible. They also liked to show off their flying skills.

The water below was glistening from the light reflected by the moon. The navigator, having checked the FMC display for distance to target, turned to Pritchard and displayed three fingers. That meant 3 minutes to the DZ. He turned to his team and did the same.

As they got to within one hundred feet of the DZ, the pilot pulled back slightly on the control column to slow the forward momentum, banking slightly as he did to turn into the wind. The increase in rotor noise was evident as they chopped through the air with a deep thud thud thud. Pritchard slid the cargo door to one side, as the pilot adjusted his trim and lowered the aircraft towards the water, hovering three feet above the now rippling watercourse as the rotors' down draught disturbed the surface. Thumbs up from the pilot was all he needed. The CRRC was pushed out into the night air, hitting the water with a splash, and then Pritchard was the first to spill from the aircraft followed by the rest of his team.

Stealthily, they entered the water with no more than a ripple.

Once the helicopter had moved from the DZ and headed back to the airbase, Pritchard waited a short while until everything was again still and quiet so that he could check whether his team had been compromised.

Satisfied that they had not, he was the first to climb in to the craft, the others followed one by one. Once in the boat he pulled out a map and compass from the map pocket inside his rubber suit, and checked his bearings and compass heading. He knew exactly where he was and the heading he should take he just wanted confirmation. He checked that the landfall, where they would cache the boat and wet suits, was two thousand yards from their present position. Using hand signals, he put up two reversed fingers, and then made a symbol of a zero three times, signifying two thousand. He also pointed the direction in which they would be going.

Pritchard powered up the 35 horse engine, which kicked in first time, and directed the craft along the river's edge in the required direction. The sound of a boat wasn't that unusual, as there were always hunters out looking for their nocturnal prey.

Five hundred metres from the cache point, he cut the outboard engine and they used small paddles for the rest of the journey. The ebbtide flowed quickly, almost causing Pritchard to overshoot the drop off point. The two paddles were thrust into the water to break the boats speed, followed by small movements to navigate towards the ramp.

They quickly but quietly stepped from the craft, pulled it onshore and stripped off their rubber suits to reveal their black all-in-one cotton fatigues. The rubber suits were placed in the boat for the return journey. Individuals who had the necessary expertise picked up communications, including SATCOM, weapons and medical supplies. Their NVG was already switched on.

Pritchard knew that it was another thousand metres to the camp in a north-westerly direction, through thick woodland. They would stay close together until they reached the perimeter fence. Satisfied that all the equipment was removed from the boat and that his team were all accounted for, Pritchard signalled his instructions to move out. He took point position and the rest followed. They covered the ground swiftly. The banks of the river were eight or nine feet high and the foliage had clearly not been cut back for years, allowing them to stay concealed from any watching eyes. Despite the absence of any vehicle, Pritchard was not convinced that the camp was unoccupied, and a careful study of the large-scale map had convinced him that this was the safest approach.

The camp, they soon discovered, was surrounded by an improvised chain fence topped with razor wire. It wasn't new, as long streaks of rust discoloured the galvanised metal, but its mere presence was effective enough to act as a useful deterrent to the idly curious. The grass was long on the outside of the camp, another way of keeping an eye on intruders. The fence continued unbroken as far as they could see, and Pritchard realized this was the fence which had shown up in the aerial photographs. It surrounded the camp. It would not be proof against a determined assault, but over the years it would have deterred curious eyes.

Using the clarity of his NVG, Pritchard was able to see that the fence was not electrified and that, as per the briefing, there were indeed four Nissen type huts within the camp. He was also able to confirm that there were two observation towers; one at the front left and one at the rear right of the fence. The satellite imagery enhancement from the military satellite (MILSAT), was exact. The area was in darkness except for light emanating from the third Nissen hut. Each tower was occupied by a single individual dressed in some kind of camouflage uniform and armed with a rifle similar to the Belgian FN or the British Army 7.62 SLR.

The main entrance gate was closed and no one seemed to be nearby. *'The gate sentry is probably in the first hut,'* thought Pritchard, as he tried to create a mental picture of the area. It all seemed rather quiet, too quiet for his liking. There was no movement of any kind.

The track from the gate continued for a hundred yards, then turned to the right away from the river. It would be good to position a two-man intercept team at least a further hundred yards along the track. He also noted that the towers were built inside the fence line. That wasn't a problem but could be time-consuming.

Jazzy music was audible, but he couldn't identify where it was coming from. Pritchard moved back to the tree line, having made his plan. He signed that

Karma four (Comms) would stay with Pritchard. Karma two and five would move on to the track to eliminate any hostile attempt from that direction, as per their briefing. Pritchard indicated by the flip of his finger for the track team to move out and to take up their position. They were to signal by radio once they were in position. The remainder adopted low profile positions, observing and listening.

Five minutes had elapsed when the radio came to life with the whisper of the track team.

"Karma one, this is Karma two in position."

"Karma one, copy that," acknowledged Pritchard

He knew nothing would come along that track now. Pritchard maintained observation of the compound. There was no movement at all, which he found rather strange. He knew from the briefing board that there was a clearing 500 yards north of the track, which would be used for the extraction of the teams and their 'objective'. Karma three and six were tasked to secure the Helicopter Landing Site (HLS), and to signal once secure. Observation of the camp would continue.

A further ten minutes had elapsed when the whisper of the extraction team came through.

"Karma one, this is Karma three, HLS secure."

Pritchard acknowledged. That was another key position taken care of. The guard in the rear tower was the next on Pritchard's agenda. He indicated to the seventh member to go around the back of the rear tower keeping within the tree line. He moved carefully, keeping at least fifty yards from the fence line.

The loud music made it easier for him to move. He adopted the position, supported by a tree, and slowly raised his 5.56mm M4 carbine with sound and flash suppresser. Using the laser-aiming module attached under the barrel, he centred the laser beam on the head of the target. His thumb twitched on to the selector, wondering whether a single or short burst would do the trick. He settled for the single shot, controlled his breathing, and with a short squeeze of the trigger, discharged the round that exploded the head of the guard. The man's legs gave way as his nervous system was paralysed, and he crumpled to the floor in a silent heap.

Pritchard gave the order for Karma eight to dispose of the guard in the front tower. From his position next to Pritchard, he was able to get a clean shot. He raised his .45 HK pistol and using the laser sight discharged a single shot. The guard fell like a rag doll. Karma seven remained at the rear of the camp.

'*Everything has gone too smoothly,*' commented Pritchard to himself. Having come to terms with the fact that there didn't appear to be any threat on the outside of the camp fence, he gave the order to Karma four to set up the SATCOMM link.

"Team Leader, this is Karma one, area secure. GO GO GO."

From leaving the airbase to sending the green light message, it had taken forty minutes to secure the area.

Copeland knew that it wouldn't take Pritchard long to secure the area, so he had ordered the remaining aircraft powered up and ready. The teams were standing alongside each of their respective Helos when Copeland received the message he'd been waiting for through his earpiece and replied:

"Received. Airborne now. Team Leader out."

Copeland walked the short distance back to his helicopter, turned and signalled 'mount up and move out'. With Copeland were Dinger and Sergeant Jose Rodriguez, leader of call-sign Viper. Sergeant Jason Lopez was airborne shortly after with his Cobra team, and Daniel Anderson with Python followed on.

"I love this shit," said Copeland, looking at Dinger as he spoke. "It reminds me of the special ops infiltration we did in Columbia, back end of last year."

"That was one hell of an op, Jack."

As they got closer to the target area, the navigators signalled three minutes to the DZ. The side doors were slid open on both sides, and the teams held the rope ready for the final signal, then came the warning of one minute to go. They were on top of the targets before they knew it, catching the pilots slightly off guard. Jostling with their aircraft, almost standing them on their tail rotors, they quickly brought them under control and into a hover.

Almost at the same time, Cobra and Python teams leapt onto the ropes and descended one by one. Half way down, the first two out of the aircraft threw percussion grenades through the side windows of the huts, and the explosion caused the huts to vibrate, shaking the ground around them and shards of window glass were blown outwards.

Once every man was on the ground, both aircraft moved away from the DZ towards the extraction zone secured by Pritchard earlier. There was still no activity. No running forms or bodies anywhere and no hostile reaction. The forty minutes of almost peace that Pritchard had endured before the assault teams moved in was blissful. All he could do now was watch and cut off any escapees or engage any hostile rebels. The MILSAT imagery, which was shown at the briefing and zoomed to its maximum resolution, showed that Hut Three was holding the objective.

Copeland was still airborne in Helo One watching events unfold before him. His mind drifted back to when he was a Captain in the Special Projects Team of the Sabre Squadron at Hereford. He lost count of the number of times he had endured the practices in the 'Killing House' until it became second nature. It was always drilled in to them that once they had mastered the basics, the drills would become more and more difficult with multiple entries and multiple targets clearing several rooms at a time and then a whole floor. Split second timing was crucial in identifying who was the bad guy and who was the innocent victim caught up in the incident before any target was engaged. The success of the operation was very much dependant on this fundamental rule. The training was as realistic as it could possibly be, using live ammo and grenades, but no matter how much care and attention to detail is paid and trained for there was always the distinct possibility of injury.

Copeland's mind went further back to his early years as Officer Commanding Sabre Squadron. It was a Hostage Retrieval Operation at Stansted Airport in the UK, storming a hijacked aircraft. A ricochet round had hit one of his team, which hadn't been fired by the terrorists, but one of their own. Since then, new types of ammunition were constantly being tested in the 'Killing House'. The latest introduction that Copeland had managed to acquire was the new fragmentation round that exploded on impact with any surface. Copeland had insisted that the new round be used during the training for this Op.

"Jack, you okay?" enquired Dinger as he shook his arm. "I've been trying to get your attention for the last few minutes."

"What, yeah I'm fine," Copeland responded as he came back to reality. He continued "How we doing so far?"

"Right on schedule," replied an enthusiastic Dinger.

Copeland continued to look across the camp ground as Cobra and Viper teams entered their respective Nissen huts: Cobra one and two were able to kick the door of the first hut, then entered with handguns drawn covering each corner between them left and right, whilst three and four gave support from the rear. As the door burst open, they saw that the percussion grenade had done its job. Three targets were flat on the floor. They were hostiles so Cobra one and two despatched them with double taps. The radios came to life:

"Team Leader Cobra one, three targets down. Objective one secure," declared Pete Petrowski.

"Team Leader, Python one, two targets down. Objective four secure," confirmed Dave Millerchip.

"Team Leader, Cobra five, six targets down. Objective two secure," said Cobra one's second in command (2IC).

"Team Leader, Python five, two targets down and one civilian in custody," reported Dave Millerchip's 2IC.

Copeland and 'Dinger' Bell had watched the events from the sky. They were pleased with the end result, but some modifications would have to be made for the next exercise.

"Team Leader to all call signs. Good job, guys. Move out to the pre-arranged HLS, and I'll see you back at the airbase," instructed Copeland. "Karma one, this is Team Leader, over," continued Copeland.

"Go ahead, Team Leader."

"Move the CRRC along the river to the area next to the HLS. Helo three will be there to meet you. I'll see you back at base."

The order given the pilot swung the yoke and headed for the base.

Helo one had landed and shut down before the remainder of the Task Force Helos arrived. Copeland looked at his watch. It was two thirty in the morning. He'd been on the go since four am the previous day. The warm air was now starting to make him tired. He could hear the thunder of the remaining birds approaching. As Helo two was about to land, Copeland's pilot caught his attention and pointed to the headphones. Copeland moved across to the helicopter.

"What's the problem?"

"There's a call from SOCOMM for you, boss," said the pilot. "It's on the SATCOM link." he added.

Copeland donned the headphones.

"Copeland here," he said.

"Jack, this is Chuck Martin," said the voice at the other end. Chuck Martin was a two star general at SOCOMM, and Copeland's immediate boss.

"What keeps you up this time of morning? And you're missing all the action. Now can you see why I don't want your job?" replied Copeland with a smile.

"Jack, I've just had the President on the line. He wants you to head over to DC tonight, and meet him and the hot shots at the DoD this afternoon."

Copeland was trying to get his head round what could be so important that the President *and* the Chiefs of Staff wanted to see him, especially at such short notice. All sorts of reasons were going through his head, but none made any sense. He'd heard on the grapevine that the DoD was being hit with budget cuts for this financial year that could mean downsizing. His own department would be under threat. Why would that involve the President, though? He would get others to pass on the bad news, surely?

"What's the noise all about, Chuck?" asked Copeland, hoping for an honest reply.

"No idea. However, you can bet your bottom dollar it won't be any picnic."

"What time's the meeting set for?" asked Copeland.

"Sixteen hundred. That should be enough time for you to get there. Talking of which, get your pilot to take you over to the Navy base and then hitch a ride in one of their Tomcats over to Andrews Air

Base. Let me know what time you expect to arrive and I'll have a car there to meet you."

Copeland glanced at his wristwatch to ascertain the time available to him and then continued; "Thanks, Chuck. You do know I haven't the uniform for the occasion? It's all back at Fort Bragg."

"It's not a fancy dress party, go dressed as you are. Take off the war paint, though, or they'll think it's an invasion! Brief me as soon as you can. Good luck, Jack."

Copeland removed his headset and walked across to Dinger.

"Go through the debrief with the guys, will you? I've been summoned to DC. I'll see you when I get back to Fort Bragg. When, I don't know."

Copeland handed his sidearm and radio microphone to Dinger. He then stepped back and saluted him to dismiss himself, and headed towards Helo one which was already starting up. Copeland climbed in to the aircraft, strapped himself in and within seconds was airborne. Dinger watched as Copeland disappeared from sight, heading in a north-easterly direction.

Hyatt Hotel, Arlington, VA – three months after arriving in the USA

Mohammed showered, dressed and breakfasted in his room, his routine every morning. He picked up the local directory from the lower half of his bedside cabinet beneath the hotel information pack. He opened it and almost straight away found what he was looking for. *'More luck than judgement,'* he thought, though it was probably the most used page in the entire book. He wrote down the information that he wanted on the pad next to the phone, tore the page off and tucked it in his trouser pocket. He moved across the room to the wardrobe, opened the folding doors, and pulled down the black holdall from the top shelf where it had remained since his arrival. He dropped the bag on the bed, opened its zipper, and then pulled the bag apart to reveal its contents. He had to get out of the hotel and he had to start to familiarize himself with what was around him.

Sitting on the edge of the bed he took out a Nikon SLR camera and a two hundred millimetre bayoneted zoom lens that he attached to the main body, and then loaded the thirty-five-millimetre colour film that he took from the side pouch of the holdall. Having attached the plain black carrying strap to the camera, he placed it back on the bed. Fishing in the bag again he pulled out a black cloth that had a knot tied at the top and placed it on his knees. He quickly assembled the parts that the cloth contained and finally tested the working mechanisms. Satisfied that he was now looking at a working model of a Sig Sauer P320, he placed the weapon behind his belt in the small of his back. It felt awkward and cold at first, but a few adjustments soon sorted that out. The cloth he put back in the bag and returned it to the top shelf. Then he grabbed the long black leather coat that was hanging beneath the shelf, picked up the camera from the bed, and left the room.

As he was leaving the hotel, a cab pulled up kerbside and dropped off his fare. Mohammed waited by the hotel door until they had almost finished paying.

It was a crisp morning but nevertheless he felt a droplet of sweat trickle down his spine as he moved forward and climbed into the waiting cab, startling the driver. Before the cabbie could say anything, Mohammed leant forward and spoke.

CHAPTER FOUR

The Pentagon always produced a feeling of awe in Copeland. Not because of its size or geometric shape, just the amount of chiefs and not enough Indians who worked there. There was a chief for a chief who looked after a chief. Everybody seemed so far up the next guys arse it sometimes was difficult to recognise who was who. He understood its function and how important and critical it was to the defence of the United States. He also knew his career could end here in a heartbeat. If somebody didn't like his method of operation, at the flick of a pen, he would be history. Assigned to the list of unemployed. His pension frozen and he'll be claiming social security. Nobody would offer him a job. He would be outcast, ostracised, and hounded by government puppets. That was the worst case scenario. He wasn't here to lose his job; well at least he didn't think so. On the other hand he didn't really know why he was here. He could only speculate. Where to begin? There were so many variables.

'*Pull yourself together, Copeland,*' he said to himself.

Colonel Jack Copeland, United States Army assigned to SOCOMM, knew that he was the best. Nobody was better than he was. It wasn't an arrogant self-appraisal, but one that came with confidence and experience. He walked up the countless steps at the front of the building on the south side, dressed in his special operations black cotton fatigues. He'd managed to remove the camouflage cream at the Naval Air Base prior to his 'fly by the seat of your pants' ride in an F-14 Tomcat. Although he was a member of the US Military, Copeland still had to go through the security desk. He didn't work there, so technically he was a visitor and as such would be issued with a visitors pass. The only difference was that he didn't need escorting. Copeland had to sign in, and he gave the name of the person to be visited as 'The President of the US'. Copeland collected his pass, clipped it to his left breast pocket and proceeded along the walkways towards the designated venue. Having negotiated seemingly countless corridors and rings, he finally arrived at the Command Briefing Room. The outer door was closed so courtesy prevailed and Copeland took a deep breath and knocked twice with his right hand. He heard a mumble from within so he twisted the door handle, pushed the door forward and entered the room, closing the door firmly behind him.

"Come in, Colonel. Take a seat." It was the President of the United States, George Kennedy, who spoke first.

Copeland observed the amount of brass and number of suits that sat around the large rectangular table.

'Court Martial? No, no JAG that I can see. Promotion? No, they are held at Fort Bragg…' Copeland was now intrigued. He moved towards the table in the direction of the only vacant seat.

"Good morning, Mr President, Gentlemen." said Copeland.

He noted that the President sat at the head of the table, and that Copeland's seat was between the US Air Force Chief of Staff and the US Naval Chief of Operations. Next to the President was the Secretary of Defence. Further round the table, Copeland noted the CIA Chief, the FBI Chief, and the National Security Advisor to the President.

'Chuck was right; this wasn't going to be a picnic. It has all the hallmarks of being a crisis meeting, though.'

This was a meeting that he would have to pay close attention to, even though he was exhausted. The President took a sip of water from the glass in front of him on the desk, and looked towards his captive audience.

"Okay, gentlemen, let's begin. You all know Colonel Jack Copeland. A member of TWaID and assigned to SOCOMM. His background speaks for itself," stated the President.

"Colonel Copeland, I really am most grateful to you for sparing so much of your valuable time to attend this meeting." Copeland wasn't sure whether he was being sarcastic or genuine, however he listened as the President continued,

"I know that you have other pressing tasks as indeed do I, but this is a situation requiring immediate action." The President paused for breath and sent a warm smile towards Copeland but again, he couldn't be sure whether it was sincere or not. He didn't really care, but there was one thing he did know, and that was he had no choice other than to attend the meeting. It was a god damned Presidential order, for Christ's sake!

The President introduced the attendees before starting his brief.

"In the light of the atrocities that took place in Africa in 1998," he continued, "Killing scores of Americans, I vowed then, as Vice-President, to bring to justice those involved. In my inaugural presidential address at the end of last year, I reiterated my intentions." The President took a deep breath before continuing:

"Up until now, SOCOMM have provided us with reactive, specially trained troops. That will continue. However, what I have proposed – and the Joint Chiefs have accepted – is that another force is required in order to augment the successful special operations that we already conduct. Those bombings, I am sure, will not be the last against US targets, intended to weaken our influence and global power. I still feel there is a major threat against our diplomatic infrastructure in the African continent and Middle-Eastern region, and most of our intelligence resources will be focussed on those areas. We cannot safeguard every single embassy: the cost would be phenomenal and unacceptable to the people of our country. The funding of this additional asset will be over and above the fiscal provisions for SOCOMM. This has already been agreed by both the Senate and the House."

Listening with interest, Copeland still had no idea where this was going or why he was at this meeting.

The President continued,

"The new arm will move in to the already established Headquarters in DC, having direct contact with all the available agencies who presently provide intel to SOCOMM. This will be a powerful organisation, answerable only to me. A scrambled line connected to my office will be supplied."

The President paused to take another drink of water before continuing:

"You'll all now be asking yourselves," as the President scanned each face in the room, "What is the purpose of this new arm? It will use the existing resources of SOCOMM with access to every conceivable item of modern equipment and technology from planes to laptops. They should want for nothing. The price of failure is high. A degradation of our foreign relations would ruin global economy, and weaken the power and strength of the US dollar, something that cannot be permitted to happen. The new arm will have the authority to carry out covert surveillance, counter espionage, infiltration and if need be, the elimination of any threat against the US or its foreign infrastructure by covert or overt means. It will also be used for major rescue operations."

Copeland listened intently to this last bit. These were the ingredients to start a goddamned war. He'd make a note of that and ask a question at the end. The President cleared his throat and continued:

"Like anything else, this new arm needs a name. The unit will be called SCORPION." The President again paused and looked at each person around the table to get a feel for their opinions.

"The only thing left to consider now is who to appoint as the Commander of this new unit. A number of names were suggested, however, in my mind there was only one person who had the right qualities and experience to be able to tackle this job head on. That's why, Colonel," he said, as he looked directly at Copeland, "I requested your attendance here this afternoon."

Copeland shifted in his seat uncomfortably. Being headhunted twice. This confirmed what he had suspected when he entered the Pentagon that afternoon.

"I would like to offer the appointment as head of Scorpion to you, Colonel Copeland. The nomination has already been agreed to by all here today prior to your arrival. It is now down to you to accept. You are the best at what you do. Should you decline the offer..." the President paused.

Copeland was thinking that this would definitely be the worst-case scenario of no job, no pension, no future.

"You would not be thought of any differently to what you were before you entered this room," he continued.

'Yeah, right! Where have I heard that one before?' Copeland thought.

"Before you make your decision, though, Colonel, I'm sure that you have some burning questions that you would like to ask me or anyone else here. Just one more thing: Scorpion is not a covert organisation. It will be known in order to act as a deterrent. Okay, go ahead..."

Copeland sat up straight in his chair and glanced over his notes.

"When am I supposed to take up this position, Mr President?" asked Copeland.

"You will clear your desk at TWaID and be at the DC office on Monday next."

"I'll need a right hand man to assist me. My choice, though," insisted Copeland.

"That's okay, Colonel. Do you have anyone in mind?" enquired the President.

"Yes, sir," replied Copeland without elaborating. He continued,

"The covert and overt actions you suggested as part of the tasks of Scorpion could be seen by some as an act of war. This could well increase intolerance of the US and escalate terrorism in our weakest areas. The very thing that you are trying to protect us from," stated Copeland.

The President gathered his thoughts.

"I am aware of that, Colonel. However, the fact remains that we have a duty to protect US property and citizens alike by whatever means are deemed necessary. Fallout from an incident is down to politicians to answer to. You will be required, of course, to clear any actions through me first but, rest assured, you will have the support of the House and myself. One last thing, though, Colonel, unless of course you have any further questions?"

Copeland shook his head.

"Because of the high profile of the position, the rank of Colonel is considered insufficient. It has been decided that the rank of Brigadier would be offered to you with immediate effect."

Copeland was amused to think that he had totally discounted the possibility of this being a promotion board: who better to bestow the rank of Brigadier on a soldier than the President of the United States himself? *'This just gets better as it goes along.'*

"I'll now open the floor to the Joint Chiefs and anybody else who'd like to have any input," said the President.

"This position, Jack, does not give you the authority to do as you please." It was Walter Zieglar, the Chairman of the Joint Chiefs.

Copeland turned his head towards him and surveyed his frame with disgust; unfit and grossly overweight for a military man, he was a physical monument to a life of over-indulgence. Copeland ignored Zieglar and turned towards the FBI Chief, Richard Garcia.

"With regards to the bombings in '98, I'll need all the investigation data that you hold, including any named suspects that you have identified. I'm going to have to build a picture here, and establish if there are any connections or future intentions by the same groups."

"It'll be on your desk Monday morning, Jack," confirmed the FBI Chief.

Copeland turned his eyes to the NSA, Phil Scott. "I'll need up to date intel on the African regions where we are most at risk. I'll also need periodic satellite photographs of the regions, as well as those covering Afghanistan."

"Why Afghanistan?" enquired the NSA.

"I have my reasons, which will become clear later," snapped Copeland, although he didn't mean to.

"You'll have that by the end of next week," confirmed the NSA. Copeland decided that there was one further question he would ask the President.

"Mr President, Sir, where do the Joint Chiefs fit into my command chain? I can't keep going straight to you. You've got a country to run," enquired Copeland.

"Good point, Colonel. Excuse me, Brigadier," the President corrected himself. "The NSA and the Chairman of the Joint Chiefs will be your direct contact in my absence or unavailability. Is that clear?" declared the President

"Straight down the line, Mr President."

The President again glanced around the table. "I would like to thank Brigadier Copeland for accepting this enormous task. There is no man I would rather trust with the lives of our people. Good luck, Copeland."

Everyone stood up as the President walked towards the door. He disappeared in a heartbeat.

'I need a stiff drink,' thought Copeland whilst he tried to get his head around what he had been asked, no, ordered to do. Copeland moved across to where the CIA Chief, Mike Goddard, was sitting.

"Mike," said Copeland, offering his hand to shake. "What did your boys find out about last year's bombings?"

"Not much really. We have an idea who was instrumental in terms of the original concept and finances, but no concrete evidence," said the disappointed CIA Chief.

"Can I have copies of your findings and any updates next week?" asked Copeland.

"Yeah, sure," acknowledged Mike.

"Not wanting to pin blame at home for anything, are there any unscrupulous people in our Government's Administration that you have identified?"

"I'm not with you, Jack," said a confused Mike.

"Are there any weak links within the staff corps who are known to be susceptible to bribery or blackmail leading to the handover of information about our diplomatic infrastructure?"

"We've managed to weed out all of those in key areas. If there are any others then they're doing a grand job of keeping it quiet."

"Thanks, Mike. I'll talk with you on the phone next week. I'm going to have to leave now, things to do. Packing, etcetera."

Copeland bade his farewells to those left in the Briefing Room and exited into the corridor for the long walk back.

Today was Wednesday. Copeland would go to Fort Bragg on Saturday to clear out his desk and return to DC on Sunday. He had two days to spare. First he needed to call Chuck Martin on the Pentagon secure phones to bring him up to speed. He then needed to call Dinger Bell to get him to clear his desk. He was coming too. He just didn't know it yet.

Business taken care of, since he was in the neighbourhood Copeland decided to make a phone call to his sister, Jennifer, who had recently moved to nearby Arlington, VA. He needed a break and he would certainly enjoy the next two days off. They would probably be his last for a while…

*   *   *

Mohammed instructed the cabbie to stop further along the road than his intended destination. He paid his fare and left the cab without any further conversation. He stood on the sidewalk for a while as the cab disappeared into the distance, and then turned around and began to walk back in the direction the cab had just brought him. Having walked about five hundred metres, he stopped and took the piece of paper out of his trouser pocket. He looked at the name that he had scribbled down in the hotel, and then looked up to confirm the name on a board above a mobile trailer that he deduced was being used as an office. MIKE'S RENTALS the sign said. Satisfied, he put the crumpled paper back in his pocket and casually looked around. A few minutes later, he headed towards the office, and noticed the door was slightly ajar; peering through the gap he saw the back of a man seated at a table and leaning slightly forward. He pushed the door, which resisted with a slight creaking noise.

"Joe, leave it outside with the keys in it. I'll sort it out later," bellowed the man confidently from inside the cabin without turning round.

Mohammed climbed the one step that brought him into the office. It looked more like a disorganised storeroom – papers were everywhere.

'How can a guy run a business like this?' he thought. Mohammed was now standing right behind him but his approach had been so quiet that the man was still completely unaware of his presence. It wasn't until he

leant to his left to pick up something from the desk that:

"For fucks sake, man! You scared the living fucking daylights out of me! Jesus!" The man was probably about two hundred and fifty pounds of fat, and a gibbering wreck.

"What the fuck you doing sneaking up on someone like that? Man, you nearly gave me a heart attack!" He stood up and walked to the percolator and poured himself a coffee, heaping three spoons of sugar into a mug that looked as though it hadn't seen clean water for months.

"What do you want?" the man said uncomfortably, as he walked back to his chair, still in a state of shock.

"That's no way to speak to your customers. I need a car."

"People normally knock! But you've come to the right place. What kind?"

"One that's not traceable."

"That's gonna cost you."

"How much?"

"Twenty-five big ones."

"That's reasonable."

"Thousand," clarified the man, seeing the expression on Mohammed's face and then continued, "That includes your false registration, licence, insurance, and unused engine and chassis numbers."

"When can you get one?"

"When do you want it for?"

"Couple of days."

"I need to get it prepared, and the paperwork done."

"Don't let me down," said Mohammed finally, as he stood up and left the trailer. He caught a cab further down the street, and headed back to the hotel, Stage One of the plan complete.

CHAPTER SIX

Spring in Washington DC had always appealed to Jack's imagination. Looking across the landscape from his 37th floor office in the heart of Washington DC, the views were both panoramic and breathtaking, even spectacular as the flowers began to bloom and the trees filled out as if being inflated. Copeland had gained respect from politicians and senior military advisors for his handling of numerous successful military operations, which in some cases had had hidden agendas. After each operation, Copeland was always invited to the White House to personally give a full account of the missions to the President and the Joint Chiefs of Staff. These successes demonstrated that there was indeed a need for a specialist unit acting independently to preserve the integrity of US Government property and its citizens.

Copeland now had the responsibility of ensuring that the United States' global interests were safeguarded by an immediate reaction team (the SAS had called this a Quick Reaction Force) on twelve hours' notice to move (NTM). A tall order by any stretch of the imagination but nevertheless a Unit which he had quietly encouraged and was determined to ensure was successful. Continuing to watch the ant-like people below and the hundreds of coloured dots on the road, vehicles going about their daily business, he thought, *'Promotion has its perks: an office with a view, no less!'*

Contemplating the considerable responsibility the President of the United States *himself* had placed on his shoulders, he startled slightly when the intercom on his large rectangular desk buzzed.

"Mr Copeland, Major Bell has arrived," said Mary Grovehurst, his personal secretary.

"Thank you, Mary. Would you send him in, please, and bring us two coffees?"

The door opened and there stood Major Dinger Bell in a suit. Copeland had never seen him wear one before. It wasn't him, but he was sure they'd both get used to it.

Copeland walked across to greet his old friend and extended his hand. Dinger reciprocated.

Mary knocked on the door and entered with two coffees.

"Thank you, Mary," Copeland said, as she turned to leave the office.

The office was quite large compared to others he had been assigned. It was a corner office, with glass on two sides. A large coffee table with soft black leather chairs positioned around it was close to one wall, and the door was centred on the other wall. Copeland had a glass desk with two computer monitors as well as a laptop on a small table behind the desk.

Copeland guided Dinger to the coffee table and they both sat down.

"You took me by surprise when you called on Wednesday. It seems too good to be true. What's the catch?" asked Dinger

"As far as I know there isn't one. Just a great burden of responsibility."

"If I took this job, I insisted I would choose my own 2IC," continued Copeland. "That was one of the stipulations. They agreed. The rest you know. We go back a long way, Dinger, and I wouldn't want anybody else. Oh, and they promoted me to Brigadier General. They've also promoted you to Colonel. Congratulations!"

"This just gets better," smiled Dinger.

Copeland stood up and moved to his desk. He moved a few files to one side, picked up the one from the FBI and returned to the comfortable chairs.

"While I was at the Pentagon, I asked the FBI Chief, Richard Garcia, for all the info he had on the '98 bombings. This is it." Copeland handed the file to Dinger.

"It's pretty vague, but they are damned sure that they know who the front man was for that op. He's also been responsible for other terrorist action in the Middle East. Nobody ever gets to see him. He's discreet, he's clever and he's bloody good."

Copeland let Dinger digest the info in the file. Then he said:

"We need to build up a profile of this character using every means. We can access all the data: we just need to ask for it. That picture that's clipped to the inside cover is pretty out of date, so he is likely to have changed appearance by now. The latest intel suggest that he has a number of people who do the work for him. If that's the case then he will have a recruiter and an organiser who the others report to. It has been suggested that the recruiter is an Iraqi and the controller Sudanese. It's my guess that the man at the top is a Saudi businessman. Money will be flowing like oil. There may also be an Iranian connection. Since they all seem to be from Arab speaking nations, they will blend into a team easily."

Dinger was impressed by the intel already to hand. "Do we know how the '98 bombings were committed?" he asked Copeland.

"The attack in Nairobi was by car bomb, but it exploded by the building next door, which toppled onto the embassy. There was also a shoot-out between the Marine guards and a number of gunmen. It is believed that two of the gunmen were killed in the blast that followed. The Tanzanian attack was also a car bomb. The vehicle was parked at the front of the embassy. It blew in the front of the building, the reception area was a heap of rubble."

"That seems to be their preferred method of attack. No limitations on parking adjacent to official buildings. Of course it also has a wider dispersal of shrapnel thus creating damage and injuries over a greater area."

"Correct, Dinger. What I need to find out from Phil Scott – the current NSA to the President – is why there was no prior warning from the intelligence services, which might have given them a heads up. As you know, each embassy has a CIA agent on staff, unofficially of course. It's his *job* to snoop around. We've got a lot to do, Dinger. We need to assess those Embassies we feel are likely to be targeted, and let them know ASAP. I'm going to arrange for you to meet the NSA this afternoon at the White House, and I'll go and see the CIA Chief, Mike Goddard, at

Langley. Get all the info he has on the Arab embassy locations. I'll get the up to date intel relating to terrorist activities in the same regions. We should be able to meet half way and come up with something."

Copeland got up from his chair and moved towards his desk. He sat down in his black leather executive chair, which reclined immediately as he sat down. Copeland picked up his phone and looked across at Dinger.

"Mary, can you get me Phil Scott, the NSA at the White House, please?"

Dinger was still reading over the files when the phone rang.

Copeland picked up the receiver.

"Mr Copeland, Phil Scott is on the line for you."

"Thanks Mary. Phil, hi, it's Jack Copeland. How you doing?"

"Fine, thanks, Jack. Hope you've settled into the office okay? What can I do for you?"

"I need for you to meet Dinger Bell, my 2IC. Preferably this afternoon."

"You know you can access my diary using your computer? It's already been configured for you."

"No, I didn't, but thanks. Dinger knows exactly what I want from you, so rather than steal his thunder I'll let him discuss the matter with you. Do you have a slot at thirteen hundred today?"

"Yeah, that's okay."

"Okay. Thanks, Phil."

Copeland replaced the handset.

"It's all set for thirteen hundred. Use one of the pool cars from the garage. Mary will let you know which ones are available. Any problems, Dinger, give me a call on my mobile."

Copeland then telephoned the CIA at Langley and arranged a similar meeting with Goddard.

*   *   *

US embassy, Khartoum, Sudan

A red Nissan pick-up van dropped off a teenage boy. The boy set up a stall with goods from the back of the pick-up. The van moved on. The boy remained, looking across the road directly at the embassy. He appeared to be scribbling.

*   *   *

US embassy, Cairo, Egypt

White post markings were painted on to the wall of the embassy, where a three-ton truck had been.

*   *   *

US embassy, Tripoli, Libya

A third man on a bike joined two having coffee. The oldest one of the three mounted the bike and left. People would come and go from the embassy. One of them wrote things down.

*   *   *

US embassy, Casablanca, Morocco

A man in a white suit approached one of the Marines at the embassy door. He asked for the Marine's photograph. He obliged. Photograph of entrance taken.

*   *   *

US embassy, Freetown, Sierra Leone

The white Mazda van turned left onto Sanders Street from Adelaide Street. It was two cars behind the black Mercedes. Both cars were heading north-east. The Mercedes turned left onto Walpole Street from Siaka, then right through the compound gates of the US embassy. The Mazda continued along Siaka, passing the embassy and moving along Stevens Street.

*   *   *

Copeland was fifteen minutes early. It was better to be that way than late. Although he had never been to Langley before, he was told to keep an eye out for twin six-storey towers joined in the middle by a four–storey core area. It was distinctive and stood out amongst the other buildings. Copeland had managed to park in the CIA visitor's car park.

'So this is the George Bush Centre for Intelligence,' he said quietly to himself. He approached the automatic door, which was released by an operator. Copeland entered and the door closed behind him. He looked back towards the door, watching as it closed. He then approached the main desk.

"Good afternoon, Sir. May I help you?" enquired the man in a grey suit behind the desk.

"Yes. I have an appointment to see your Chief at thirteen hundred hours."

"May I ask your name, Sir?"

"Jack Copeland."

"Thank you. I'll just let him know you're here."

Very formal, noted Copeland as he turned and looked away from the desk. Forty-five seconds later, Copeland heard the lift (*'elevator'*, he reminded himself,) bong as it arrived. The door opened and Mike Goddard strode towards him. They shook hands in greeting.

"Jack. Welcome to the CIA. How was the journey from DC?"

"Lunchtime traffic's a bitch, but I allowed for that."

"Come on, let's go up to my office."

The two men moved towards the central elevator. The door was still open from when Mike had landed moments earlier. They both stepped inside, Copeland first. Mike pressed the button for the fourth floor, and the elevator responded immediately with such smooth acceleration it felt like you weren't moving at all. The only indication was the number on the small screen increasing as they passed each floor.

"Easy question to start with, Mike: what is the CIA responsible for?"

"As Director of the CIA and the US Intelligence Committee, I am responsible to the President and accountable to the American public through the

Intelligence Oversight Committee of the US Congress. We have no jurisdiction on home soil."

"Okay, that's the text book answer. What happens in reality? The assassination plots, the botched coups, and the drug experiments?" queried Copeland with a smile.

"That was pre-cold war, Jack, but I'm sure a few policy makers would like to see a return to those days. The problem now, of course, is that it is widely believed on 'the Hill', and in the intelligence community generally, that the years of scandals have made us overly cautious. 'Risk aversion' has taken hold. Having said that, we gather global intelligence on everything. Nothing can move or breathe without us knowing about it."

"The '98 bombings caught you out."

"That was an area we thought was relatively safe. Just goes to show that nothing is safe. I reckon it's high time we looked in our own back yard, too, before we're caught with our pants down."

Reaching the fourth floor, the door opened and both Mike and Copeland stepped out into a wide space populated by desks and computer terminals. Mike directed Copeland to the far corner and into an office.

"Take a seat," instructed Goddard, as he gestured to the vacant chair.

"Would you like coffee, Jack?"

"Yeah. White, one sugar please."

Mike picked up the phone, and pressed a few buttons.

"Could I have two coffees to my office, please?" he requested.

"Have you settled in okay? It's your first day, but I can see you're keen."

"I've got a few things rolling already. I don't believe in waiting until tomorrow. That's valuable time wasted."

"So: what can the CIA and I do for you, Jack?"

"I'm focussing my attention on the Middle East because I feel that that is where our main problems abroad are. What I want to do, Mike, is build up profiles of terrorist groups who are known and active in the region. That is where you come in."

There was a knock at the door.

"Yeah?"

A young woman dressed in a blue blazer jacket, white blouse, and a light beige knee length skirt, with long brown hair, entered with two cups of coffee, sugar and milk on a silver tray, and placed them on Goddard's desk. She left with a slight glance back at Copeland, who obliged her with a smile as she closed the door. Copeland admired her poise. If he was somewhat younger the chase would've been on.

"That's one of our bright young field agents, Kathy Price. Nice kid: must have wanted to see you close up," Goddard said, noticing Copeland's attention had wandered slightly...

"Now, where were we?"

Copeland continued, "If you would give me a complete list of global terrorist organisations plus their profiles, I'll will sift through them, and identify those which probably have current offensive tendencies."

"Yeah. That's not a problem. I have a department called the Directorate of Intelligence headed by Joanne Wiley, which deals with that angle. I'll give her a call."

Mike punched in the four digits which would connect him to the Office of the Directorate of Intelligence. There was no answer. He cancelled the call with a frown.

"Now that *is* odd. Leave it with me, Jack. When do you want the info?"

"ASAP. There will be a lot of sifting to do so the sooner, the better. You can fax it to me at the Scorpion offices. Did you really get no whispers at all before the '98 bomb, Mike?"

"I swear to you we didn't. It caught us on the hop."

"I find that hard to believe. With all the hi-tech gear and listening stations you have, not to mention satellites, I can't even fart in my own bathroom without you lot knowing about it."

"We're not that obvious, are we? No, straight up, Jack, we'd moved our source to another area four months previously."

"That was a costly mistake."

"Don't I know it and I'm still paying for it today; constant reminders and it was a huge blow to our credibility. And, although the old Soviet Union is no longer our 'Hard Target', terrorism is in some ways even harder to crack. We keep on being told that we need more and better spies who can penetrate terrorist cells and the secretive regimes of rogue states like Iraq and Libya. But I'd best stop bitching or they'll have me shuffling paper in the Department of Transportation for the rest of my career. Is there anything else we – or I – can do for you, Jack?"

"Not at the moment. You've been a great help, Mike. Thanks."

Mike stood up from behind his desk, which prompted Copeland to do the same.

"I'll get those documents faxed to you tomorrow. Anyhow, I'll walk with you to the elevator."

Once summoned, the elevator arrived. Mike extended his hand and Copeland reciprocated.

"Nice to see you again."

"I'll give you a call if I need any more info on those groups."

"Do that. Bye."

The elevator door closed and Mike returned to his desk to ascertain the whereabouts of the Head of the Directorate of Intelligence.

Copeland arrived at the ground floor level, exited the elevator, and walked through the opened automatic door back to his car.

At least it wasn't rush hour back to DC. He'd take a leisurely drive so that he could mull over what he had accomplished this afternoon. He didn't expect to see Dinger until tomorrow morning when hopefully a piece or two of the jigsaw could be put in place. He'd wait until the fax arrived…

*   *   *

Mike input the four digits of the extension to the Directorate of Intelligence (DoI) again: still no answer. He accessed the CIA intranet and Joanne's diary file. According to her schedule, she had no appointments that afternoon and should have been in the office. He would go down the hall to her office

51

later. Perhaps she had a personal commitment or was in the powder room. There would be a reasonable explanation, he was sure.

*   *   *

Copeland looked at his watch. It was four fifteen pm. Twenty minutes ago he had left Langley. He dialled Mary at the Scorpion offices. His secretary picked up after a few rings.

"Mary, hi, it's Jack. Have you heard from Dinger yet?"

"No. He did say that he would call as he was leaving the White House."

"Thanks. Have there been any messages for me or any mail this afternoon?"

"No messages, but I've put the mail on your desk, Nothing urgent."

"Thanks. If I'm not back at the office by five pm, lock up and I'll see you in the morning."

"Thanks, Jack."

"See you tomorrow. 'Night, Mary."

"Goodnight, Jack."

Copeland hung up and decided to enjoy the drive. There was nothing else he could do tonight.

*   *   *

Joanne S Wiley was thirty-four, single and one of the youngest agents to be promoted to her level at the CIA. Head of the Directorate of Intelligence was a high-status post. She was also very attractive with shoulder length blonde hair and blue eyes. She had a body to die for and she knew it, but she had never had a long-term relationship. She had graduated from Harvard with a top degree and had enhanced her educational qualifications by gaining a top up degree. She was fluent in four languages, French, Russian, German and Spanish. She also had an MSc in Computer Science. She was ambitious and intended to go all the way to the top. Success had brought her a lifestyle to go with it. A four bedroom detached house in the wealthy suburb along the Belle View Blvd in Alexandria, VA, which she shared with her mother. She had recently procured a BMW 540 as fitting her station. Her journey to work was twenty minutes and sixteen point nine miles. As Head of the Directorate of Intelligence she had the responsibility of leading the analytical branch of the CIA, which was responsible for the collection, evaluation and dissemination of all available intelligence on key foreign issues. It was a powerful position that allowed her access to sensitive and secret information.

Joanne S Wiley was normally in the office between eight and eight thirty AM. At thirteen hundred hours, the phone rang in her office.

"Wiley."

"Is this Joanne Wiley of Belle View Boulevard?" said the caller.

"Yes, it is. Who am I speaking to?" demanded Joanne.

"This is the Alexandria Police Precinct. Your mother has been assaulted at your house, and we think it may have been an attempted burglary. We'd like you to attend the scene to establish if any items are missing."

"Yes, of course. I'll be there in thirty minutes."

Joanne left her desk, collecting her coat on the way out. She hadn't stopped to think how the caller had known her CIA direct line number. Her car was in the secure car park. She climbed in and drove along her usual homeward route. She arrived home to find neither a police officer nor a police car.

'*He could be inside,*' she said to herself.

She walked towards the front door. The door opened slowly. Joanne was now facing her mother.

"Why are you home so early, dear?" asked her mother

"Are you okay?" demanded Joanne.

"Of course. Why shouldn't I be?" asked her mother, looking curious.

"Have you had a police officer round this morning?"

"What do you take me for? Why would I want one?" she asked rhetorically. "Your father was all I needed. Rest his soul. What the devil is going on, Joanne?"

"Nothing. I'll speak to you later. Lock all the doors whilst I'm out. Don't open them to anybody until I get back tonight. Understood?"

"Yes. Stop fussing. You're frightening me. Has something happened?"

"I'm not sure. I had a mysterious phone call at work, that's all. Just another prank, I imagine. I'll see you later, mother," Joanne said. She heard her mother lock and chain the front door. Joanne climbed back into her BMW and drove along Belle View Blvd towards the George Washington Memorial Parkway. Having crossed Chain Bridge, she left the Parkway in the direction of McLean, and then onto Dolley Madison Blvd.

The time was 14.15 hours. She was travelling faster than she normally did. As she turned off Dolley Madison Blvd, she hadn't seen the car that pulled out in front of her from the junction with Waverly Way off Dogue Hill Lane, the road leading to the Langley HQ. She braked, skidded, and hit the rear right of the other car causing it to spin. Both cars came to a halt within a short distance. Considering the impact, there appeared little damage to both cars. The occupant of the other vehicle, a dark handsome well-dressed man in his 30s, got out and approached the BMW. He didn't appear injured but knocked on Joanne's window.

"Are you okay?" he said in a soft voice.

Joanne was a bit shaky but uninjured. She hoped. She had noticed his dark eyes and black hair and how well-groomed he was. She stabilised her thinking enough to say to herself:

'He's gorgeous!'

"Yes, I think so."

The man opened Joanne's car door and helped her out by holding her arm.

"It was all my fault," she said.

"It was actually mine. I didn't look properly. I am just visiting Alexandria, and I haven't worked out my way round yet."

Joanne noted that he had the wiry black hair of a Middle-Eastern person. He also had the soft accent to go with his looks.

"Listen, there's not much damage to either car, so I'll give you my insurance details for you to get yours repaired. Mine's a hire car so that will be done automatically. There's no need to involve the police on a trivial matter such as this."

He finished noting his insurance details and handed them over to Joanne.

"I would also like to give you my address here in Alexandria. I would like for us to have dinner together. My way of apologising. Think about it. My number's on the note too."

Joanne thought, *'He's a bit forward. He never even asked if I was married or was living with someone!'*

"By the way, my name is Mohammed Abdul Naseer."

"I'm sorry. I'm Joanne Wiley," she said, extending her hand.

Mohammed began to walk back to his car. Before climbing in he turned to Joanne.

"Give me a call when you are free. I would like to see you in better circumstances! 'Bye."

"'Bye," said Joanne, moving back towards her car.

She climbed into the BMW and watched as Mohammed drove in the opposite direction. She then resumed her interrupted drive back and left her car, as always, in the security car park. Having switched the engine off, she paused before opening her door and picked up Mohammed's note from the passenger seat and thought to herself, *'Why not. I need some spice in my life."*

*   *   *

Mike decided to walk over to Joanne's office. As he was crossing the elevator lobby, Joanne almost ran him down.

"I'm sorry, Mike," said a rushed and flustered Joanne.

"Whoa… Where's the fire, Joanne?"

Both Mike and Joanne began walking in the direction of her office.

"I had a phone call in to my office this morning, which hadn't been routed through the switchboard. I thought nothing of it at the time but the caller said that he was from the police. They were saying that my mother had been assaulted, and the house broken into. They asked that I get to the house as quickly as possible to establish if anything was missing."

"How's your mom, Joanne?"

"She's fine but the strange thing is when I got there, there was nothing wrong at all. My mother wasn't hurt, nor had the house been burgled. There hadn't even been a police car or police officer at the house."

"Did the caller say from which police station he was calling?"

"Alexandria Police Precinct"

"I'll give them a call later to see what they're playing at."

"Thanks."

"Don't mention it."

"The other annoying thing was that I was rushing back to the office when a car came out of a side street off Madison Boulevard and I T-boned it."

"Are you okay?"

"Yes, I'm fine, Thanks."

"How's the car? We could give you a pool one for the time being."

"It's still driveable, but I will have to get it repaired soon."

Joanne omitted to tell Mike about Mohammed. As far as she was concerned, that was personal.

"Oh, Joanne, do you remember me mentioning to you last week about that new organisation the President has set up, Scorpion?"

"Yes, I do."

"Well, I had Jack Copeland over this afternoon. I tried your number whilst he was here since he wanted something that your office can provide for him."

"What's that?"

"He's trying to build up profiles of middle-eastern terrorist groups which may pose a direct threat to our assets in that region. Can you dig it out for him this afternoon? I said that I would fax it to him by morning."

"No problem."

"I think it would be best that he directs his enquiries to you, Joanne, for anything else. I'm sure his angle will be inclined towards your department."

"Fine."

"I'll let you get on, Joanne. Let me have those files later, will you?"

"Sure."

"Are you okay? It's just…you look different, but I can't pinpoint why."

"Yep, I'm okay," she said with a smile.

Mike left Joanne's office and returned to his own.

*   *   *

Copeland was in his office by 07.00 the next morning. Mary, his secretary, still hadn't arrived. He didn't expect her until 08.00. Mike had sent the fax on the terrorist groups as requested and Copeland collected it from the fax machine before entering his office. He sat down at his desk and began to read the comprehensive list of groups.

'I hadn't realised there were that many,' he thought to himself.

Some Copeland discounted immediately and scored a line through their names. Others he placed to one side to be considered. At 08.00 sharp Mary entered his office.

"Morning, Jack. Would you like some coffee?"

"That would be nice, Mary. Thank you. Dinger should be here shortly."

Mary turned and left Copeland's office, closing the door behind her. At 08.15 Dinger entered the office

"Morning, Jack. Did you have a good day yesterday?"

"Not bad. How about you?"

"The NSA gave me some good info."

"I got my intel on the groups, which I've been sifting through this morning."

There was a knock at the door. It opened and Mary entered with two coffees and placed them on the coffee table. She turned and left to go back to her office, closing the door behind her.

"I've eliminated quite a few of the groups so far," said Copeland. "However, I still have this pile to consider."

Dinger moved over to the coffee table and sat on one of the leather chairs, drinking his coffee before he began.

"Do you want me to go first, Jack?"

"Sure. Crack on, Dinger."

"The embassy in Khartoum is on a main road, so is vulnerable from a frontal attack. There are no side streets adjacent to the building, but there is an access point at the rear."

"Khartoum. Hasn't that just re-opened?"

"Yeah. It's been closed for nineteen months and the government's reason for re-opening it is to ratchet up the pressure on Sudan to respond to the international community on terrorism, human rights, and the civil war in Juba."

"That looks like politicians bowing to pressure."

"Well, not exactly, Jack. With Iran under a new moderate government and Libya behaving itself, the willingness of Sudan to moderate its behaviour could be a critical contribution to stability in the region. The re-opening should not be seen as a sign of weakness; rather, it is a reward for modified behaviour."

"Okay, I get your point. What's next?"

"The embassy in Tripoli. It is a detached building accessible on all four sides. No fencing, no cameras, no parking restrictions. They do have the usual Marine guard. It is also overlooked by a block of flats. I rate this as extremely vulnerable. The next one is Morocco. This again is a detached building, which has five floors. It is on a main route. It has a Marine guard posted out front. It has a vehicle compound to one side, accessible through an electronic gate controlled by the guard. The side streets, particularly, render it vulnerable to attack."

"Can't you give me any good news, Dinger?"

"Not really, Jack. Money has been the hindrance for quite a while, thus badly needed security upgrades have been on hold. I think there is a naive reliance on local intel to tip us off about incidents before they happen."

"Do any of these posts have CIA agents in place?"

"Now they do, yes. These have all been increased since the '98 bombings."

"Okay. What's next?"

"Cairo. This is a three story building built amongst others so is safe on its sides. The front however is on a main road and the rear is vulnerable too."

"Why do they build them on main roads?" asked Copeland rhetorically.

"Because…"

"I know the answer, Dinger. I was just asking myself. Do they have any kind of security at these places?"

"They all have a Marine guard whether he is outside or in the lobby. They all have bulletproof glass protecting the receptionist from attack. The receptionist also controls an airlock system, which prevents undesirables from entering the inner rooms of the embassies."

"Is that it?"

"Afraid so."

"It's not much of a defence is it? It sounds like a compromise?"

"Not really. However, there hasn't been much call for anything else until recently. Bear in mind the US Government wants to make all their Embassies accessible to everyone to encourage people to visit or work in the States. What they don't want is a fortress-like edifice which might give people the wrong impressions about the US."

"I see your point. Anything else?"

"Sierra Leone. This again is a detached building. It has steps up to the main door. Marine guard posted out front. Has a vehicle compound adjacent to the rear. Has a main road to its front and a side street. Again it is assessed as being vulnerable."

"Okay, Dinger, I'm starting to get the picture here. I don't think this organisation could protect all these assets even if we wanted to. There are just too many gaps to plug. Do all the embassies have a security officer?"

"Yes, normally ex-military. They draft local orders in respect of security measures. They also disseminate government legislation and policy to its staff."

"I don't know why 'Dinger,' but I have a gut feeling that something is going to happen in one or all of these regions, probably because they are such easy targets. I want you to inform all the relevant security officers to get their staff briefed and to be extra vigilant. The reporting of things should now be second nature no matter how trivial. It's better to be that way than to say *if only*. Get a telex drafted for transmission to each one that you have identified."

"I'm on to it now," Dinger said as he left the office

Having briefed Mary on what the document should contain, Dinger returned to the office.

"Let's move on to the terrorist profiles," said Copeland, sifting through the pile.

"I've had another look through the pile of possibilities and have whittled it down a little further. I now have five probables"

Copeland lifted each piece of paper from the pile and handed a copy to Dinger.

"The first one – Al Jihad although they come in various guises. They are basically an Egyptian Islamic extremist group divided into two separate factions. One is in Afghanistan and is a key player in terrorist financier Osama bin Laden's new World Islamic Front, the other is the Vanguards of Conquest led by Ahmad Husayn Agiza. They have an increasing willingness to target US interests in Egypt. They tend to operate in the Cairo area, but have a network outside Egypt, including Afghanistan and Sudan."

"Are they still active?"

"They haven't conducted an attack in Egypt since nineteen ninety-three, but they have threatened to retaliate against the US for the incarceration of a number of their members."

Copeland shifted the paper to the next group.

"The next one of interest is Hezbollah – The Party of God. Although not active in our targeted regions, they were responsible for the bombings of the US Embassy and US Marine Barracks in Beirut in

October '83, and the US Embassy annex in Beirut in September '84. They were also responsible for the kidnapping of a US diplomat in Lebanon. They receive substantial amounts of finance, training, and weapons from Iran and Syria. This is a group we shouldn't discount. It may be dormant at the moment, but it doesn't take much to make it an active unit."

"What's their current strength?"

"Several thousand."

"Who pulls the strings?"

"Well, they are closely linked and allied with and often directed by Iran, but may conduct operations not approved by Tehran."

Copeland flipped over another sheet of paper.

"The next group, which still remains dormant at this time but cannot be discounted, is the Al Fatah group headed by no less than Yasser Arafat himself. They disappeared into many other middle-eastern countries during the Israeli invasion of Lebanon in '82."

"Any idea to where?"

"Tunisia, Yemen, Algeria, Iraq and others. They have a headquarters in Tunisia, with bases in Lebanon."

"Who pulls the strings on this outfit?"

"They have close political and financial ties with Saudi Arabia, Kuwait and other middle-eastern Gulf States. As I said, it's one to watch. This last one interests me. It is a group called Al-Jama'a Al-Islamiyya, otherwise known as the Islamic Group. This is Egypt's largest militant group, active since the late '70's. The thing that stands out is the connection with Bin Laden of Saudi Arabia. In 1998 they signed a statement calling for attacks against US civil property, but have denied support for Bin Laden. The group brings us back again to Afghanistan where they receive support from militant organisations. This is at the top of my list at the moment."

"What's their most recent activity?"

"In 1997, November, they killed fifty-eight foreign tourists in Luxor. They have also claimed responsibility for the attempted assassination of the Egyptian President, Mubarak.

"Have they attacked any US facilities?"

"Not specifically, but they've made many threats to do so."

"What's their current strength?"

"Unknown, but probably several thousand hard-core members and another several thousand sympathisers. I should get the weekly MILSAT of Afghanistan this week."

"What will that reveal?" enquired Dinger

"Well, I'd like to do comparisons to look at shift patterns and displacements etcetera. Anyway, that's all of the groups of interest to me. Mike over at Langley asked that I liaise directly with his Directorate of Intelligence regarding any further intel. I think I'll bring her up to date now."

"Oh, it's a she, is it?" enquired Dinger.

"Yep. It's a sign of the times – equality and all that."

CHAPTER SEVEN

Joanne Wiley sat in her office looking at a piece of paper with a stranger's phone number on it. She kept looking at it debating whether or not to arrange a date. She wasn't used to the dating game. Her career had dominated most of her life. She had no regrets, of course, but she was missing that something special – a relationship. At thirty-four she didn't want to be over the hill and remain unsettled in the long term. Children for her were not an issue. She could do with or without them. Eventually, courage overcame pride. She picked up the telephone and dialled the number.

"Mohammed," said the voice at the other end.

"Hi, this is Joanne Wiley. I don't know if you remember me or not but we bumped in to each other the other day, excuse the pun?"

"Of course I do. How could I forget such a beautiful lady?"

"Thanks," she said, embarrassed.

"Have you managed to sort out the damage to your car?"

"Not yet. Haven't had the time, what about you?"

"I've collected another car. They were quite good about it."

"Mohammed, I was ringing to see what you were doing this weekend?"

Joanne was nervous as the words came out. She wasn't normally this forward, especially with someone she had met so briefly! But he seemed different: polite, handsome and probably great to be with.

"I'm free all weekend. Why do you ask?"

"I just thought we could get together," said Joanne, finding it oddly difficult to string a sentence together.

"How about dinner Saturday night? I know a marvellous Italian restaurant nearby."

"Okay. That sounds great. You haven't been here that long, so how do you know it's excellent?"

"Asking a question like that makes you sound like a Police Officer. You're not, are you?"

"Good heavens, no. Nothing like that."

"Good. I know the restaurant because it has been my main source of food since arriving here. I can certainly recommend it."

"Italian it is, then. What time shall we meet there?"

"Let's say eight pm."

"Fine. I'll see you there. Silly me. I don't know where it is?"

Mohammed gave the directions to Joanne who wrote them down.

"Any problems finding it, please give me a call."

"I will, and thanks. 'Bye."

"'Bye," said Mohammed.

Joanne Wiley couldn't believe she had had the courage to call. She felt easier now, but was still nervous about her first date in…how long? She couldn't remember. Her hands began to shake; was this excitement at the thought of something good or had she made a mistake that would be hard to get out of? Only time would tell, she tried to convince herself.

*　　　*　　　*

"Yes," said Ibrahim Khalil, answering the phone.

"It's all set for the first meeting on Saturday evening," said the voice at the other end.

"Good. Well done. Brief me when you have any further information."

Ibrahim put the phone down on its cradle. Good, he thought. The next stage had begun.

*　　　*　　　*

"Mary, can you get me Joanne Wiley at Langley, please?" requested Copeland.

"Sure."

Moments later the phone rang in the Scorpion offices of Jack Copeland.

"Copeland," he answered.

"Jack, this is Joanne Wiley, the Directorate of Intelligence at Langley. You wanted to speak with me?"

"Nice to talk with you at last, Joanne. Did Mike bring you up to speed about our liaison?"

"That I am to provide you with whatever you require, yes."

"Good. Joanne, have any of the embassies in the regions that concern me reported any unusual activities as of late?"

"No. Nothing filed here. Why do you ask?"

"I feel that something major is about to happen, but I just can't pin-point it. It may be one or multiple sites. It's a gut feeling. Can you speak with your agents at the embassies and see what you can get from them?"

"Yes, sure."

"The smallest piece of information, however insignificant, could be the vital clue and the piece of the jigsaw that I've been waiting for."

"No problem. As soon as I have something, Jack, I'll let you know."

"Thanks, Joanne. Perhaps we could get together sometime for a drink?"

"Maybe."

"Speak to you soon. 'Bye."

"'Bye," said Joanne.

*   *   *

Joanne did *not* know what to wear for her date. She had a wardrobe full of clothes, but they were her working attire. She had asked her mother for her opinion, but the reply wasn't particularly helpful. She finally decided on a black skirt and white blouse. That was smart enough without revealing too much. Time was running short. She had spent so long deciding on what to wear that she only had time for a shower instead of a bath. Finally dressing herself and applying a little makeup, she looked in the tall free standing mirror on the floor, and said to herself *'You're putting on a little weight, Joanne,'* patting her stomach. She then went downstairs.

"Mom, you will be alright, won't you?"

"Of course. Stop fussing. You have a good night. You haven't been out for ages."

"I will, thanks. I'll be back around ten-thirty."

Joanne gave her mother a kiss on the cheek, collected her handbag and raincoat, then stepped outside and closed the door behind her. She started her car, and reversed out of the driveway. She had Mohammed's instructions next to her. Following them to the letter, a forty-five minute drive brought her to the restaurant. She checked her watch: seven minutes early. She would wait. It was, after all, her prerogative. Only a handful of people entered the restaurant during her short wait. She hadn't seen Mohammed. Perhaps he was already in there. Joanne had started to feel nervous again. Her stomach began to tighten and beads of sweat appeared on her top lip. It's now-or-never time, she thought. Joanne stepped from her car, locked it using the remote sensor, and walked towards the restaurant. She noted the name above the large window: *'DON BENI'*.

She pulled the restaurant door towards her, stepped inside and immediately swept the room for Mohammed. It took a second look for her to spot him: in the corner at a table for two. She moved towards him, and he looked up then stood up from his seat.

"Good evening, Joanne. You had no problem finding the restaurant, I see?"

"None at all. Your directions were spot on."

"Good. May I take your coat?"

"Thank you."

Joanne opened her coat and started to remove it. Mohammed stepped behind her and slid it off her shoulders. He then passed it to one of the waiters.

"You look absolutely beautiful again," Mohammed commented.

"Thank you. You're quite smart yourself."

"Would you like a drink, perhaps?"

"Yes, please. Red wine."

"Okay."

Mohammed raised his arm and attracted the attention of a waiter. "Could I have the wine list please?"

"Certainly, sir," replied the waiter

The waiter brought the wine list that Mohammed immediately glanced through. "A bottle of the Chianti Flask Francesca, please."

"A very good choice, sir," said the waiter, as he retreated.

"So, how is your car? Is it still driveable?"

"Yes. I'll have to have it repaired, though, once I manage to get some time off work."

"What line of business are you in?"

"I work for the government – nothing important really."

"I would have thought that any work for the government would be important?"

"It can be, depending on where you are."

"Do you work in Washington DC?" enquired Mohammed.

"No, but not far from here actually."

The waiter reappeared with the red wine. He opened the bottle and poured a taster into Mohammed's glass.

"Yes, that's fine, thanks."

The waiter filled both red wine glasses, placed the bottle on the table and withdrew.

"Do you work at Langley, then?" tested Mohammed.

"Yes, I do." Joanne was surprised at how easily the answer came out. She usually stuck to her cover story.

"Isn't that where…?" said Mohammed slowly.

"Yes, it is," said Joanne cautiously, wondering where the conversation might be going.

"Ah! So you're a spy! I didn't know there were any lady James Bonds?"

"Mohammed, James Bond is a make-believe English spy. He's a figment of Ian Fleming's imagination loosely based on his work with MI6. We work differently over here," said Joanne, laughing.

"I'm sorry, I hadn't realised," he said innocently. "Are you ready to order?"

"Sure. What would you recommend?"

"They do a great pasta with bolognaise sauce."

"That's settled then."

Mohammed gained the attention of the waiter by raising his hand.

"Are you ready to order, sir?" asked the waiter.

"Yes, please. We would both like the pasta with the bolognaise sauce."

The waiter collected the menus from his customers and disappeared into the kitchen.

Mohammed raised his glass. "I would like to propose a toast, Joanne."

"To what?" Joanne raised her glass.

"A chance meeting. Without that we wouldn't be sitting opposite each other this evening."

"Okay," replied Joanne with a slight smile.

"To a chance meeting," they declared, and chinked their glasses together.

"How rude of me, Joanne, but I haven't asked if you are married. Somebody as beautiful as you must be, surely?"

"I'm not sure I would be here if I was. No, I'm still single."

"The right person still hasn't come along yet?"

'Perhaps he has now,' Joanne thought to herself.

"I've always put my career first, which makes any kind of relationship tricky."

"That must have been difficult for you?"

"Sometimes, yes. Seeing all my friends happily married, some of them already parents, and here am I: still single and living with my mother."

"I'm sure your mother is a pillar of strength to you?"

"Yes, she is, bless her."

"What about your father?"

"He died of a heart attack six years ago. I couldn't leave my mother on her own, so I decided to take her in. She has been company for me."

"I'm sorry to hear about your father. It's not easy losing a close member of the family. I take it you were close?"

"Oh, yes. I was the apple of his eye. He was so proud of me graduating from Harvard and getting a job at Langley."

The waiter returned with both orders "Enjoy your meal, ma'am, sir."

"This looks really nice," observed Joanne. "What brings you to the US, Mohammed?"

"Well, I work for a telecommunications company, which is based in Saudi Arabia. We are trying to expand the network with an alliance amongst other countries. The US is one such country. Perhaps you could assist me to persuade your government to help?"

"I don't work for that side of the government, unfortunately."

"Pity. It would have made my visit that much easier. I could then have spent more time with you."

Joanne was flattered, but there was nothing she could do to help him. "How long are you staying in the US?"

"Possibly four weeks, maybe more, maybe less."

"Do you visit here often?" said Joanne, starting to smile.

"What's funny, Joanne?"

"Well, that statement is normally used as a chat-up line when approaching a stranger."

"I've got a lot to learn about these customs."

"You're not doing too badly."

Joanne and Mohammed finished their meals at almost the same time.

"That was wonderful. Thank you, Mohammed."

"My pleasure. I hope it isn't the last time we can do this?"

"I hope not," said Joanne looking at her watch "My goodness, look at the time!" It was ten twenty pm, she noted. "I promised my mother I would be home by ten thirty at the latest!"

"You're not a child any more, Joanne. You are entitled to your own life now."

"I know, and this has been a wonderful evening. It's just that this is the first time I've left her on her own."

"Okay."

Mohammed raised his hand again, attracting the attention of the waiter. He settled the bill.

"Do you have any plans for tomorrow?" Mohammed asked.

"Not specifically. No. Why do you ask?"

"I thought you might like to show me around this beautiful town of yours?"

"Yes, I would. That would be nice."

The waiter brought Joanne's coat and Mohammed assisted her with it. They both stepped outside.

"It's chilly tonight, especially coming out from a warm restaurant," commented Joanne.

"Yes, it is. Where have you parked your car?"

"Just over there." Joanne pointed.

"Let me walk with you," insisted Mohammed.

"I've had a lovely evening, Mohammed. Thank you."

"It was my pleasure."

Joanne reached her car, then used the remote sensor to de-activate the alarm and central locking. She opened the driver's door. Mohammed bent towards Joanne and kissed her on both cheeks. This felt strange, but she didn't resist.

"Goodnight, Joanne. I will see you tomorrow. Small detail, but where shall we meet?"

"Do you know the George Washington Memorial?"

"Yes, I do."

"I'll see you there, at eleven am sharp."

"That's great. Goodnight and drive safely."

"I will. Goodnight."

Joanne climbed in to her car, started the engine, and drove away.

Mohammed moved towards his car, thinking, *'So far so good.'*

*　　　*　　　*

The Next Day – 1000 hours

Joanne looked out from her bedroom window across the manicured front lawn. The sky was blue, the sun shining and the birds were singing. She felt so much happier. She might have found the missing piece of her life, though only time would tell. It was only a twenty-minute drive to the Memorial. She wouldn't leave until ten-forty: she didn't want to appear *too* keen. Joanne was already dressed in stone-washed jeans and a loose fit cream sweater. She felt this enhanced her feminine features. She was proud of her body. She had good shaped hips and a moderate size bust, and at five feet seven tall she considered this to be proportionate. She walked downstairs to the kitchen.

"Tell me about last night then, dear?" asked her mom.

"Nothing to tell, really."

"What is he like?"

"Charming and polite."

"Is he American?"

"No. He's from the Middle East. Saudi Arabia, I think."

"I think they're too smooth for my liking. Keep an eye on him, though, Joanne. Don't be fooled by appearances."

"Oh, mother. The only time I have really been out with someone in ages, and I can already hear resentment."

"I just want you to be careful. I don't want to see you hurt. That's all."

"Thanks, mother. I'm meeting him at the Memorial Park at eleven am. I don't think I'll be late back."

"It's okay, I can manage!"

"Don't think that I will neglect you or start drifting away, it's just that I need a social life…" said Joanne reassuringly.

"I know, dear. You go and enjoy yourself."

"Thanks, I will, now."

Joanne left the house, and pointed her car in the direction of the Memorial. Mohammed was already at the car park by the time she arrived. She found him quite easily and parked as close to his car as possible. Mohammed came over and opened her door. She climbed out.

"Morning, Joanne. What a lovely day."

"Morning, Mohammed. Yes, it is." she said smiling.

"You look absolutely radiant again."

"Thank you," she said, blushing slightly but liking the compliment.

"Where shall we walk to? I'm in your capable hands. I'm the tourist and you're the guide."

"Okay. Let's walk this way." Joanne pointed as they began to walk.

"So what is the history behind the park, then?"

Joanne felt like a teenager on her first date, but was excited at the opportunity to impart her local knowledge.

"The Memorial Parkway is an area of natural beauty running along the Potomac River. It connects sites such as Mount Vernon, where George Washington once lived, passes through the nation's capital, which he founded, and ends at the great falls of the Potomac."

"How do you know all this?"

"Living here it is hard not to know the history. There are reminders everywhere."

"That's fascinating. You have so much to do here in America. It seems a shame that weekends are so short. You will be back at work tomorrow?"

"Yes, unfortunately."

"Why do you say that?"

"No particular reason."

"Do you enjoy your work?"

"At times, yes, but there are so many demands on the agency that I don't seem to make any headway."

"If you ever want to talk about it, I will always listen."

"Thanks, Mohammed, but you probably wouldn't understand."

"Try me," tested Mohammed.

"Some other time, maybe."

"Sure."

"Let's sit on that bench and take in these marvellous views." Joanne led the way to the bench and sat down first.

"I read in the news that the government has set up a new organisation. What is it called – Lizard, no?" said Mohammed teasing Joanne.

"Scorpion," chuckled Joanne.

"That's it."

"There are so many organisations here in the US. What is their function then, amongst all these other departments?" tested Naseer.

"Well, it's no secret really. They gather intelligence on terrorist groups who may have an undesirable interest in US assets."

"That sounds really exciting. Are you involved?"

"Yes. Not with the organisation, just as a liaison officer."

"So what is happening in the world of terrorism, then, Joanne? It must be a fascinating area?"

"There are some interesting developments, but I can't say what they are."

"Top secret, eh?"

"No. The agency doesn't overlap with Scorpion. They just ask us for help."

"What kind of help?"

"Finding information for them including from our assets abroad."

Although Joanne knew that she shouldn't be revealing this kind of information to Mohammed, she felt so comfortable with him that it seemed there wasn't anything to be concerned about – even if he was from the Middle East. He seemed honest and sincere. She'd now breached her personal boundaries as well as the work ones.

"Is it like the spy movies where the CIA has an agent at every embassy?"

"Something like that, yes. Can we change the subject, Mohammed, please?"

"Yes, I'm sorry, Joanne. How long have you lived around here?"

"Since I was a child. I was raised in this neighbourhood. My roots are here, and it would be difficult if I had to leave."

"Is there a chance of that? Promotion or something?"

"Promotion. No. I'm already at the top of my department. The only reason would be marriage, I suppose."

"Do you have a business card Joanne?"

"Why do you ask?" enquired Joanne.

"So that I can look at your name every day."

Joanne opened her purse, pulled out her card wallet and extracted a laminated card with the CIA logo emblazoned on it.

"Here you are."

"Thank you."

Mohammed looked at the card and noticed that under the name of Joanne S Wiley was the department she headed – Directorate of Intelligence. They both began to head back towards the car park.

"Thanks for another wonderful day, Joanne."

"I've enjoyed it too."

"Shall I call you in the week to arrange another time?"

"That would be nice. You don't have my number, though."

"I do now," said a confident Mohammed, flourishing her card.

Mohammed opened Joanne's car door. He kissed her on both cheeks again, and watched as she drove away. He pulled out his mobile phone and made a call.

*   *   *

Somewhere in the Kingdom of Saudi Arabia

The telephone rang in the flat of Ibrahim Khalil

"Yes," said Khalil in Arabic.

"The contact is the Directorate of Intelligence at Langley."

"Good. Anything else?"

"She has a direct link to Scorpion regarding operations."

"Anything else?"

"Not yet."

"You don't have a great deal of time to obtain what we need. Move more quickly," demanded Khalil.

"I'll see what I can do…"

Khalil hung up on him, and immediately dialled again: another international call.

"Things are moving according to plan," said Khalil.

"Everything must be in place in four weeks' time," said his contact.

"They will be," said Khalil hoping that his voice sounded confident enough.

"Keep me informed…" said the voice and cut the connection.

CHAPTER EIGHT

Copeland was still shuffling through the terrorist profiles hoping that something would stand out from the rest. No matter how hard he tried he just couldn't 'pick one'. His office phone rang, startling him.

"Jack, Joanne Wiley is on the line from Langley," said Mary.

"Thanks, Mary. Hello, Joanne, this is a nice surprise. To what do I owe the honour?"

"You asked me to ring you if anything came out of the embassies."

"Yes, I did. What have you got?"

"Well, the Marine Guard at the Khartoum embassy reported that a single vehicle has been taking undue interest in the front of the building: passing it several times. The passenger appeared to be drawing or making notes…"

"Recce or tourists?" he said to himself aloud, interrupting Joanne.

"What was that, Jack?"

"Just talking to myself. Anything else?"

"The same Marine noted that a man was standing on the corner across from the embassy taking photographs of the front entrance."

"We often get those, though. Did he say what he looked like? African or European, for instance?"

"No."

"What about the other locations, Joanne?"

"Nothing reported as yet."

"That's good. However, I was expecting more signs of unusual activity. There probably have been such, just not noticed yet... These people are good, Joanne, we're up against pros here. We need to be just as good – better yet, keep one step ahead. Joanne, I may have to call upon some of your agents to go deep to try and infiltrate some of the terrorist camps."

"That's no problem. We already have agents in these theaters of operation, all they need is a prod to wake them up."

"Thanks. I *have* managed to narrow the list of groups down to four."

"Only four from that list I gave you?"

"Yep. These fit the profiles of possibilities but the one which I am really interested in is a group called *AL-JAMA'A AL ISLAMIYYA* otherwise known as the Islamic Group."

"Why them in particular?"

"They have connections to the Bin Laden School of Terrorism out of Afghanistan. This is Egypt's largest terrorist group with funding from Saudi Arabia. They support attacks against US assets and facilities."

"There was a Bin Laden connection to the '98 bombings, wasn't there?" asked Joanne.

"Indeed. They haven't claimed responsibility, but I know they were involved somehow. What we don't have is any concrete evidence to point the finger. That's where I'm hoping some of your agents could help."

Joanne was thinking all of this through. What Copeland was asking was no small thing. She had never before been in a position where she had to activate agents in foreign areas.

"Regarding the active use of our agents, Jack, I will have to refer the matter to the Director, Mike, for his approval. I'm sure it will be okay, but you know how much bureaucracy and red tape we have here?"

"Sure, I understand. Get Mike to ring me if there is a problem."

"I will. Anything else, Jack?"

"No. Thanks again." Copeland put the phone down.

'Why only Khartoum?' Copeland asked himself and pondered a little longer: *'It's only just re-opened.'*

*   *   *

Mohammed Abdul Naseer had been a member of the Islamic Group – *AL JAMA'A AL ISLAMIYYA* – for eight years. Egyptian by birth, he now lived in Riyadh, Saudi Arabia. He had a degree from Cairo University in World Studies, and was spotted during his study years as a potential candidate for the group. Subsequently, he was recruited into the group in the early '90s as an intelligence officer. He had the responsibility of obtaining information on the vulnerability and accessibility of particular targets.

That was then. Now, he had been a sleeper in the US for the last four months. He knew that it was only a matter of time before he would be activated. His cover story, if the authorities ever questioned him, was that he was working for the Saudi Telecommunications Cartel initiative to expand into the global market of cellular phones. This was backed up by documentation. His credentials had to be watertight to stand up to the test of time and the inquisitive nature of any contacts. Prior to arriving in the US from Saudi via Cairo he had been instructed to make contact with the Intelligence Chief at CIA Headquarters in Langley, Virginia, when the time was right. The order had duly come through, and that was when he orchestrated the accident between himself and Joanne Wiley. He wasn't so sure about his latest instructions to move quickly. The timing just wasn't right. It was too soon after the initial contact. He might frighten her off and the time he had invested in the US solidifying his cover story would have been for nothing. He looked at Joanne's card and decided to make a call.

"Wiley," she answered.

"Joanne, it's Mohammed. How are you?"

"I'm fine. This is a nice surprise."

"I was ringing to see if you were free anytime this week?"

"My social calendar is so hectic these days! I'll have to check my diary."

"Well, if it's a problem, Joanne…"

"I was only kidding you, Mohammed. It would be nice to get together. What day did you have in mind?"

"Friday?"

"Sure. What if I cook us something special at my house? You can get to meet my mother. She's curious about you."

'I bet she is,' said Mohammed to himself. Being from the Middle East always raised a few Western eyebrows.

"Yes, that would be nice. I'll need directions…"

Joanne duly instructed him how to get from his hotel to her house. Mohammed already knew where she lived, but needed to maintain the fiction that they had met accidentally.

"I'll see you on Friday about eight pm. Enjoy the rest of your day."

"I will, and thanks for calling. 'Bye."

Joanne looked at the phone as she put it down. *'That was a nice surprise,'* she said to herself with a smile. Emotions now accompanied Mohammed when she thought of him. Friday could be special, and she intended to ensure it was. This could be the next turning point in her life. She hoped so, since a relationship had eluded her for so long. It was time to feel like a woman again.

*   *   *

The secure phone rang in the offices of Scorpion.

"Copeland."

"Jack, it's Mike over at Langley."

"Yes, Mike, what can I do for you?"

"Joanne briefed me on your request for a couple of agents. I only wish I could, Jack. Turn back the clock to the good old days during the Cold War era, and I would have had more than enough assets or foreign nationals on the CIA payroll. As you are probably aware, the agency hasn't escaped federal budget cuts, which is making us accountable for a lot more these days than we ever had been previously. Some of our operations, especially the clandestine ones have left a bad taste amongst the intelligence community and in particular the bill payers on the hill. This of course has left me with fewer resources. We throw money at a problem in the hope that at some point we will have a successful outcome. Some we do and some we don't but we are measured on our success rate. Though the Soviet Union is no longer our target, terrorism is in some ways harder to crack. We need more and better spies who can penetrate terrorist cells and the secretive regimes of Rogue States like Iraq and Libya. We're not as effective as we used to be, and past Presidential Administrations have all tried to distance themselves from our activities so that if anything goes wrong they can honestly put up their little mitts and swear that they knew nothing about it. It sucks, Jack. I figure all this bureaucracy, and their mistrust of the agency stems from when Presidents, frustrated by diplomats or the military, turned to spies and asked them to do the impossible. You know: those Presidents in the 1970's who ran the CIA through its worst scandals, and denied all knowledge. Now Presidents who believe in covert action as a tool of statecraft make sure to have a hands off policy. I'm surprised Scorpion exists at all."

"Jesus, Mike I hadn't realised it was that bad. Forget my request, it was a long shot in any case. You've got other, more important things on your mind. Thanks for trying, anyhow," offered Copeland, realizing his request was no small ask.

"Jack, with all the problems we have I've only just scratched the surface. The country can't do without us and yet all this government stonewalling and gibberish is so restrictive we can't get anywhere! The security of our great nation is at terrible risk unless we can get a handle on what is going on…"

"You might get that sooner than you think," said Copeland. "I'm sure that, whatever it is, it's imminent and it's going to be somewhere we are especially vulnerable," he continued.

"Even if I *could* help you, Jack, you know yourself that it takes time to infiltrate organisations and to build trust. There might not be enough time for that if you're looking at a short time hit. Also, this puts the lives of agents at risk if it isn't planned correctly, coupled with the fact that if we blow it, it will make infiltration harder in the future: our reputation for botching would undoubtedly precede us."

"I do get your point, Mike."

"Just thought I needed you to know the agency's position on this, Jack."

"Thanks for filling in the details, Director. 'Bye."

Copeland knew very well that it would be difficult to get any intel from within these groups in the time span he'd projected, but it had been worth a try. To do nothing to decrease vulnerability would inevitably keep the US wide open to attack: doing something (anything?) changed the situation from one of reaction to one of action. It was reactive situations that cost lives and produced panic rather than a reasoned response.

*   *   *

At eight pm sharp, Mohammed pulled into Joanne's driveway. Dressed in chino's, a light blue V-necked sweater and black polo shirt, he stepped out of his car, collecting a bunch of roses and a bottle of red wine from the front seat as he went. A knock at the door brought an immediate response from Joanne.

"Hi. No problem with the instructions then?"

"None at all."

"Come on in, Mohammed," invited Joanne.

Mohammed noted that Joanne was wearing a beige skirt above the knee and a black blouse. Her shoulder-length blonde hair was flowing. She looked stunning.

"Joanne, these are for you," said Mohammed, as he handed over the flowers. "The wine is for everyone," he continued.

"Thank you, Mohammed," said Joanne, with a broad smile of appreciation. She moved quickly into the kitchen to find a vase. She returned and placed flowers and vase on the dining table.

"They look really nice. Mohammed, I'd like you to meet my mother," Joanne said, directing Mohammed towards the sitting room.

"Mum, this is Mohammed Naseer, the gentleman I was telling you about."

"Pleased to meet you, young man. Joanne has told me so much about you," said Mrs Wiley, as she stood up from her chair.

"It's my pleasure, Mrs Wiley. I hope it was all good?" enquired Mohammed. "And I can see where Joanne gets her looks from," he said, teasing both Wiley ladies.

"You're making me blush now," said Mrs Wiley.

Joanne looked at her mom, who seemed to be favourably impressed by Mohammed. As long as Joanne could win the approval of her mother she would have no problems.

"I'll leave you two together for a few moments while I finish preparing the food," said Joanne as she returned to the kitchen.

Mrs Wiley and Mohammed talked quite comfortably whilst Joanne brought out the hot dishes from the kitchen onto the table.

"Okay, everyone, supper's ready."

Both Mohammed and Mrs Wiley joined Joanne at the table.

"This smells and looks really good, Joanne," commented Mohammed.

"You haven't tasted it yet," quipped Joanne.

Mohammed let Joanne and her mom help themselves to their portions before filling his own plate.

"So, Mohammed, where do you live when you are not in the States?" asked Mrs Wiley.

"Riyadh in Saudi Arabia. That's the capital city."

"What kind of job do you have?"

"I work for the Saudi Telecommunications Company."

"America is a long way from Saudi. What brings you here?"

"Mom, give Mohammed a breather, will you? I'm sure he doesn't want to be interrogated whilst he's eating!" interrupted Joanne.

"It's only a mother doing her duty for her daughter," said a defensive Mrs Wiley.

"No, it's okay, Joanne, really. Going back to your question, Mrs Wiley, I am over here to try to obtain some assistance from the American government to enable our country to expand its national and international infrastructure for cellular phones."

"Don't you have mobile phones in Saudi?" enquired Mrs Wiley.

"We do, but the network is not as robust as yours and the cost of calls is still very high. We are trying for a tripartite cartel to assist us in moving forward."

"I would have thought that with all the money from oil you would be a very developed country?"

"Money doesn't buy everything but it sometimes falls in to the wrong hands. We do not have the expertise to create the things that we need. We seek help from other countries such as yours and the UK."

"Were you born in Saudi, Mohammed?"

"No. Cairo, actually."

"You speak very good English."

"English is a subject taught in all our schools, and one in which you have to gain a qualification."

Mohammed turned to Joanne. "This is really nice, Joanne. Not only do you have beauty, but you are an excellent cook."

"It didn't take long to prepare," said a coy Joanne.

Joanne, Mrs Wiley and Mohammed finished eating almost simultaneously.

"Anyone for coffee?" asked Joanne.

"Please," replied Mohammed.

"Yes, dear," said Mrs Wiley.

Joanne left the table and returned with a coffeepot, milk, and sugar on a tray. She poured three cups, passing two of them to her guest and her mom.

"Shall we move over to the soft chairs?" enquired Joanne.

"Sure," agreed Mohammed.

"I'll just move these pots from the table, dear," said Mrs Wiley, without looking at either of them.

"Leave them, mom. We'll use the dish washer later."

"You two get sat down. I'll be with you soon."

Both Joanne and Mohammed moved across to the sofa and sat companionably together drinking their coffee.

"What kind of week have you had?" asked Joanne.

"Not very good, really."

"Oh? Why is that?"

"I haven't been able to progress any further with this cellular phone business. I'm under pressure to move quickly and obtain the right information. But I feel that if I rush things, then the end result will not be as expected and the effort that I have put in to it will have been a waste of time."

"Does that mean you could be here a little longer?"

"Maybe. I hope so," he added, knowing full well that once the targets had been destroyed his work would have been completed, and it would be time for him to extract himself back to Saudi or Cairo or wherever his next mission was going to be. He wasn't sure. He hadn't received those instructions yet. Mrs

Wiley had finished clearing the plates and returned to the lounge.

"I think it's past my bedtime, Joanne. I'll leave you two together. It was nice to meet you, Mohammed."

"My pleasure, Mrs Wiley."

"Goodnight, everyone. See you tomorrow. Joanne."

"Goodnight, mom."

Joanne waited until her mother got to the top of the stairs before continuing,

"Would you like some wine, Mohammed?"

"Please."

Joanne departed to the kitchen, returning with two glasses and the wine. She passed the wine and corkscrew to Mohammed.

"Would you do the honours?"

"Yes, of course."

With the cork removed, Mohammed poured two glasses of wine, passing one to Joanne.

"Let's have a toast," suggested Mohammed.

"Okay. To what?" enquired Joanne.

"To us," responded Mohammed.

"To us," said both Mohammed and Joanne, as they clinked glasses together.

"So, what do you think of my mom?"

"Wonderful woman. You resemble her in many ways."

Joanne placed her glass on the coffee table, and then sat back looking admiringly at Mohammed.

"What's wrong, Joanne?"

"Nothing, I was just thinking…it doesn't matter."

"Yes, it does. What's on your mind?"

"I can't help but think that our chance meeting, the day we bumped in to each other, was fate. I feel so comfortable with you around…" She paused, and then continued, "No it's silly really."

Mohammed leant forward to place his glass on the coffee table. He moved closer to Joanne, placing his arm behind her and across her shoulder. He then leant towards her and began to kiss her on the neck. Joanne responded by tilting her head backwards. He sensed a little nervousness in her body language, but was confident this could be overcome. He could hear her breathing change as excitement took over. He moved towards her ear lobes, teasing them with his tongue then directed himself to her lips, kissing them softly at first, then with passion. She was breathing more heavily now. He moved his right hand to her blouse and began to loosen the top buttons. He placed his hand inside her blouse and cupped her left breast. He teased her nipple with his fingers and it responded immediately through the lace material of her bra. She was excited now.

"Are you sure you want to do this, Joanne?"

"I've waited a long time for this moment. Let's enjoy this together."

Mohammed managed to unhook her bra. He lifted it over her head, and Joanne arched her back, emphasising her breasts. Mohammed cupped her breasts together, kissing each one in turn. He then teased each nipple until they were hard and their owner almost panting. Joanne lifted herself up and untucked his shirt from Mohammed's trousers. She slid her hand down his chest towards his groin. She noted that he was also excited, which increased her own arousal. Joanne stood up, shedding the remainder of her clothes whilst Mohammed looked on as this lithe tantalising act revealed all her wonderfully curvaceous charms.

Mohammed stood up so they could cooperate in removing the remainder of *his* clothes. They held each other close, taking comfort from each other in their vulnerable nakedness. Then they entwined and made sweet passionate love on the sitting room rug.

Afterwards, Joanne happily lay in the arms of her marvellous lover. It had been a long time since she had experienced lovemaking like that. She felt wonderful. She felt like a woman again. She also felt complete. Mohammed knew that this deepening bond would be difficult to break when the time came for him to leave. He wasn't quite sure which way he would go. Joanne leaned across Mohammed and kissed him on the lips.

"Thank you, Mohammed. That was wonderful."

Joanne stood up and walked towards the stairs. Mohammed admired this feminine form. She had a perfect body, sculpted by a skilled artist. Joanne returned clad in her dressing gown.

"Would you like some coffee?" asked Joanne.

"Please. Decaffeinated if you have any."

"No problem."

Mohammed could see that Joanne had relaxed and was now wearing a gentle smile. She was obviously feeling happy, but he was getting confused and out of focus. He mustn't let his emotions affect what he had to do! The time would soon come when he would have to make that judgement call. Joanne returned with the coffee.

"Thanks, Joanne."

"You're welcome."

Joanne sat down on the floor and leaned back into Mohammed's arms. She felt protected, secure. She also felt that this was, somehow, *right*.

Mohammed thought that this might be a good time to ask a few more questions. He would have to be careful in the structuring and presentation of his enquiries, so as not to make Joanne suspicious.

"So what kind of day have *you* had, Miss Joanne Wiley?"

"Pretty quiet, really. That's how I like it to be."

"What's happening with Scorpion?"

"How do you mean?"

"I'm just curious about these secret groups."

"Well they're not secret, just careful. Being from the Middle-East, Mohammed…"

"It's that obvious is it?" he asked, rhetorically.

Joanne chuckled "You will have heard about the Islamic Group?"

Mohammed raised an eyebrow. This was the kind of thing he was trying to get from Joanne, but hadn't expected it to be so readily offered!

"As far as I know they are an Egyptian terrorist group who have carried out numerous atrocities. Why do you ask, Joanne?"

"It's just a name that has cropped up at the office."

"Are Scorpion interested in this group?"

"Maybe."

"Who is in charge of the team?"

"Jack Copeland. His background is in Special Forces. Let's move away from work."

"I'm quite fascinated by all this, you know."

"There are things that I shouldn't be telling you. Are you married, Mohammed? Have someone waiting for you back home?"

"No and no. Like you, I haven't had the time to build a special relationship. I suppose that, at our ages, we should make some effort towards social interaction."

Mohammed looked at his watch. It showed 2.14 am.

"Joanne, I think I had better start making a move."

"Oh dear. I would ask you to stay but an inquisitive mother would make it a little awkward…"

"I fully understand."

Mohammed finished his coffee, dressed and then held out his arms to Joanne. She responded by moving in to the proffered hug. He cuddled her and pressed a kiss on her lips. The embrace seemed to last an eternity.

"I've had a wonderful evening, Joanne. Unfortunately all good things must come to an end."

"I hope not. I'll give you a call during the week."

"Okay. 'Bye," said Mohammed, as he stepped out of the house towards his car.

"'Bye," Joanne whispered.

Mohammed waved to her as he drove away. She responded, and then closed the front door. She stood there with her back to the door in a dream, thinking of Mohammed and what they had just experienced together. She cleared the cups into the kitchen, turned off the remaining lights, and took herself off to bed.

Joanne lay on the bed, still in her dressing gown and wondering why Mohammed had an interest in Scorpion. It *might* be the result of her offering the information in the first place, or, perhaps, he was just interested in its Middle-East role, since he was from that part of the world. '*Yes, that was probably it,*' she said to herself. Having resolved that burning question, Joanne removed her robe and climbed between the sheets. She quickly fell asleep.

*   *   *

The telephone rang in the apartment of Ibrahim Khalil.

"Yes," said Khalil half-asleep.

"Scorpion is taking an interest in our group. I think they have zeroed in on us."

"Good work. Well done, but stay calm."

"When do I leave?"

"When the time is right and when Allah wants you back. Anything else?"

"Not at the moment."

"Keep in touch." Khalil cut the connection.

Khalil made the usual follow-on call: "Scorpion are taking an interest in us," he said.

"What are they doing?" asked the voice at the end of the phone.

"I'm not sure, but…" Khalil was interrupted.

"What do you mean you're not sure? I pay you to get this information, and so far you haven't given me a great deal. Time is running short. Your next call better have what I need!" said the voice before the connection was severed.

'Imbecile. Does he not realise it all takes time?' Khalil complained to himself.

CHAPTER NINE

Copeland was looking over the satellite imagery provided by the recent MILSAT cross-over of Afghanistan. What he didn't have were comparisons. But he could get them…

"Mary, can you get me Phil Scott, please?"

Moments later the office phone rang, and Copeland pressed the hands free button allowing the call to come over the speaker.

"Copeland."

"Jack, it's Phil Scott. What can I do for you?"

"Thanks for the recent imagery of Afghanistan."

"No problem."

"How often are these photos taken?"

"Weekly."

"On the same day?"

"Yeah."

"Can I have the last three photographs of the site?" enquired Copeland.

"Sure, but what are you looking for?"

"I'll show you as soon as I've looked at the others."

"When do you want them?"

"This afternoon?" asked Copeland, thinking it was a tall order.

"Sure. I'll get the office to drop them off to you."

"It's OK, Phil, just give me a call and I'll pop over."

"Ok. Do you have anything that I might be able to brief the President on?"

"I'm trying to piece everything together at the moment. As soon as I do, I'll let you know. Thanks for your help, Phil."

"Don't mention it."

Dinger had heard Copeland's side of the conversation with Phil Scott.

"What was all that about, Jack?"

"These pictures definitely tell a story. The problem is they all tell the same story."

"I'm not with you."

"I bet the other ones that I have asked for show exactly the same details and information as this latest one. Do you know why?"

"They are taken of the same region?" said Dinger, stabbing in the proverbial dark.

"No. Well, yes, they are taken of the same region but that's not the real reason. The reason is that they are taken at the same time on the same day every week."

"Which gives those on the ground time to clear things away?"

"Correct, well done, Dinger. What needs to happen is a realignment of the satellite to take pictures on different days. That way you get a better perspective; it catches them off guard thereby creating more productive comparisons. I hope…"

"Dinger, give Captain Short a call and see how the lads are doing. Let's get an update on their operational status. Just in case."

Captain Short was the replacement for Dinger at TWaID. He was the one now responsible for the operational effectiveness of Jack's old command. Captain Short knew these highly trained individuals were to be available to Scorpion on VERY short notice. Copeland didn't want to lose all connection with the unit that had been his command for so long. These were the boys he would call upon to counter any insurgent attack. He wanted to make sure they were ready. In the far corner by the coffee table, Copeland had a twenty-eight inch wide-screen television for the sole purpose of keeping himself up-to-date with global news. It was often the case that news reporters knew what was going on before the intelligence services had any hard intel, so he tended to rely on the media for up to the minute bulletins. He switched the set on and flicked to the CNN channel. Onscreen was a report on the most recent conflict between the Palestinians and Israelis, with casualties rising daily. He noted the name of the reporter, Elisabeth Young. He'd seen her before, but couldn't place her. There was something about her that kept him staring at the screen totally oblivious of the report being made.

'*She must be the Middle-East correspondent for CNN,*' he thought. He was sure he would meet her one day.

Dinger re-entered the office with a brown envelope in his hand.

"Jack, this just arrived from the NSA. It must be the MILSAT photographs you were after," said Dinger as he handed the envelope over to Copeland.

"That was quick, thanks."

"What did Captain Short have to say?"

"The lads are in peak shape, just raring to see some action."

"They'll get their chance soon enough; I'm sure of it."

Copeland opened the envelope and extracted four oversized photographs taken by an orbiting MILSAT. He walked to the middle of the office and laid them on the floor. He picked up the one he had received that week and laid that next to the last one in chronological order.

"Dinger, what do you see in these photographs?"

"They all seem to show the same image to me."

"Exactly. That's why we need to reschedule the shots. This is a complete waste of time and resources. I'll speak with Joanne Wiley, she should be able to sort this out."

Copeland buzzed Mary.

"Mary can you get me Joanne Wiley over at Langley, please?"

Moments later the office telephone came to life.

"Copeland."

"Jack, it's Joanne at Langley. What can we do for you?"

"The MILSAT images that are obtained over Afghanistan are done weekly, right?"

"Yep," said Joanne, wondering where this conversation was leading.

"I've just had four sent over from Phil Scott; no wonder you guys can't see anything unusual."

"I don't follow."

"They all show the same thing. Nothing."

"Probably because nothing *is* happening."

"There's plenty happening out there, it's just that you're predictable. You take a shot at the same time and on the same day every week! The guys whose picture you're taking can read you like a book. They adjust their schedule accordingly."

"So, what are you saying, Jack?"

"Change it up. Re-align the MILSAT. Give it a new set of instructions and we'll catch these bastards with their pants down. There is something going on, Joanne, but with what you have at the moment we're blind."

"D'you know what it takes to reprogram the satellite?"

"No, but I do know it's not impossible. We need that info for analysis, Joanne."

"What part of Afghanistan are you primarily interested in?"

"The Hindu Kush Mountain range near Nuristan Provence north-east of Kabul. I appreciate that the mountain range is some 500 miles long and it'll be like looking for a needle in a hay stack but…"

"Okay I'll get on to it right away."

"Can you let me know when you expect the new program to take effect?"

"Sure. Anything else I can do for you?"

"No, that's all, Joanne. Thanks."

Copeland put the phone down and turned towards Dinger with a look of satisfaction on his face.

"You'd think I was asking for the world the way these people go on," complained Copeland.

"I suppose the agency thinks that no-one in that region would be intelligent enough to monitor and predict our satellite patterns."

"I'm inclined to agree. There are evil minds at work plotting god knows what from this desolate corner of our planet. We're talking about the international school of terrorism here. The region is vast which makes it ideal for those callous bastards to conceal themselves in the mountainous regions."

"What do you hope to find on the new images, Jack?"

"I'm hoping it will show movement of vehicles and people. If we can enhance the image and really zoom in, we should be able to get some clue as to where their hideout is located. Once we've ascertained that I want to concentrate on the area in and around Kabul."

"For what?"

"There are flat plains here so it is my guess that somewhere in this area there are training camps. The CIA hasn't picked up on this before, so they're breaking new ground. It's a long shot, but they've got all this fancy equipment so we may as well maximise its potential and swing it in our favour for once. It'll keep the wolves away from the door for a little while longer, and the tax payer happy."

"You're gonna piss a few people off by changing routines."

"It's routines that keep us predictable and get us nowhere. However, I can tell you what it does give us, and that's trouble, with a capital 'T'. When you're predictable, people can easily second-guess your next move. It should be the other way round. *We* should be predicting *theirs*. I would like to think that the intelligence services of this great country of ours holds all the aces. Sometimes I'm not so sure. The '98 bombings caught them napping."

"The thing is, Jack, we simply can't monitor every single inch of the globe."

"Where America has interests, why the hell not? If they kept their eyes and ears to the ground a bit more…it's amazing what you can pick up. I'm still concerned that nothing has been reported out of the Middle-East embassies."

"Perhaps there's nothing to report."

"There is. It's just that they haven't seen it yet. I don't want to recommend a heightened security condition until something else comes in. My other concern is that it may already be too late. Do some background digging on this character Osama bin Mohammed bin Awad bin Laden, would you?"

"Bit of a mouthful. Anything in particular?"

"Everything. He's got plenty of skeletons in the cupboard."

Dinger frowned at that last statement, but didn't ask. He had his orders and would get on to it right away.

*   *   *

US Embassy, Freetown, Sierra Leone

The black Mercedes stopped by the road works on Sanders Street. The man controlling the red and green flags looked casually towards the car. There were three people inside, two in the front and one in the rear. He made a mental note. He raised the green flag. The Mercedes drove on towards Siaka.

*   *   *

US Embassy, Khartoum, Sudan

A Red Mazda van containing two Arabs stopped in front of the embassy. One man stepped out and walked across to the stall opposite. The vendor passed a piece of paper to the man who retreated and climbed back into the vehicle before it drove away.

*   *   *

US Embassy, Cairo, Egypt

A white Toyota pick-up had been parked adjacent to the embassy wall for two days. Its occupant had watched from the Market Square opposite, in the event that embassy staff might take an interest. None taken. He would report this.

*   *   *

US Embassy, Tripoli, Libya

A man on a Suzuki motorcycle pulled up on the road outside the front of the embassy. He began to take photographs of the buildings either side of the embassy, and the front of the embassy itself. He was not challenged. He would report this.

*   *   *

US Embassy, Casablanca, Morocco

A group of people demonstrated at the front of the embassy. Two Marine Guards were posted outside the front door. Demonstrators were not challenged or moved on by local police. Vehicles were parked in front of the embassy.

*   *   *

CIA Headquarters, Langley, VA – Office of the Directorate of Intelligence

Mike stepped into Joanne's office.

"Joanne, Anne and I are having a party over at our place on Friday night. Can you make it?" asked Mike, as he entered Joanne's office.

Anne was Mike's wife of fifteen years. She was forty-four years old, and they had two boys aged twelve and ten. Mike had asked her to give up her career as a secretary at Langley when they got married. She reluctantly agreed and was now eager to restore her pride and return to employment at Langley. The sooner the better: she was becoming bored being at home. She missed the human interaction that is common in today's modern workplace. She seemed to be losing some of her social skills, and was hoping that a party would help her polish up some long-unused skills.

"Sorry, Mike, but I may be busy this weekend."

"That's the first time I've heard you turn down an invitation."

"I do have a life of my own outside Langley, you know," snapped Joanne.

"It must be serious?" said Mike defensively.

"What do you mean?" quizzed Joanne.

"Well, for you to retort like that, there must be someone in your life."

"If you must know, it is someone who I met by accident – in its literal sense."

"I thought you were determined to remain the most eligible spinster in town! Come on, then, I'm intrigued now. Who is he?"

Joanne felt that she needed to be cautious here as to how much she gave away. But what the hell, she was feeling much happier than ever before.

"Do you remember the day I received a call saying that my mom had been attacked?"

"Yeah, that was about three or four weeks ago, wasn't it?"

"Right. Well, on the way back do you recall that I mentioned having an accident?"

"Sure."

"Well, the driver of the other car is the person I've been dating."

"You dark horse, Joanne. What's his name?" teased Mike.

"Mohammed Naseer."

"That's not American, is it?"

"Very astute of you. Now I can see why you're the Director of the Agency," said a sarcastic Joanne before continuing, "No, it's of Middle Eastern origin."

"May I ask where?"

"Saudi Arabia," replied a cagey Joanne.

"Is he rich?"

"Why all the questions?"

"I'm just curious as to who he is and how he managed to win you over so quickly. That's all."

"He's charming and fun to be with."

"What's he doing in the States?"

Joanne was talking fluidly now. Out of annoyance more than anything else. She didn't mind divulging information on her new acquaintance. The office banter was bound to be harder to deal with.

"He works for the Saudi Telecommunications Company. He's here to get some assistance from our government to help expand their cellular network. Apparently, there is a three-party involvement, US, UK and Saudi who hope to bring the best heads together to create a better framework."

"I think I read something about that. Have you checked him out?"

"No. Why should I?" said Joanne defensively.

"Because you are the Head of the Directorate of Intelligence, Joanne, and he's from the Middle East. Do you not think that it was more than a chance meeting? That it could have been orchestrated, for instance?"

Joanne stared at Mike. He was now casting doubt on Mohammed's credentials. The night Joanne and Mohammed made love, she had thought then that he was taking an unusual interest in Scorpion for someone who worked for a telecommunications company. However, Joanne was starting to fall in love, and her reasoning was emotionally skewed. Had she made the right decision to get involved, or was this a *really* bad judgment call and the beginning of a disastrous sequence of events?

"The accident was actually my fault, Mike. I was travelling too fast when his car came out of the side street. I couldn't avoid hitting his car."

"Do you remember you said to me that you had had a call from the police over at Arlington Precinct?"

"Yes, I do."

"I checked on your behalf as I said I would do, and there was no such call made from the precinct. What do you make of that?"

Joanne didn't reply. Everything was moving too quickly and things were starting to stack up against Mohammed.

"How deeply are you involved with him?"

"That's none of your goddamned business, Mike."

"If it involves National Security then I think you will find it is. The first person to come into your life in ages and you get so emotionally involved that you've forgotten the basic rules."

"Why do you think everybody's bad, Mike? There are some good people around. I'm just trying to add something to my life that has been missing for a really long time. I do believe that I have found love. Would you deny me that?"

"All I'm saying, Joanne, is be careful, and do some background checks on this guy. Okay?"

"Alright," said Joanne, knowing that she probably wouldn't.

"Has Jack Copeland been in touch lately?"

"Yeah. He's asked for the MILSAT to be reprogrammed to take some more snaps over Afghanistan. The ones he has already are next to useless."

"Why those ones?"

"He wouldn't tell me. He must have his reasons, and, of course, he has the President's authority."

"Has it been reprogrammed yet?"

"I've submitted the new co-ordinates, but it will take a couple of hours to change position."

"Finish early this afternoon and take the rest of the day off. Get your life sorted out, Joanne. You can't be too careful in your position."

"Thanks, but let me be the judge of that."

"You're destined for greater things in the agency. You could even be tipped to take over as Director. It's well within your ability. Don't throw that away. See you later."

Mike left Joanne's office and returned to his. He made a series of phone calls. He arranged twenty-four-hour surveillance of Joanne and the monitoring of her cell, home and office phones. Mike couldn't take any chances. If nothing abnormal was reported then national security should still be intact, but if it went the other way, then… Mike didn't want to think about it. It meant that the agency had been betrayed by one of its own, and he would have to act accordingly. He really hoped that it wouldn't come to that. He knew Joanne was a professional and dedicated to her job, but love can make people do things that they would otherwise think twice about doing. He would wait to see what would be reported.

*   *   *

Joanne still hadn't memorised Mohammed's phone number, so she rummaged in her purse, and rang him on the office phone.

"Mohammed Naseer," said the voice at the other end.

"Mohammed, it's Joanne. We need to speak," she said anxiously.

"It's nice to hear your voice too. What's the panic?"

"I can't tell you at the moment. Can we meet this afternoon?"

"Sure. Name the place."

"The car park at the George Washington Memorial at four pm."

"Okay. See you then."

Joanne had started to perspire. Beads of sweat formed on her top lip, reminiscent of her first date with Mohammed. She needed to resolve certain issues with him before their relationship could develop any further.

*   *   *

Office of the Director, CIA, Langley, VA

The telephone rang.

"Sir, we've intercepted an outgoing call made from the office of the DoI. She has made contact with the target and a meeting has been set for four pm today at the George Washington Memorial car park."

"Keep me posted," said Mike.

He was feeling a little disappointed in Joanne. He hadn't expected her to act so quickly. He would monitor the situation.

*   *   *

Joanne left the office at three-thirty and headed for her car, parked in the lower ground secure parking lot below Langley

She climbed in and drove through the control barriers onto the freeway. At the same time, a second car left Langley from the surface car park, remaining three cars and a discreet distance behind hers. Its two occupants would be in constant contact with the Director at Langley. The car park at the George Washington Memorial was unusually busy for that time of day. Joanne parked in the first available slot she could find. She climbed out and began to walk along the roadside line of parked cars, looking for Mohammed. She didn't see him in his car, causing Mohammed to jump out quickly and run after her. As luck would have it, he caught up with her in the area the surveillance team had chosen. The gun microphone had an operational distance of a hundred metres and was plugged into a state-of-the-art tape recorder. The video camera had a downlink to Langley and was covertly deployed within the car.

"Hey, Joanne. What's the urgency?" enquired Mohammed.

"Mohammed, I'm worried. I've had a roasting from my boss today concerning us. He thinks you're some kind of terrorist because you come from the Middle East. All that stuff I told you about Scorpion was because I thought you were genuinely interested."

"I was very much interested in what you had to say, but you don't honestly believe that I am a terrorist, do you?"

"I don't know what to believe. I need some assurance from you that you're not linked in any way with terrorist groups. Can you honestly promise me that?"

"I'm over here on official business for the Saudi Telecommunications Company. Nothing else."

"I'm sorry to doubt you, Mohammed, but my position is very delicate. I don't want to spoil what we have together, but I need to be sure that you will be honest with me about *everything*. Deal?"

"Okay."

Mohammed felt uncomfortable now. Joanne was beginning to lose trust in him. It might well be harder to gain the information that he required from her. But he wasn't about to give up.

"How are Scorpion doing, anyway?" he teased.

"You're impossible, Mohammed," said Joanne, laughing before continuing, "They're looking at Afghanistan now, so it looks like Saudi is off the menu."

"That's good to hear. I would like to know more about Scorpion when you have more time. I'm very interested in things like that."

"I've been given the afternoon off, so do you fancy coming back to my place for coffee?"

"I'd best not Joanne. Can we get together later in the week?"

"Yes, sure. Give me a call and we'll arrange something."

"I will."

Mohammed and Joanne began walking back to her car. They hugged and kissed before Joanne climbed into her car and drove off. Mohammed waited until she had disappeared from view before making a phone call.

"I think they're on to me," said Mohammed to his control.

"Are you sure?" said Ibrahim.

"Yes. I haven't been identified but it will only be a matter of time. Some information for you: Scorpion are concentrating on Afghanistan."

"That's good. It keeps them away from our targets. We don't have much time left before Allah seeks revenge. Keep in touch," and Ibrahim hung up, as usual.

*   *   *

Operations Room, CIA Langley, VA

Mike was sitting in the ops room at the agency watching the live link from the surveillance unit at the George Washington Memorial monitoring the conversation between the target, Mohammed Naseer, and an unknown via a cellular phone. Mike had already obtained the cell phone number of the target from the phone intercept on Joanne's office telephone. He had initiated a trace of the number being called. The call was cut short, ensuring any attempt to trace the recipient would fail. What *was* known was that it was an international call; the dialling prefix that of Saudi Arabia.

Mike picked up his phone and punched in the number that connected him directly with Scorpion.

"Copeland," said the voice.

"Jack, it's Mike over at Langley, how you doing?"

"I can see why I refused promotion in the military with all this paperwork shuffling. That's not why you called, though, is it?"

"No. We may have a problem."

"How big?"

"One of my people has come into contact with a possible undesirable. It's containable at the moment, but some information regarding Scorpion may have been leaked."

"By what source?"

"I can't say at the moment. There may be a connection with Saudi Arabia. I have surveillance on the leak and target but I thought you ought to know."

"Where is this target?"

"Nearby."

"He or she?"

"He."

"Thanks, Mike. I think we may be heading in the right direction after all. Let me know as soon as you have anything else. Oh by the way, is Joanne in this afternoon?"

"No. I sent her home early. Why?"

"I just wanted to know if any other security issues have been reported out of the Middle-East Embassies?"

"She'll be back in the morning."

"Okay. 'Bye."

Copeland wondered if the target was a sleeper and what his mission might be. These questions would have to be answered. Mike would undoubtedly brief him with only what he wanted Copeland to know, but Jack would push him for more information since he knew that Mike would withhold information as any true intelligence officer would.

Copeland pressed the intercom for his secretary.

"Mary, can you get me Dinger, please?"

Moments later the phone rang. "Copeland."

"Jack, it's Dinger, what's happening?"

"Where are you at the moment?"

"Stuck in the evening rush hour. Probably take me about forty-five minutes to get to you. Is it urgent?"

"Come straight back to the office. I've got some intel for you from Langley."

"See you in about an hour then."

Dinger was true to his word. He parked his car in the basement car park, and took the elevator to the thirty seventh floor, arriving on the hour.

"What's the urgency, Jack?"

"I had a call from Mike this afternoon. One of their agents has made contact with a possible undesirable from Saudi Arabia."

"Professionally or socially?" enquired Dinger.

"Not yet verified, but it seems that information regarding our operation may have been leaked."

"To what extent?"

"Not known. Mike has initiated surveillance on both target and source. This could be the breakthrough we've been waiting for. My concern at the moment is why is he here in the US? My focus has been the Middle East."

"Where is the target at the moment?"

"Local. That's *it*, Dinger! What would I do without you? It makes complete sense that he is here: where better to source information about Scorpion than on our doorstep?"

"Why don't Langley pull him and the source in at the same time, and find out what the hell is happening?"

"Let's see what develops. Now, what have you got in relation to Bin Laden?"

Dinger ruffled through his notes before he began:

"He has a number of aliases. Sometimes he is called 'The Prince', 'The Emir', 'Abu Abdallah', 'Mujahid Shaykh', 'Hajj', and 'The Director'. I thought to have one name was bad enough, but this guy must get confused trying to remember who he is from one day to the next. He was born in 1957 in Saudi Arabia. Height is six four to six six, weighing approximately one hundred and sixty pounds. Thin build, brown hair, brown eyes, olive complexion. Whereabouts presently unknown. He's a popular guy, Jack."

"Why do you say that?"

"Our government have offered a bounty of five million for information leading to his capture or conviction."

"What about any involvement in terrorist attacks?"

"He's been linked to some of the most notorious events from '93 through to the present day."

"Go on, you've got my attention now."

"The '93 World Trade Centre bombing in New York left six dead and thousands injured. In Manila in 1994 there was an attempt planned on President Clinton's life. It was abandoned after a bomb factory caught fire. 1998 saw the bombing of the Khoban Towers in Saudi Arabia killing nineteen US military personnel. '98 was also the year in which the US Embassies in Nairobi and Tanzania were targeted, killing more than two hundred and twenty people in total. Still in '98, another planned assassination attempt on President Clinton in Pakistan was thwarted when his trip was cancelled. That's it."

"He can run, Dinger, but he can't hide. What about finances?"

"He is reported to be receiving millions of dollars from Saudi businessmen. What is interesting is that our intelligence services have obtained an audit report showing recent transfers from Saudi Arabia's largest bank to charities that serve as fronts for Bin Laden."

"Any idea what these are used for?" enquired Copeland.

"Said to be 'Protection Money' aimed at staving off attacks on businessmen's properties. Uses? No concrete data."

"Is he married?"

"It is reported that he is estranged from his family, which runs Saudi Arabia's largest construction company. He's obviously not happy with his own country."

"How do you mean?"

"He has called for the overthrow of the Saudi government."

"He doesn't pick small fry does he? Taking on the Saudi government is not a simple thing. I think we've got a damned good picture of this guy, Osama bin Laden. Well done, Dinger. The only thing that we don't know about him is his current whereabouts. That's why I asked for a re-programming of the MILSAT over Afghan. I think we can safely say, Dinger, we're getting close to something, but what that is I don't yet know. It's getting late now, so let's knock it on the head and resume in the morning."

"That's the best thing I've heard all day," sighed an exhausted Dinger.

CHAPTER TEN

Mohammed left his hotel room on the sixth floor and walked the long corridor to the waiting elevator. Depressing the G button, the elevator responded and stopped as requested at the ground floor. The doors parted with the fluidity of a well-oiled machine. Stepping out, Mohammed quickly scanned the foyer and reception area, taking in what he saw and dismissing what he thought was irrelevant. There was a well-built older man standing to the right of the reception desk in a dark blue business suit that looked a little tight around his waist. He was busy talking on his cellphone: probably arranging his next client meeting or wrapping up the day's events with his secretary. Two men in jeans and casual tops sat on couches that had been set out in a square in front of the reception desk. Both were reading the New York Times and neither looked in his direction. Satisfied, he approached the receptionist who sensed his approach. She looked up:

"Good evening, Sir."

He looked into her eyes. They were brown, but large and strikingly beautiful. He loved beautiful women but they were a distraction. Composing himself, he needed to respond and began in a soft voice.

"Good evening, umm…Jane" picking out her name from the badge on her left lapel. "Where can I get an Arabic newspaper?" he continued.

The receptionist replied with a courteous smile. "If you step out onto the sidewalk, turn left and continue down to the next block you should be able to pick one up there."

"You're very kind. Thank you." Mohammed turned towards the exit doors.

"You're welcome," she responded with a coy smile.

He made his way towards the revolving door but decided to use the single door to the right of it instead. There's no way out if you get trapped, whether accidentally or otherwise. Mohammed glanced back to see Jane smile at him as he left the hotel. Stepping onto the sidewalk, he stopped by the kerb. It was cold, the bitter chill in the air making the temperature feel lower than it was. He rubbed his hands together to encourage the blood flow in his fingers, and then blew warm air into his cupped hands. He pulled his coat tightly around him, and pulled up the collar to keep out that evening air. He glanced up and down the street. First one way then the next. The traffic was pretty heavy, but free flowing. There were a number of cars parked nearby along the kerb, on both sides of the road. Most appeared to be empty but he was interested in the ones that had two up. No one looked in his direction. Not that he expected them to. Mohammed was sure that, by now, someone somewhere would be watching him, noting and reporting his every move.

Thrusting his hands deep into his coat pockets, he turned and began to slowly walk away from the hotel in the direction the receptionist had indicated. Subconsciously, he wanted to hear the sound of a car door opening to convince him that he wasn't being paranoid. He heard plenty of noises, but not that one. He didn't want to turn round, but did and noticed a tall lean man with a dark grey trench coat stepping out of a car some fifty yards away. The sidewalk was fairly busy but he would find it difficult to hide if he had to. Mohammed stopped at the corner for what seemed like ages as the crossing lights changed to 'Walk', and then back to 'Don't Walk'. The man he saw step out of the car continued past him and across the road. Having watched him reach the other side, Mohammed turned around and approached the street vendor. The vendor looked cold and bored, but had the company of a steaming polystyrene cup of coffee perched atop a bundle of tied newspapers. Mohammed saw what he was looking for, and picked up the Al-Hayat newspaper from the rack at the front of the stall, folding it and placing it under his left arm, whilst he fumbled for change with his other. He handed over a five-dollar bill.

"Keep the change," he said as he walked away.

He began to retrace his steps, heading back towards the warmth, comfort and relative security of the hotel, stopping periodically and looking over his shoulder – *nothing*. They were either very good, which he was sure they would be, or there was genuinely nothing there at all. He re-entered the lobby and headed straight to the elevators without even a glance towards the receptionist who looked a little disappointed. He took the middle elevator and as it ascended, he opened the newspaper to the personal section, as he did each week, but this time something caught his eye.

'AS A RESULT OF NEW DEVELOPMENTS, THE SAUDI COMMUNICATIONS REPRESENTATIVE IN THE UNITED STATES IS TO CONTACT HIS OFFICE URGENTLY AND WITHOUT DELAY.'

The elevator door opened and he closed the paper and walked back to his room. He quickly swiped the key card and entered the room, closing the door behind him where he stood for several minutes. His heart was racing and although it was freezing outside, he had beads of sweat on his upper lip. He felt uncomfortable but he didn't know why. Was it the possibility that he was being watched or was it because he now had to make a call, which in effect would mean that he would have to carry out the task that he had come to do? He wasn't sure if he was ready for this yet. He pulled out his cell phone and looked at it as if expecting it to come to life. He scrolled through the address book to the number he wanted, paused, and then dialled.

*   *   *

Office of the CIA Director, Langley.

Mike's cell phone rang. He looked at the screen and accepted the call, but had to wait for the scramblers to kick in before he could speak. It was one of the analysts.

"Yes, Douglas."

"We've intercepted a call made by Mohammed. Again to the same country and the same number."

"That's probably his controller. Were you able to pinpoint where it was received?"

"No. He wasn't on long enough."

"Did you tape the conversation?"

"Yes. He was told to watch a CNN broadcast at four ten in the morning, to move more quickly on his contact and to find out more about this new task force, strengths and capabilities etcetera."

"Anything else?"

"No. It was severed after that. Another newspaper was picked up again. Same routine."

"Have it handed in to the Middle-East desk for translation."

"Already done."

*   *   *

He lay on top of the hotel bed and decided to get a few hours' sleep before watching the news broadcast. It wasn't long before he dropped off. Mohammed wasn't privy to the overall plan, but he could sense the increase in activity. There was also the urgent need for information from his contact. A loud shrill from his alarm woke him at four in the morning after seven hours sleep.

His body reluctantly moved to the en-suite and a splash of cold water brought some life back into him. He switched on the TV and found CNN. Right on cue, CNN crossed live to Qatar television. He recognised the two men on the screen and once the statement had been given he knew exactly what had to be done. Mohammed was getting used to the way of life in the States. It had been so relaxing and easy going over the previous weeks and months. Now he was about to do something that would jeopardise all that. He knew it would be a testing time in the friendship he had formed with Joanne. He wouldn't admit it to anyone else, but he was beginning to become fond of her. That was the hardest part.

*   *   *

Copeland was in a deep slumber, but was subconsciously aware of a loud ringing noise. He fumbled for his alarm and pushed all the buttons. Nothing happened. The noise still continued unabated. He checked his watch alarm then realised it was the phone on his bedside cabinet. Through blurry eyes, he looked at the red LED display on his alarm clock. 4.05 am. He switched on the table lamp and eventually picked up the secure receiver.

"Yeah," he said, half asleep and eyes squinting against the light.

"Jack, it's Mike."

"Who?"

"Mike over at Langley."

"Don't you people ever sleep? D'you know what time it is?" He knew that Mike would be aware of the time, but he had to ask him.

"Switch on your TV, and tune in to the CNN channel."

"Nobody in the world is awake at this time in the morning, except for those nocturnal creatures who crave the excitement of the graveyard shift."

Copeland almost fell out of bed. He staggered over to the TV, picked up the remote and pressed the power button that brought the TV to life. It was already set to CNN. Rubbing the sleep from his eyes, he tried to focus. Mike was still on the phone line so Copeland picked up the handset.

"Is that who I think it is?" asked Copeland.

"You've got it in one. Osama bin Laden," confirmed Mike.

"What's he doing?"

"Playing dumb at the moment. The other guy that's speaking is his top lieutenant, Ahmed Bin Khalid."

The TV screen now had Copeland's full attention as the statement was read out.

"We have declared Jihad against the US Government, because the US Government is unjust, criminal and tyrannical. It has committed acts that are extremely unjust, hideous and criminal whether directly or through support of the Israeli occupation of the Prophet's Night Travel Land (Palestine). And we believe the US is directly responsible for those who were killed in Palestine, Lebanon and Iraq."

The most important statement was left to the end to so that it had the impact it was intended to give, and had everyone on the edge of their seats:

"IT IS NOW TIME TO TAKE ACTION AGAINST THE INIQUITOUS AND FAITHLESS US IN THE MIDDLE EAST".

The broadcast was being transmitted live by the Qatar TV Network. Copeland noticed that Bin

Laden, dressed in traditional Yemeni robes and sporting a traditional dagger, looked on approvingly as his lieutenant gave the statement. Was the Saudi militant unleashing his terror operatives? Copeland spoke into the telephone handset.

"Since we don't know his intended targets, push out a cascade warning, under the umbrella of SECRET to all our assets in the Middle East from embassies to troops to ships."

"Already being drafted. Do you want to call the NSA?"

"Yep. I'm gonna have to on this one. Thanks for the call, Mike."

"No problem."

Copeland went into the bathroom and swilled his face with cold water. He dried off then returned to his bedroom. He picked up his secure phone, and dialled the secure number for the National Security Advisor to the President of the United States. Connection was made almost immediately, but there was a delay in the recipient answering the call.

"Phil Scott," said the NSA. Copeland knew that he was trying to sound fully awake, but he would be in the same condition that Copeland was when he received his call from Langley.

"Phil, it's Copeland."

"Jack. What time is it?"

"Four twenty-five."

"Am or pm?"

"You should be so lucky. It's am."

"What have I done to deserve a call at this ungodly hour of the morning? Has war broken out?"

"Not yet."

"So, what's so important?"

"CNN have relayed a live picture broadcast from Qatar TV involving Osama bin Laden. Although he didn't speak, his sidekick, Ahmed bin Khalid, read out a statement saying it was time to take action against the US in the Middle East."

"What do you make of it?"

"Given his past history, I don't think it is an idle threat. He didn't identify what the targets were, so that's a pretty grey area. If we put everything on a heightened state of alert for god knows how long, it would strain everyone."

"Any suggestions, Jack?"

"Langley are alerting all US assets in the Middle East to a possible terrorist strike, the sponsor being Bin Laden. They are urged to be fully alert as to any unusual activity and to report back to Langley."

"Sounds good to me. I'll brief the President. He'll probably want to speak with you sooner rather than later. Anything else?"

"Not yet."

"Thanks for the call. You may have been right after all."

Copeland hated being right because nobody ever believed you no matter how convincing your arguments were. People just went into denial in the hope that the problem would go away or would not exacerbate. The danger now was that an endless stream of often-contradictory cables, informant tip-offs and electronic intercepts would overwhelm the intelligence service. Analysts would have to analyse all in-coming traffic, and then prioritise action on those that seemed to be likely targets. This all takes time. Time that Copeland knew he didn't have.

*   *   *

Five hours later Mohammed made another call from his hotel room.

"Wiley," said Joanne, as she picked up her telephone handset in her office.

"Joanne, it's Mohammed,"

"How are you on this fine crisp spring morning?"

"I'm fine, thank you. You're up nice and early. What's the occasion?"

"I was ringing to ask if you were free this evening?"

"Well, actually, Mohammed, I have to take mom to see her friends. I tell you what; I'll drop her off and then get straight back home. You can meet me there about 8 pm if you like. Is that okay?"

"That's fine, Joanne. Are you sure that's no trouble?"

"Just accept it or I might change my mind!"

"I like a domineering woman."

"You ain't seen nothing yet. Anyway it'll be nice to see you again. See you later."

"Sure. 'Bye."

*   *   *

CIA, Langley

Mike decided to sleep in the office as it was late and he didn't want to disturb his wife as he stumbled through the door at an ungodly hour. She understood, but it was difficult. The silence of the night was broken when his telephone rang.

"Yeah," said Mike half asleep

"Sir, we've intercepted a call in to the DOIs office from the target," reported the duty analyst.

"Yeah and?"

"She's meeting him at eight pm tonight at her house."

"Thanks."

*   *   *

The Next Day

The telephone began to ring in the offices of Scorpion. "Copeland."

"Jack, I have the President on line two," said Mary.

"Thanks, Mary," said Copeland as he pressed line two. "Good morning, Mr President," continued Copeland.

"Morning, Jack. Phil Scott has briefed me on the events last night. Quite a show, wasn't it? What do you make of it?"

"He cites the Middle East, but where in the Middle East? It's one hell of a region, Mr President. I wouldn't know where to start looking. We have a lot of assets from buildings through airbases through naval hardware scattered all over the Middle East. Why couldn't he have been more specific?"

"That would be too easy for us."

"I get the feeling that he is trying to scare us in to shuttering all our embassies in a bid to weaken US foreign relations," said Copeland.

"That's how I interpret this as well. What do you suggest?"

"We can't do anything. Close the embassies and you give in to terrorism. Your position as President would be untenable. You would be forced out of office."

"I have to be seen to be doing *something*, god damn it!" exclaimed the President.

"A security memo has already been sent to all Middle East assets asking them to be more aware of their surroundings. We can't do anything else at the moment. You can't put everything on a heightened state of alert for a time frame that we don't know. That would just weaken morale. The down side to this, Mr President, is that we may have to accept the prospect of losing some of our assets, including people and materials. We don't know what his MO is, so until something happens we can't get a clear picture as to his intentions. After that we can act and hopefully save any further losses."

"I see your point, Jack. Thanks for the briefing. I just hope we can do something to help those people so far from home."

"So do I, Mr President. So do I."

*   *   *

Outside the house of Joanne Wiley – 2000 hours

Mohammed sat in his car outside Joanne's house. She hadn't yet returned. There were a number of other cars parked along the kerb. This was natural for a residential area, so he paid no attention to them. Moments later, he saw a set of headlights moving towards him. He hoped it was Joanne. His hopes were confirmed when the car turned in to the driveway. She stepped out of her car and walked towards Mohammed. They hugged and kissed and then they both walked towards the front door. He put his arm around her shoulders.

"It's chilly tonight, isn't it?" he said

"Yes. Would you like a cup of tea, wine or beer?" asked Joanne as she inserted her key in to the front door lock.

"Tea would be nice, thanks."

They entered the house and Mohammed closed the door behind him. Joanne removed her coat and hung it on the coat peg by the front door. Mohammed did the same with his. He then followed Joanne into the kitchen, where she began preparing the tea.

"What time do you have to collect your mom, Joanne?"

"Not until ten pm. Why?"

"I just need some time with you, that's all."

"It must be serious. We'll talk in the front room."

Joanne finished making the tea and handed a cup to Mohammed. They both moved in to the sitting room.

"So what kind of day have you had?" asked Mohammed

"Pretty quiet, really. How about you?"

"Same. There doesn't seem to be much activity at the moment. It's as if I've hit a brick wall and can't move any further forward."

"That must be frustrating for you?"

"It is. At least I get some free time to be able to see you."

"Any news on when you are likely to return home?"

"Not yet. I hope I don't, really. I'm quite happy here, with you."

"Do you really mean that?"

"Yes," said Mohammed looking directly in to Joanne's eyes.

They closed the small gap between them and kissed, sensuously at first, then with true passion.

Joanne broke off, then took Mohammed's hand and led him upstairs to her bedroom. This time there would be no inhibitions, or any doubt. She stood by the bed looking at his face and into his eyes. She was looking for that commitment. There was no hesitation in either of them. Mohammed began to undo the front buttons of Joanne's blouse, whilst she helped him remove his jumper and shirt. He had a well-defined body. He obviously looked after himself.

Mohammed removed the blouse from Joanne's shoulders then unhooked her bra, removing it completely. He cupped both breasts in his hands and teased each nipple with his tongue until they became pert. Joanne began to move her body, sensing the excitement. He gently laid her down on the bed, removing her skirt and then admiring her body as she lay there. He removed the remainder of his garments, and then he lay on top of her, gently caressing every part of her body. This sent Joanne into spasms.

"Make love to me now, Mohammed," demanded Joanne.

Their bodies entwined and they moved in beautiful harmony. The passion that both had enjoyed had made their skins shine with perspiration. Now Joanne and Mohammed lay on the bed together beneath the cotton sheets. Holding each other in silence. They were thinking about what had just happened. Mohammed was thinking that he was getting more deeply involved with Joanne, whilst Joanne was thinking that this cemented their relationship, and she would approach discussing that when the time was right. Mohammed had to focus on the real reason why he was with Joanne this evening, but didn't know when the time would be right to ask her questions. There probably wouldn't be a right time.

"Joanne."

"Yes."

"This Scorpion group led by this man, Copeland."

"You're not still on about them are you?"

"I'm just curious that's all."

"About what?"

"The security of the United States is in the hands of this group of people, but how many of them are there? Can they actually prevent something happening?" enquired Mohammed.

"Not really, but they have at their disposal all the Special Forces-trained people and the equipment and transport to be able to move into hostile areas."

"That's a lot of people then?"

"Yeah, probably all of fifty people including pilots and ground crew."

"Wow, so many. What about their current assignments?"

"I can't really tell you that."

"Oh, I'm sorry for asking, Joanne."

"I don't actually know. They were looking at Afghanistan before. Now, I just don't know."

"Okay. I won't ask you any more questions about Scorpion. Well, not yet, anyway."

Joanne leaned forward pulling her pillow from behind her and struck out at Mohammed in a playful swing. This brought them together again. They both kissed and then Joanne looked at her bed-side clock: it showed nine thirty.

"Mohammed, I'm going to have to get dressed and go to pick up my mom. Thanks for another wonderful evening."

They climbed out of bed and dressed. Mohammed followed Joanne downstairs, collecting their coats as they moved towards the front door. They both stepped outside and immediately put on their coats to protect against the evening chill. They shared a kiss and went their separate ways towards their cars.

"I'll call you in the week," said Mohammed.

Joanne waved and blew a kiss in his direction. They drove away at the same time, but in different directions.

*　　　*　　　*

Mohammed stopped the car outside his hotel and made a call.

"It's Mohammed."

"Any news?" asked Ibrahim

"The strength of Scorpion involves some fifty people from the Special Forces, which includes their pilots."

"What else?" demanded Ibrahim.

"I get the impression that they can go anywhere at a moment's notice."

"What about current objectives?"

"It looks like they are still concentrating on the Afghan region. Is that good or bad?"

"You don't need to know. The less you do know the better it will be for you."

"Are you expecting some trouble in the States?"

"Just be prepared in case you are questioned."

"Questioned by who?"

"The FBI."

"This was never mentioned in my brief! There was no indication that I would be caught!"

"It was always a risk, particularly given the high profile contact that you've made."

"What will happen to my contact?"

"That's of no concern to you. You were sent to get the information and you have done well. Soon it will be time for Allah to take his revenge."

*　　　*　　　*

CIA Headquarters, Langley

The duty analyst called Mike on his home number.

"Sir, the guys on surveillance outside the DoI's house have recorded dialogue between target and source. They say it makes good listening. They've also sent video images on the downlink of the two of them outside her house. There's also been a break through, sir. The target made another call at approx. ten thirteen pm. He stayed on longer and guess what?"

"Bingo. Right, I'm on my way in. Have all the stuff ready for me when I get there." said Mike.

Goddard arrived at Langley thirty minutes later.

"Okay, give it to me straight."

The analyst rewound the video link and replayed it. Mike watched with disappointment at how easily Joanne had been sucked in by the charm of this…he'd think of a suitable description soon.

"The audio tape is on its way as we speak."

"Good. Give me the news that I want to hear. Where was the call to?"

"He stayed on just long enough for us to get a fix. You were right about Saudi Arabia. It was triangulated to the capital, Riyadh."

"Now, why doesn't that surprise me?" said Mike rhetorically. "What about any follow on calls from Saudi to somewhere else? Can we get a fix on those?"

"We're one step ahead of you. We used the recipient's number, and locked it in to the comms satellite. He wasn't that clever because he made a follow on call to a mobile number in Afghanistan."

"Great work, guys. The Saudi must be the middleman, the organiser, and the connection in Afghanistan could be the one who's pulling all the strings – Osama bin Laden at a guess."

The surveillance audiotape had arrived and was being played to Goddard. It was specific and digitally clear, picking up every sound in Joanne's house. He skipped the emotional part and listened with interest and annoyance at the detail that she was so casually giving away concerning Scorpion. He would now have to be ruthless. He had warned her of the consequences. The situation had reached point where it threatened National Security. There was only one thing he could do – which he did with reluctance.

Mike called the home number of the Director of the FBI, Richard Garcia.

"Richard, it's Mike over at Langley. Sorry to disturb you at this time of night, but I need an arrest warrant issued for two subjects."

"What have they done to piss you off?"

"Let's just say it's in the interests of National Security."

"Any names?"

"The first one is Mohammed Abdul Naseer, residing at the Hyatt Arlington and the other one is," Mike paused, took a deep breath then continued, "One of my own people, I'm sorry to say. Joanne Wiley."

"Joanne Wiley? Are you sure?"

"I wish I wasn't. It took me by surprise as well, but I want them both lifted at the same time, so that neither has the chance to make any calls."

"Who do you want to make the arrests, Mike? Our guys or yours?"

"We'd best make this Federal," insisted Mike.

"Sure. I'll get on to it right away. They'll be brought back to the federal building in DC for questioning. Do you want to be in on it as well?"

"Sure. I have the evidence that will need to be produced. I also want Jack Copeland to be involved since this is about his organisation."

"Does he know?"

"No, not yet."

*   *   *

Mike rang the out of office number for Jack Copeland

"Copeland."

"Jack, it's Mike, sorry to disturb you but something major has come up."

"Don't keep me in suspense, then. Go on, what is it?"

"Do you remember the brief I gave regarding the leak at the agency, and that the info was being passed to a Middle Eastern connection?"

"Yes, and?"

"Well, I've requested two arrest warrants from the FBI to detain both the source and target."

"Who are they?"

"One is Mohammed Abdul Naseer from Saudi Arabia, and the other is," Mike paused while he came to terms with the situation. He continued, "Joanne Wiley, from DoI."

"My, they aim high. Who'd have laid odds on it being Joanne? Has anything been leaked that would jeopardise our operation?"

"Yes and no."

"That's a contradiction in terms, Mike. It either has or hasn't. There are no grey areas."

"The two of them are to be taken over to the federal building tonight and we will begin the questioning tomorrow. I'd like you to be there. I have all the tapes recorded during our surveillance, which will need to be produced as evidence during the interviews. You might learn something."

Copeland was as surprised as the next person that Joanne Wiley could stoop so low and jeopardise the National Security of her country. That was the very thing that she had vowed to protect when she first joined the agency. She was very nearly at the pinnacle of her profession, outranked only by the Director. The higher you go the harder the fall. In Joanne's case, if she were found guilty her lifestyle would be dramatically changed. He would find out during the next few days or weeks why she would throw away such a glittering career. Nothing could top that, surely?

∗   ∗   ∗

As if it had been choreographed, the FBI had arrived simultaneously at the residences of Joanne Wiley and Mohammed Abdul Naseer. There was no uniformed presence of police officers at Joanne's house, only four FBI agents, but four armed officers plus a further four FBI agents approached

Mohammed's hotel room. Both Joanne and Mohammed were arrested without any resistance and taken to FBI Headquarters at the Federal Plaza building on Pennsylvania Avenue.

"Why have I been brought here?" demanded Joanne.

"You will be interviewed in the morning on suspicion of being involved with terrorism, and undermining the National Security of the United States."

"This is absurd. I want my lawyer here now. I want to make the phone call that I'm entitled to."

The FBI agent passed Joanne a telephone. She made a call.

"Mom. It's Joanne."

"Are you okay? What's going on?"

"It's a long story, but I'm being held by the FBI in DC. They say I've been involved in some kind of terrorism. It's okay, Mom, I've done nothing wrong. Can you give Wendy Cox a call? She's my lawyer. Get her to come over to the FBI headquarters tonight, please."

"Sure. Is there anything else I can do for you?"

"Just pray, please, that this has all been a mistake."

"Has it something to do with Mohammed?"

"I don't know where he is."

Wendy Cox was unable to attend Joanne on the night of her arrest, but the next morning she was waiting for her outside the interview room.

"Just give me a few minutes with my client, please," said Wendy to the FBI agent. Wendy and Joanne were given privacy in the interview room.

"You look awful, Joanne. What's going on?"

"I've been arrested on a charge of being involved with terrorism and undermining the National Security of the US! It's all absurd, Wendy, really."

"They must have had some evidence to arrest you in the first place. Think what it might be. Somebody you've met recently, or spoken to? You have a powerful position at the agency, Joanne. You must have an idea, surely."

"In fact, thinking about it, there is one person. No, surely it can't be."

"Who is it, Joanne? Tell me?"

"Someone with whom I had a fender bender – Mohammed Abdul Naseer. He's from the Middle East. He's the only person I can think of. Come to think of it he did keep on asking me about Scorpion."

"Okay, Joanne. We'll stop there. The FBI will have to take over from here. I'll be with you every step of the way. Okay?"

Joanne nodded and then started to cry. She had never been on the wrong side of the law before. At the agency she had called the shots, but this was a whole new ball game. Others were now in control of her future. These were people who would demand answers; answers to questions that would be intrusive and embarrassing. They would stop at nothing until the truth was known. The whole situation and scenario was spinning around Joanne's head as she tried to come to terms with what was happening. She wanted to think straight and get everything into perspective. She would tell them everything they wanted to know. If need be, she would take a polygraph test just to prove her innocence. She was starting to realise what was at stake. The agency had been her life since leaving Harvard, and she wasn't about to throw that away without a fight, no matter how stupid she had been. The FBI agent returned.

"Okay, we're ready for you now," he said.

Looking into the room through a two-way mirror were two other FBI agents, together with Copeland and Goddard. To their right through a second two-way mirror was Mohammed.

"I have a suggestion, Mike. We may be able to use Joanne to our advantage," said Special Agent Larson.

"How do you mean?" Mike asked.

"Look at it this way. Mohammed doesn't know that Joanne has been brought in nor does Joanne know that Mohammed is also here. What we can do is use Joanne to go along with what Mohammed has been asking her about Scorpion, and hopefully the tables will be turned. He then starts singing like a bird. That's the theory, anyhow. The practicalities are that Joanne would have to agree. It could be dangerous for her but, given her situation, I think she'll oblige."

"She's a strong willed woman normally, but this time she has allowed her emotions to cloud her professional judgment. It's worth a try. What do you think, Jack?" asked Mike, turning towards Copeland.

"Great idea. We need to know which organisation he is working for, that way we can narrow the field." Copeland looked towards Special Agent Larson.

"How do you want to play this?"

"We'll give a full brief first. We'll also have to continue to monitor her movements and that of the target. We'll have to use long-range microphones just in case something goes wrong. That way we can have agents on hand ASAP."

"Okay, let's get on with it."

Special Agent Larson and his colleague, Special Agent Jackson, left the observation room and headed in to the interview room currently occupied by Joanne and her lawyer. Copeland and Mike continued to watch from the observation room.

"Good morning, Miss Wiley. My name is Special Agent-in-charge Mike Larson and my colleague is Special Agent Ralph Johnson. Can I get you a drink or something?"

"No, thank you. I just want to get this over and done with."

"Sure. The charges against you are quite serious, and the position you hold within the agency demands that the penalty, if found guilty, would warrant sentencing you to the maximum penalty allowed by the courts."

"What am I supposed to have done?"

"We have both audio and video tapes which show you in compromising positions with a Middle Eastern undesirable, Mohammed Abdul Naseer. The tapes are very detailed. What we need to know, firstly, is how your relationship with him is developing?"

Joanne began to recite the events as they happened from the day of the phone call, to the accident, and to their sexual encounters.

"Has he ever mentioned his connection or involvement with terrorism?"

"No, never. In fact when I did ask him he denied any involvement."

"Has he ever spoken to you about his family?"

"No."

"Do you not find that strange?"

"We just never got around to discussing the finer details," Joanne snapped.

"Listening to the tapes you seem to have gained his trust pretty quickly considering the amount of information you have offered concerning Scorpion. It could undermine its operational effectiveness."

"Scorpion isn't a secret organisation. The President himself said so."

"The name and its existence is not, but how it operates has to be protected."

"I realise now that I may have acted with indiscretion, but I truly believed that he was genuinely interested in its existence."

"He was definitely interested, but not in the way that you had hoped. Were you aware of any telephone calls made by Mohammed to other destinations after your meetings with him?"

"No."

"After your meetings when you went your separate ways, he would make several calls to Saudi Arabia."

"That's not a surprise since the company he works for is located there."

"We traced the number but as yet haven't been able to pin point an address. However, a follow on call was made to Afghanistan. What do you say to that?"

"I did tell Mohammed that Scorpion were interested in Afghanistan, so maybe the call has a connection with that. I don't know. Where is Mohammed?"

"That will be explained to you shortly."

Both Mike and Copeland continued to watch through the glass as the interview progressed. Mike was of the opinion that Joanne genuinely believed that Mohammed was not a terrorist. Also, he wanted to believe that the information that she had passed on regarding Scorpion was done innocently. Mike could not, however, forgive her for abusing the position and trust that he and the agency – and ultimately the country – had given her. However, if what was about to be suggested was successful, then both the courts and the agency could be swayed to being more lenient in their sentencing. Nevertheless her career would inevitably be over and the trappings of success gone. It would take a miracle for it to be any other way. Mike looked towards Joanne and he noticed that the ordeal was starting to take its toll. She looked like a shell of her former self. Mike entered the interview room.

"Hi, Joanne. How are you feeling?"

"I'm sorry, Mike. If only I had taken your advice sooner. I've let both you and the agency down badly. I don't know what to say."

"It's a good job we caught it when we did, otherwise who knows what could have been disclosed. Your intuition took you in the wrong direction."

"I truly thought that I had found someone who loved me as a person and not for my job.."

Mike looked at Special Agent Larson, and then glanced back to Joanne and Wendy.

"What's wrong?" asked Joanne as she saw people looking at each other in the room.

"Joanne, the FBI and the agency would like to try something. You could do something for us that might save your hide."

"Whatever it takes, Mike. My whole life is the agency. I don't want to throw that away. What is it you want me to do?"

Mike explained to Joanne the need for her to continue to gain Mohammed's trust, and to find out more about his background. His credentials *would* be verified.

"It could be dangerous for you to get more involved, but Scorpion need to be certain who and what he is. The agency and the FBI also need answers. Are you up for it, Joanne?"

Joanne looked at Wendy.

"This is the only way you can redeem yourself, Joanne," said an approving Wendy.

"Okay, but how does this affect my chances of returning to the agency?"

"Your duties will be downgraded to lower level intelligence until this whole affair is resolved. Any information that you require in pursuance of your task will be given to you either by the deputy director Kurt Simmonds or myself. Is that understood?"

"Yes."

"Mohammed doesn't know that you are here and I would like it to remain that way. Once you leave this building you are not to mention this conversation to anyone. We will of course continue to monitor the movements of the pair of you."

"I can't get physically intimate with him again, knowing that you are listening to everything."

"We will use discretion, Joanne, but it will be for your own protection."

"Against what?"

"Just in case it turns nasty. There will always be agents outside your house whilst you're there. That's all you need to know. Do you have any questions before we release you?"

"How often do I need to make contact with him?"

"Good question. As often as you wish until you have all the information."

"How will I know?"

"We'll tell you. Oh, and by the way, Mohammed is being held in the next interview room. He'll be released shortly after you so that you can initiate contact."

Joanne was feeling a little easier now. The problem didn't seem as insurmountable as it did before, but she would have to tread with caution. This could be her only real chance of repairing the damage and embarrassment she had caused. She wasn't about to mess this up.

Whilst her release was being processed, Mohammed continued to be questioned. He had said when and where he had entered the US, and stuck to his cover story. He maintained his innocence as far as involvement with terrorist groups. His affair with Joanne was for emotional reasons and nothing to do with her appointment at the agency. The FBI was not convinced by his story and hoped that further surveillance in the coming weeks would bring out the truth. Mohammed would be released on the grounds of insufficient evidence in order for him to pursue his relationship with Joanne. He would be watched every step of the way.

*   *   *

Arlington Hyatt Hotel, VA – Later that day

"Ibrahim, it's Mohammed. I think they're onto me."

"How do you know?"

"I was arrested by the FBI last night, and questioned this morning."

"Where are you now?"

"Back at my hotel."

"What did you tell them?"

"I stuck to my cover story."

"Keep doing that. Nothing can leak out until after the event. Is that understood?"

"Yes, but what event?"

"You will see soon enough. The time is almost upon us as our leader has prophesied. Have the FBI charged you with anything?"

"No. They released me on the grounds of insufficient evidence."

"Be careful, Mohammed, in what you do and say. We have all the information we need, but if there are any changes to what you have reported, then you must call me."

*   *   *

After Joanne and Mohammed were released, Copeland entered the interview room.

"Do you think she'll play ball, Jack?" asked Mike.

"She has no choice. All the cards are currently stacked against her. If she doesn't then she gets prosecuted; even if she does there's no guarantee that she won't be. It's that simple."

"Yeah, I'd hate to see her destroyed because of a moment of weakness. She had a bright future at the agency. People like her are hard to find."

"Let's not start getting sentimental here, Mike. She may have done irreparable harm to our operational effectiveness, only time will tell. However, if we are still able to fulfil our security roles and she comes up trumps with this strategy, then you could negotiate for clemency. I'm sure the President has *some* influence," said Copeland, wryly.

*   *   *

Somewhere in Afghanistan

"Khalil, it's Ibrahim."

"Yes."

"Our connection in the US is becoming nervous."

"His time is almost at an end."

"What do you mean?" queried Ibrahim.

"He's disposable, is he not?"

"Well, yes, but…"

"You know what to do."

"What about the girl?"

"Casualties of war. Don't go soft on me or you will leave *me* no choice."

Ibrahim was starting to shake. He hadn't expected Bin Laden would be this ruthless to one of his own. Reality was starting to hit home. His own position was not as secure as he thought. He too was expendable. If he didn't carry out his orders, then he himself would become the hunted. That wasn't an option he wanted to consider.

Khalil made the call to put his plans in motion.

CHAPTER ELEVEN

B elle View Boulevard was busier than normal with traffic travelling to and from work. As was the case most mornings, people used this road as a through route to the Parkway. Travelling amongst the traffic was a white Chevrolet van with signs on its sides reading *TV/Aerial Installations*. On its roof was a set of extendable ladders. The vehicle travelled slowly along the road, to the annoyance of other traffic, with both its occupants scanning both left and right as if looking for an address.

"There it is," said the passenger, pointing.

The driver slowed even more, and turned into the driveway. Both men stepped out of the vehicle and, carrying toolboxes, approached the front door. The driver knocked, but there was no response. This wasn't a surprise, merely confirmation of what was already known. Both men moved to the back of the house. The driver bent down, opened his toolbox and removed a set of skeleton keys. Using these he gained access through the back door and into the kitchen. His passenger followed. They then moved into the sitting room where they stood still for a few moments looking around.

"Wow, what a place. I'm in the wrong job," said the driver before he continued, "We need to go upstairs. Come on."

Both men ran upstairs into the master bedroom. The passenger lay on the floor and shuffled himself under the bed. He opened his toolbox and removed a cylindrical object. He gently moved it towards the bedsprings and affixed it using its magnetic connections. The last thing he did was to pull the pin from the side of the object before he shuffled back out from under the bed. Both men then collected their toolboxes and left by the same method they had entered the house. They then drove away, re-joining the traffic. It had all taken less than 5 minutes.

*   *   *

Mohammed, having now been released from FBI custody, sought the comfort of Joanne. He wanted to make amends and give her the real reason for him being in the United States. He made the call to her office.

"Joanne, its Mohammed, how are you?" said Mohammed, calling from his hotel room.

"Fine, thanks. How are you?"

"Great. I need to see you though," confirmed Mohammed.

"I was thinking about asking you over tonight for a meal. Are you free?"

"Yeah, sure. I could do with some decent food. This hotel stuff is getting a bit stodgy. What time?"

"Seven thirty sharp. Don't be late. Mom's gone to her friends for the week, so we can have some time to ourselves."

"See you later then. 'Bye."

"'Bye."

Joanne was fully aware that her boss would know of this meeting, but she wanted to tell him herself. She punched in the Director's office number.

"I've just had a call from Mohammed. A meeting is set for tonight."

"Good. The wheels are in motion," said Mike. "Be careful, though, Joanne, won't you?"

Joanne left work at five pm as usual. She was now conscious of the car travelling three behind hers. It was, in a way, a comforting sight. She felt secure but she also knew that her private life would be invaded, and nothing would return to any semblance of normality until this whole business was concluded. She pulled into her driveway and the escort car continued along the street before turning around and parking short of Joanne's driveway. Joanne walked towards her front door, then took a cursory glance back at the two men who were there for her protection. This seemed to elevate her confidence, but she really wasn't keen on playing to an audience. She had no choice. The stakes were high, the penalty severe. Having entered the house, she busied herself in the kitchen preparing the food for their meal that evening. She would then change in to something more appropriate for a cosy evening in. As Joanne came out in to the sitting room and began to walk upstairs, she smelt something rather peculiar. It was a smell that hadn't been there before. She didn't recognise the odour. She walked in to her bedroom and the smell seemed to be stronger. She would report the matter in the morning. It could perhaps be the drains? Joanne slipped out of her work clothes, entered the bathroom and switched on the shower.

Having entered the cubicle, she began to lather herself over every inch of her body. As she did so she began to feel the same sensations as the times that they had made love.

Her hands were becoming his. She began to drift into a dream and visualise the excitement that Mohammed had teased from her body. He began to touch her breasts, which excited her, making her moan. She was brought back to reality as the telephone in her bedroom began to ring. She stepped out of the cubicle, wrapped herself in a bathrobe, and then picked up the phone on the bedside cabinet. The phone had stopped ringing as she picked it up from its cradle. Joanne thought nothing of it she replaced it and went back into the bathroom. She dried her hair, applied moisturising lotion and makeup and finally walked into her walk-in wardrobe to decide on her attire for the evening. Even though she had been warned that Mohammed might be a member of a terrorist gang, this in no way affected her feelings for him. She still found him sexy and was feeling sexy herself that evening. Something appropriate to her mood was a particular daywear dress which was neither too flirtatious nor too revealing. She sprayed perfume in all the right places and went back downstairs to continue with the meal.

At 7.28 pm Mohammed pulled his car in behind Joanne's. His escort continued along the road, having already been seen by the static car outside Joanne's.

Mohammed knocked on the door. "Good evening, Joanne. You look stunning."

"Thanks. Come in," said Joanne as she looked over Mohammed's shoulder for a reassuring glimpse of the surveillance cars outside.

"Would you like something to drink?"

"Wine would be nice, thanks."

Joanne retreated into the kitchen and Mohammed followed her. He put his arms around Joanne's waist and began to nibble at her neck. She turned towards him and her response was electric. Both kissed as if there was no tomorrow. Joanne hadn't expected this, nor was she resisting. She eventually released herself.

"Steady, tiger. You must be hungry?"

"Starving. I'll be hunting my prey later."

"Go and sit down, whilst I bring out the dishes."

"Can I help?"

"No, Mohammed, you're the guest. Do as you're told."

Joanne brought all the dishes out so they could help themselves.

"This looks delicious, Joanne. Chicken has always been one of my favourite foods outside of Saudi Arabia. We're not supposed to eat meat, and if we do it has to be halal but I can make an exception here."

"I am sorry, Mohammed I hadn't realised it was your custom not to eat meat. I've still got some learning to do."

"You weren't to know."

"So, what kind of day have you had?"

"I was arrested by the FBI last night on some trumped up charge of being a member of a terrorist group. I mean, do I look like a terrorist?"

"What happened?"

Mohammed explained how he was arrested, taken to the FBI headquarters and questioned. He also added that they thought he had become friends with Joanne because of her position at Langley.

"That's absurd, Mohammed. My position at Langley has nothing to do with our relationship."

"Have they not questioned you at all?"

"No, do you think they will?"

"Maybe. Do you ever get this feeling that you're being watched?"

"That's how you become paranoid. You'll end up in a psychiatric wing."

"What's that?"

"Where people…oh, never mind," said Joanne, smiling. "There's plenty more food, Mohammed," she continued.

"I'm pretty full now. That was sensational. Can I give you a hand to clear up?"

"That can wait until later," said Joanne as she moved across to where Mohammed was sitting.

"Tell me about your parents?"

"They both died in a terrorist incident in Cairo when I was very young. I don't remember much about them, really. I was brought up by family friends."

"What did you do after you left school?"

"I went to Cairo University. Then I was headhunted to work in Saudi."

"With the Telecommunications Company?"

"Yes," said Mohammed nervously.

"Why do I sense that what you are telling me may not be the truth, Mohammed?"

"Joanne, I'm falling in love with you and I cannot tell you anything about my past. It will only get you into trouble."

"I want to help you. You have to trust me."

"I suppose it doesn't matter now. My mission is complete. When I left University I was recruited by Egypt's most powerful terrorist group – Al Jama'a Al Islamiyya, better known as the Islamic Group. I have been with them for eight years."

"Is Mohammed bin Laden a member of this group?"

"I'm not sure."

"Answer me this question, Mohammed. Why did you come to the United States?"

Mohammed began to recount how he arrived in the States and the real reason why he was there. Joanne continued:

"What about our relationship?"

"That is real, Joanne. I didn't want it to happen, but you are so beautiful and sexy. Just what every man dreams about."

"What happens to you now that your mission is complete?"

"I await instructions telling me how I return to Saudi."

"How do you get your instructions?"

"They are generally published in our Arabic newspaper, the Al Hayat. Have I got you in to any trouble at all?"

"Yes, but I'm sure I can resolve it, with your help."

"I don't know how I can help you."

"You already have."

161

Joanne held Mohammed's hand, and led him upstairs into the main bedroom. Mohammed inched his way towards the bed then turned around. Joanne kissed him on the lips.

"I'll just nip in to the bathroom and freshen up. Don't go away," said a smitten Joanne.

Mohammed was starting to appreciate how lucky he was to have literally bumped in to Joanne. His friendship with her was becoming important to his existence. He would like to settle in the United States, but after all of this he wasn't quite so sure whether that would be the right move. His thoughts came back to Joanne and he began to undress. He could hear Joanne about to step out from the bathroom, so he quickly climbed between the sheets.

The explosion blew the roof off the bedroom and the floor collapsed onto the lower level. Debris flew several hundred metres in all directions. The bathroom Joanne was about to leave was destroyed. There was no sign of either Mohammed or Joanne. The exclusive detached residence was no more. The gas mains were spouting flames, and the water mains created a fountain of water that cascaded onto the front of the house. The upper storey was engulfed in flames that spread quickly through the remainder of the house.

*   *   *

The two FBI agents outside Joanne's residence had settled in for the evening. Their job was to monitor comings and goings, and to challenge anything that seemed out of the ordinary.

"She's a nice looking woman is Joanne. It's a pity she got mixed up in this. That's one sure way to mess up your career *and* your life," said the passenger.

"What do you think of this boyfriend of hers?"

"Too smooth for me. To look at him you would think there was…shit, what the hell was that?" said the passenger shouting as a loud explosion buffeted the car.

Both got out and were appalled to see that Joanne's house had almost disappeared. Debris was still raining down into the road and onto the car. The driver reached into the car and rang the emergency services. Then he called Langley and FBI HQ. The crew of the second FBI car came running forward.

"What the hell happened?" asked the third agent.

"Probably a gas explosion."

All the agents went as close as they could to try to locate Mohammed and Joanne.

The second agent shouted,

"Over here! Got one!"

The body of Mohammed was lying in a crumpled mess virtually unrecognisable on the front lawn. Joanne was nowhere to be seen. The sound of sirens became closer by the second. Soon three fire appliances, two paramedic units, and four police patrol cars arrived. The agents swiftly briefed the police and the fire chief as to what had happened. The fire rescue ladder was positioned against what was left of the front wall, and a hose was extended to dampen the raging fire that had taken hold on the first floor. Other firemen were trying to locate the gas mains to switch off the substance feeding the raging flames. As the fire was beginning to die down, a body was seen, by the fireman on the ladder, in a small room, lying on the floor.

"I've found something!" shouted the fireman down to his chief.

"What is it, John?" asked the fire chief to the fireman on the ladder.

"Looks like a body, chief."

"Is it alive?"

"Hard to tell from here. You'll have to get access from inside. There's no floor here to move on to. Put up a ladder on the inside and you should be able to reach it."

The fire chief instructed two firemen to don their oxygen masks, and to use a small extendable ladder to reach the body. Shortly thereafter, they returned with the body of a female and laid her on the ground. The paramedics were immediately on hand and quickly took over.

"She's alive, only barely, but she's hanging in there," shouted the elated paramedic. The body of Mohammed had already been removed from the lawn and put into one of the two ambulances. Joanne was gently moved into the other ambulance and was immediately rushed to the emergency department with life sustaining first aid being administered en-route.

Mike arrived at the scene twenty-eight minutes later and was briefed by the agents assigned to look after Joanne.

"What the hell happened, guys? You were here to make sure nothing like this *could* happen."

"We don't yet know what caused the explosion. Probably a gas main."

"What about casualties?"

"One male fried, and the female is in a bad way. She's been taken to emergency."

"Will she survive?"

"Your guess is as good as mine. The paramedic thinks she will. So there's some hope."

The flames had now died down, only burning embers continued to smoulder. Mike went across to speak with the fire chief.

"Chief, how's it looking from your point of view?"

"Too early to say at the moment. The fractured gas pipe was over there, but the damage seems to have been focused on the first floor. That doesn't make sense. I'm not going to speculate, but I should have some idea in the morning. Give me a call tomorrow."

"Sure. Thanks, chief."

The police secured the area and would maintain a watch on the premises and possible crime scene until first light when the forensic unit would be able to do a more detailed investigation.

The two FBI agents outside Joanne's house caught the attention of Mike.

"Sir, before the explosion we managed to record a conversation between Miss Wiley and the target, which seems to provide the answers we couldn't get from him at the bureau this morning."

"Where's the tape now?"

"In the car."

"I'll take it. I'm off to the hospital to see if there is any news on Joanne. You guys start making some door-to-door enquiries. See if anyone saw anything unusual this morning or this afternoon. Delivery vehicles, that kind of thing."

"Are you suggesting that a device may have been planted?" asked one of the agents.

"No. I'm just keeping an open mind," retorted Mike.

One of the agents recovered the tape from the car and handed it to Mike. As he was leaving, they started to make their door-to-door enquiries. Mike wasn't hopeful that anything positive would come from these enquiries, but it was one of those police routines that had to be done at or near a crime scene.

He drove to the Arlington Hospital on North George Mason Drive and parked in the underground car park near block one six three five. He walked through into the Emergency Department and approached the reception desk.

"My name is Mike Goddard, Director of the CIA at Langley. I understand you had a female brought in this evening who was badly burned?"

"What's her name?" asked the receptionist

"Joanne Wiley."

"Are you a relative?"

"No. She's one of my senior agents."

"Okay. Yes we did. She's in surgery at the moment."

"Can I see her?"

"Not for a while."

"If there are any changes to her condition would you please let me know on this number straight away?" said Mike, as he handed over his official card.

"Certainly."

Mike decided to return to the command room at Langley. He wasn't able to do anything at the hospital, so he might as well make himself useful elsewhere.

He instructed the duty analyst to play the tape given to him by the agents at Joanne's. She had done well in such a short time. They now had a group to work on. Mike made a phone call.

"Jack, it's Mike, some good and some bad news, I'm afraid."

"Give me the bad news first."

Copeland was waiting for the bottom of the earth to drop out, which it invariably did when anybody mentioned bad news.

"Joanne's house exploded this evening."

"Was any one inside?"

"Both Joanne and Mohammed."

"Casualties?"

"Mohammed is dead and Joanne is critical at the Arlington Hospital with major burns."

"How was this allowed to happen, Mike? There were enough agents detailed to protect her. We said we would, and now we've let her down."

"Let's not jump to conclusions, Jack. We still don't know what caused the explosion. The fire chief and the forensic boys will go over the crime scene tomorrow. We should then have a better idea as to which direction the investigation will take. The other thing is the good news. Prior to the explosion, the agents detailed to Joanne recorded a conversation that she had with Mohammed. He admits to being a member of a terrorist group, Al Jama'a Al Islamiyya."

"The Islamic Group."

"The one and only" confirmed Mike, "and if I was a betting man then I would bet a dollar to a pinch of salt that this group had something to do with the explosion tonight."

"Go with your instincts Mike and get your boys to bear that in mind when they start sifting through the rubble tomorrow. If as you suspect, then there will be some evidence of their involvement. Everyone leaves a piece of something behind. Keep me posted on that front will you?" asked Jack.

"Yeah, sure."

"What about Joanne? Is she taking any visitors at the hospital?"

"Not yet. She's still in surgery. I should think it'll be a couple of days before we can speak with her. She may be able to throw some light on what happened. I knew it would be a dangerous assignment for her, but never in my wildest dreams did I envisage anything like this. "

"Neither did I. What about her mum? Has anyone tried to contact her?" asked Jack

"Not sure where she is at the moment. We know she wasn't in the house at the time so we're trying to make contact with as many connections as we know. All of her known friends and relatives that we have on file will all be contacted. If she sees it first on the news she'll get in touch with the agency."

"I wonder who the main target was, Mohammed, Joanne or both? I don't think we'll ever know the answer to that one. It'll be one of those mysteries that will stay with us forever. Thanks for letting me know, Mike. Appreciate it. Good night."

*   *   *

The FBI agents detailed by Mike to make door-to-door enquiries had visited every house bar one. This house was directly opposite Joanne's, but nobody appeared to be at home. They would make a note of that and return the next day. Nothing had been reported to the agents as being out of the ordinary. Most occupants had either left early for work, dropped their kids off at school, or were wrapped up in their own life.

'What ever happened to nosey neighbours?' asked one of the agents of himself. There was nothing further they could do that evening. They would report in, and return the next morning to continue their enquiries.

*   *   *

The fire department, FBI forensic teams, FBI agents, and additional police officers arrived outside Joanne's house as dawn was breaking. A lot of questions needed answering this morning. The fire chief, along with the forensic team, began a careful detailed examination of the house, trying to ascertain the seat of the explosion. Two FBI agents returned to the house opposite Joanne's and knocked on the door.

"Good morning, madam. I'm Special Agent Wainwright from the FBI," he said, producing his credentials. "And this is Special Agent Curtis. We'd like to ask you some questions concerning the incident across the street."

"How are they? That was awful. We'd been out most of the day, and returned late last night and saw this. What happened?"

"Do you know your neighbour at all?"

"Yes, it's Kate Jenkins. Lovely lady and lives with her mom." Joanne had obviously given a good cover story to deflect any questions from nosey neighbours.

"Do you know much about her?"

"A high flier in Washington I believe. Not really discussed it with her."

"What time did you leave your house yesterday morning?"

"We were going to leave about eight-thirty, but as the traffic seemed far busier than normal we delayed our departure until ten o'clock. Why?"

"Did you see any unusual activity along the street or in Joanne's driveway yesterday morning?"

"No, not really. What kind of unusual activity are you talking about?"

"Delivery vehicles, people. Were there any visitors to the house that you saw before you left?"

"Now you ask, I remember there was a white van in the driveway. It didn't look odd because it had *TV/Aerial Installation* on the side, and there are a lot of people changing to the digital network along the street."

"How many people were the van?"

"Just two. They were dressed in white overalls."

"Were they carrying anything?"

"I can't remember. Wait a minute, I think one of them may have had something in his hand that looked like a toolbox."

"You've done well so far, but do you remember what they were doing? Did they stay at the front of the house, go around the back at all or climb up onto the roof? Anything at all would be most helpful. Take your time…"

"We were loading the car, you know, in and out of the house and all that. I do remember though, that one minute I looked across and they were both at the front of the house, and then the next minute they weren't anywhere to be seen. I guess they were in their van having a coffee or something. You know what workers are like these days."

"It's a long shot, but I don't suppose you got the licence number, did you?"

"No, I'm sorry. I have trouble remembering my own."

"What time did the van turn up yesterday morning?"

"Maybe about eight fifty. Somewhere around then."

"Well, thank-you, you've been a great help. If there is anything else that you remember later, then please ring me on this number," said Special Agent Wainwright, as he handed his business card over.

Both Agents walked back across the road to Joanne's house, and attracted the attention of the fire chief.

"Chief, we may have a breakthrough. The lady across the road noticed a white van in the driveway yesterday morning, with two characters who were there one minute and gone the next. You might want to look for something other than gas leaks."

"Thanks. It was always on my to-do list in any case," said the fire chief as he returned to his task.

*   *   *

CIA Headquarters, Langley, VA

"Mike, it's Richard Garcia. A couple of my agents who were continuing the door to door enquiries this morning over at Belle View Boulevard came across a neighbour who noticed a white *TV/Aerial Installations* van in Joanne's driveway yesterday morning."

"Did she say how many people were on board?"

"Two males. No descriptions other than they were wearing white overalls. She also said that one minute they were at the front door, then the next they had disappeared. Maybe went around the back, she isn't quite sure on that. It's a head start though, Mike."

"Maybe it wasn't a gas leak after all. It doesn't make it any easier on Joanne, though, does it? Thanks for that, Richard. Talk to you soon."

*   *   *

Offices of Scorpion, Washington DC

"Jack, Mike Goddard is on line five."
Copeland depressed the flashing line-five button.
"Morning, Mike, any developments?"

"It's too early to speculate at the moment, but the FBI may have to change the direction of their enquiries."

"From what to what?"

"From routine to a possible terrorist connection. Once the fire chief has finished his examination of the scene, and the forensic boys have dusted their bits, we will then hopefully have a clearer indication."

"What did I tell you, Mike? Any more news on Joanne?"

"Nothing yet. No news is good news apparently. I'll go down and see her tomorrow."

"Give her my regards and best wishes."

"Sure thing."

Copeland then pressed the internal switch on his telephone console.

"Mary, can you get me Phil Scott, please?"

Moments later the phone rang. "Phil Scott on line one, Jack."

"Thanks, Mary." Copeland pressed line one.

"Morning, Phil. You've heard about the incident last night, I take it?"

"Yes. What happened? How is she?"

"Joanne is still undergoing surgery, I believe. She was badly burned, so that's going take a few major operations. As to what happened, the reason I called is because I need to speak with the President."

"Ah. Briefing on the situation?"

"Yes. Last night's incident and some other data to hand. Is there a slot in his itinerary for this afternoon or tomorrow?"

"Tomorrow at eleven am."

"Yeah, that's fine."

*　　*　　*

CIA Headquarters, Langley, VA – Office of the Director

"Mike, it's the fire chief over at Belle View, you'd best get your ass over here real quick."

Mike arrived twenty-five minutes later. "What is it, chief?"

"Come over here," said the fire chief, as he led the way. "At first I thought it was nothing, then I realised this was more than a gas leak."

"Okay, chief, you've got my attention. Can we get straight to the point without the technical stuff?"

"It was an incendiary device with a tilt switch mechanism. It's my guess it was attached to the underside of the bed. I don't know how the young lady escaped with her life, but she should have been in the same ambulance as her boyfriend. That's for you Feds to figure out."

"What is the evidence for this theory?"

"The bed is inverted and badly charred. This shows that it absorbed a great deal of heat, which suggests to me that this was the seat of the explosion. Also, a number of fragments have been recovered, which appear to be pieces of the device. The bedroom floor was blown downwards and the bed upwards. The blast had to go somewhere. There's your answer, Mike. It'll all be in my report."

"Thanks, chief."

Mike made a mobile phone call to Scorpion, and was put through by his secretary.

"Jack, it's Mike, we have a development."

"Go on."

"It is the suggestion of the fire chief that the house was destroyed by an incendiary device with a tilt switch mechanism. It seems that it may have been attached to Joanne's bed."

"That's definitely a weapon of terror. Not many people survive that type of bomb. Joanne was lucky, if you can call being almost burned alive lucky. At least she escaped with her life. I'm seeing the President in the morning, Mike, to bring him up to speed and discuss the way forward."

"Well, good luck to you," Mike said, as he terminated the call.

*   *   *

The White House, Pennsylvania Avenue, Washington DC – Next Day

"Morning, Mr President," said Copeland, as he entered the Oval Office.

"Morning, Jack. Take a seat."

Copeland noticed that Phil Scott was present as well as the Joint Chiefs Chairman, General Walter Zieglar.

"So, Jack, Phil tells me you have something urgent to discuss?"

"Last night's incident involving the Head of the Directorate of Intelligence, Joanne Wiley, was an act of terrorism and not, as first thought, a gas leak. The fire chief has spent most of yesterday sifting through the rubble and those were his findings. Fragments have been taken away for analysis which should identify what kind of device it was."

"Do you have any indication as to who would do this?" asked the President.

Copeland related the conversation he had had with Mike, and the probability that it was the work of the Islamic Group.

"How was last night's incident allowed to happen, Jack?"

"There was nothing anyone could have done, Mr President. Joanne is waiting to be interviewed once she's cleared for visitors. Hopefully she'll be able to shed some light on all this."

"Mr President, I would like to ask Jack what Scorpion has achieved since its inception. Things still seem to be happening globally, and there hasn't been a reaction from them. The Joint Chiefs are getting a little impatient with their failure to react, especially since they have at their disposal all of the Special Forces and the associated hardware. They could prove to be an expensive item?" asked General Walter Zieglar.

"Mr President, General Zieglar, Scorpion was set up to react to incidents. With all due respect, General, you've got your head up your arse. We can't go somewhere on a 'Just in Case' scenario, we don't have the resources for that. Something has to happen for us to react. We will of course use all available assets to try and be one step ahead of our opponents, and gain valuable intelligence that could work in our favour."

"What do you know about the incident last night, Jack?" asked Phil Scott.

"It is the understanding of both the CIA and Scorpion that the fundamentalist Islamic Group was behind the incident at Joanne's house. Mohammed Abdul Naseer, who was with Joanne when the explosion occurred, was a member of that group. Coincidence or not, he was in the US to gather information and report on the capabilities of Scorpion through Joanne given her position at the agency."

"Do you think Scorpion has been compromised, Jack?" asked the President

"No. They don't know our tactics or full capabilities. They were told that Scorpion was concentrating on the Afghan region, which is true in part, but it's the Middle East that I'm interested in. Mr President, something will happen soon in that region. I'm convinced of that." Copeland turned to General Zieglar,

"That is something we can't pre-empt. The playing field is far too big." Copeland turned back to the President:

"Mr President, you sanctioned the creation of Scorpion, it will, of course, be your call to disestablish it should you feel it is no longer useful."

"I have every confidence in you, Jack, and the team at Scorpion. You will have my full support in whatever activities Scorpion are involved in. You will also receive the support of the Joint Chiefs." The President looked towards General Zieglar; "Is that understood, Walter?"

"Yes, Mr President," General Zieglar said, reluctantly.

"If you don't, I'll accept your resignation without recourse."

General Zieglar was backed in to a corner. As the Chairman of the Joint Chiefs, he felt as though power and control were starting to escape him. Since the President himself gave full support and backing to the activities of Scorpion, it would be difficult for him to withdraw assistance to them. When the time came, though, he would return control to SOCOMM. General Zieglar was Copeland's senior officer and should report to <u>him</u> if military protocol was followed. This was no ordinary organisation. It had the full blessing of the President. Zieglar was hoping that Scorpion and Copeland would fail together and he would then be able to saunter back to the President, and have the power his position vested in him rather than merely 'advise'.

Copeland left the White House and returned to his office uneasily aware his position was not safe. He didn't want any conflict between the President who placed him as the head of Scorpion and the chief who was the one who would sanction the equipment he would request. What he needed was a real mission to demonstrate the capabilities of this fighting machine. Only then would the true value of Scorpion be realised.

$$* \qquad * \qquad *$$

Offices of Scorpion – The same day

"Mary has just told me about Joanne. It's that bad, is it?" asked Dinger.

"It could have been worse. She might not have been here at all. We lost her companion, Mohammed Abdul Naseer. He was killed in the explosion. The FBI got a taped conversation where he admitted to being a member of the Islamic Group. It all fits, Dinger. This is surely the group that will initiate what Bin Laden's sidekick was saying in his statement. The thing is, I don't know where to start, and I'm not going to admit that to the President or the Joint Chiefs! As far as they know every thing's under control," replied Copeland.

"How was your chat with the President?"

"We still have the President's unqualified support, but the Joint Chiefs are after my head and the downfall of Scorpion. It's these power crazy generals. We can requisition any- and everything. All it takes is a quick phone call and personnel and materiel are mobilised. The Joint Chiefs still have to ask the President, as their Commander in Chief, for his authorisation. They don't like that."

"You *are* bitter, aren't you, Jack? I'd put it down to old-fashioned jealousy on their part. You're in a high profile position here, getting the attention and all that. You've probably been photographed more times than the President and you wouldn't even have known it. They're thinking it's making you more powerful than they are. That's a hell of a lot to live up to. Let's just hope we get it right first time."

"We need to be extra prepared, Dinger. You know that the best laid plans rarely survive contact with the enemy! There is always something that hasn't been considered. A spanner in the works that makes you think on the move. That's the best thing about a military operation, you never know what the enemy are gonna to do next." The last sentence was accompanied by a wry grin.

"Any news from the embassies, Jack?"

"That reminds me,"

Copeland made a call to Mike to find out whether any further information had come in from the Middle Eastern US embassies. The reply was: nothing of any substance. Copeland was beginning to think that he might be barking up the wrong tree or looking in the wrong direction. His gut feeling, though, told him to stay focused on the key points he had already identified. If he got this wrong, it would only add more ammunition to the already bulging arsenal of the Joint Chiefs, who were ready to unleash a salvo in his general direction, given any opportunity. He wasn't about to give them that chance.

Copeland was running low on information concerning the terrorist group to which Mohammed Abdul Naseer had belonged. The Middle Eastern desk at Langley had limited data and no more was coming in. There was, however, one other avenue that he hadn't yet explored. That is, up until now. He would make the call first thing in the morning.

*   *   *

Immediately he arrived at work Copeland called the offices of the International News Gathering Desk at CNN Headquarters in Atlanta, Georgia. What he needed to know was the whereabouts of their Middle Eastern Bureau Chief, Elisabeth Young. Having identified himself, the information was swiftly offered.

"She's presently on assignment in Sierra Leone. You can get hold of her there," said the voice, concluding by giving Copeland the direct call number.

'Great,' thought Copeland to himself. He looked at his watch. Sierra Leone would be six hours ahead of Washington time. He made another call and after being connected, re-routed and on hold for what seemed like an eternity, Copeland was finally put through to the news desk.

"Elisabeth Young, please."

"May I ask who is calling?" asked the woman.

"General Jack Copeland, US Army."

"If you can hold, I'll try and locate her for you."

"Appreciate it. Thanks."

Moments later, he heard a female voice.

"What can I do for you, General?"

"Elisabeth Young?" Copeland asked for confirmation.

"Yeah."

"Forget the formalities, call me Jack," insisted Copeland.

"Okay, Jack. What can I do for you?"

Copeland detected a little sarcasm in her voice. He sensed that she didn't get on with the military, probably a professional conflict in the past. He could understand why, since the media could never get a straight answer from military chiefs. They were always accused of cover-ups, concealing the real truth with their own style of propaganda. He knew he would have to pull out his personal charm to win her trust. *'This will be difficult, but not impossible,'* Copeland thought to himself.

"May I call you Elisabeth?"

"Well, considering I don't have any other name, that's probably a good place to start."

"I get the impression military personnel are not high on your list of good guys."

"Not all. Some, yes. It depends on what you do, as to which category you fit in to."

"Have you heard of a government organisation called Scorpion?"

"Yeah. You work for them?"

"I head the team."

"So to what do I owe the honour of the Head of Scorpion calling me, Jack?"

"I'm a great fan of yours, Elisabeth. I watch your news reports whenever I can. The information you provide tends to be more accurate than that offered by our own intelligence services. I must say that wherever trouble is brewing in the world there is one guarantee in life, and that is that CNN reporter Elisabeth Young can always be found there!"

"That's what makes news. You have to be in the thick of it to create the right atmosphere. Small talk wasn't the reason you called, though, was it?"

"You don't pull any punches, do you? You're right. I didn't call to make small talk. The reason I called is to ask for your help, which means I have to gain your trust, Elisabeth. Of course, trust goes both ways. Some things that I am about to reveal to you cannot be repeated outside of our conversation. You understand that, I'm sure, since the government is rather paranoid about National Security, and at times we have to deny people information or distort the truth to prevent mass panic. If you reveal any of our conversation, then that is what you will create, and it will be on your conscience should things go wrong."

"And I suppose it's attached to the usual bullshit that you'll deny everything, having said what you're about to say? I have a duty to report, Jack. People need to know what is happening at home and abroad and if you tell me anything that they should know…"

"I understand that, however, this is one area where you will have to be discreet. I hope I can convince you to trust me on this one." replied Copeland.

"So, what's the big deal then?"

Copeland wanted to get off to a good start with Elisabeth, so he gave her all the information he had concerning the Islamic group, including the involvement of Mohammed, and his serious concerns about possible terror campaigns in the Middle East.

"Wow! That is <u>some</u> story, Jack. You're basing a strike on a gut feeling? You must have some strong guts. Have you told anybody else about your predictions?"

"Of course, but nobody wants to accept that that is where it's gonna happen."

"I'm not surprised, Jack."

"Yeah, by the time they do believe me it will be too late. I've been in the military a long time, I have a pretty strong case, and I'm prepared to lay my career on the ground. If I'm wrong, then I will do the honourable thing and step down, but if I'm right, then I'll probably get a pat on the back and a new company car."

"So, where do I fit in to this equation?"

Copeland knew that it was only a matter of time before he would be stone-walled by bureaucrats in Washington. This would strangle his ability to retrieve information, resulting in crippling the operational effectiveness of Scorpion. Its demise would therefore be inevitable. He wanted to secure this channel of information even if it *was* outside of Scorpion's structure. He had no choice. This was a cry for help.

"I personally believe that the media have a vast library of information regarding all aspects of world affairs."

"That is generally true. Yeah."

"I'm looking initially for any information you may have on the Islamic Group, Al-Jama'a al-Islamiyya." Copeland had to spell the name out to Elisabeth since he was having difficulty in pronouncing it.

"Anything else?"

"The embassies that I mentioned to you, do you have media crews in that area all the time?"

"No. We haven't the resources to do that. Of course, should anything happen in a given area, we have the transport to deploy them swiftly to practically anywhere. Why do you want to know, Jack?"

"No particular reason," said Copeland, not very convincingly.

"Why do I get the feeling you're holding out on me? You mentioned trust before."

"Nothing gets past you, does it? I was just going to ask that whenever any of your crews drive past our embassies that they keep an eye out for anything unusual. Media crews can smell things before they even materialise. That was all. Would you do that?"

"I suppose we can manage that. What do I get out of this for helping you?"

"A dinner date when I see you."

"Judging by your concerns that may be sooner than you think. I'll hold you to that. Listen, I'm sorry to have been a bit cranky earlier, but I've had a real shit of a day. I shouldn't be taking it out on you."

"Apology accepted."

Copeland gave her the office number of Scorpion so that Elisabeth could pass on any information she discovered in their records. He hoped that she would call, now that the ice had been broken. He was sure that if a chance meeting brought them together then interactions would be much more informal.

*   *   *

Two Days later – The offices of Scorpion

"Jack, it's Mike, I have the latest MILSAT pictures from Afghanistan after today's sweep. I have to admit you were right again. It does show movement. The satellite will only be over the region for another half-hour. What do you want us to do?"

"Download the photos to the main server. Can we enlarge it down here?"

"We'll have a go."

"I'll be over in two hours."

*　　　*　　　*

CIA Headquarters, Langley, VA – Two hours later

Mike reloaded the images for the benefit of Copeland. "These are the ones taken last week and these are today's. Notice the difference?" asked Mike

"There are things moving on this one," replied Copeland. Copeland pointed to what looked like a convoy of vehicles. "Zoom in on this would you?"

Mike nodded to the analyst who, after a few keystrokes on the keyboard, produced a greatly magnified image.

"There, look," said Copeland as he pointed to the vehicles; "I bet Bin Laden is being escorted in one of those."

"That's a bit of a stretch, Jack. It's not as if we can see his face."

Copeland ignored his comment.

"You saw where the vehicles came from: out of that hole. I need the map reference, Mike. I've got a hunch."

"Your hunches mean that trouble is about to happen."

"Yeah, but it keeps you lot on your toes! In the next sweep, Kent needs to snap this region and the desert areas around Kabul."

"You've got it. Jack, I've got something else to tell you. You are *not* going to believe this."

"Try me," quipped Copeland.

"Let's go in to my office."

Both Copeland and Mike headed along the corridors to the Director's office.

"Take a seat, Jack," said Mike.

"We've got a profile, through a song bird who's seeking security in the US for information that he's offering."

"What's his name, this song bird?" asked a curious Copeland

"Sultan bin Salman."

"Name doesn't mean anything. What's on offer?"

"He's a thirty-eight year old Sudanese, who spent two years in the US in the mid 1980's before going off to join the Mujahideen fighting Soviet occupation in Afghanistan. He walked into the US embassy there in mid 1996 saying that he wanted to inform on his terrorist boss. His statements included things like he had been a member of a group in Afghanistan that wanted to make war against our country. Also, he warned then that his boss might try to do something inside the US or try to attack some embassies."

"When was this warning received?" asked Copeland.

"Well, this *very vague* warning came two years before the explosions in Kenya and Tanzania."

"Great, we get a warning and because nothing happens for two years it gets ignored."

"Something like that, yeah."

"Is he directly linked with the '98 bombings, then?"

"Quite possibly but we don't have any hard evidence. His information sounds credible since he was on the run from the organisation after stealing funds from them over a number of years. We've got something else, Jack, which will interest you."

"Go on, then, it can't get any worse," said Copeland. But, looking at Mike's face, questioned "Can it?"

"An Egyptian born, naturalized US citizen managed to infiltrate the US Army during the early '80's. He rose through the ranks to reach sergeant, and was then assigned to Special Forces at Fort Bragg during the late '80's."

"What was he doing there?"

"Teaching the elite unit on Islamic Politics, culture and Middle-Eastern warfare. It now transpires that at that time he was already working for the Egyptian Islamic Jihad group, which, as you know, has close links with Al Qaeda."

"That's just great. Where is he now?" demanded Copeland.

"After leaving the Army in 1989 he took his know-how to Afghanistan where he began training Bin Laden's men in explosives. Soon afterwards he was helping to set up the terrorist cell in Nairobi."

"How the hell did he get so close to our Special Forces? He's had access to how we operate, training *and* strategy."

"Well, if they have a convincing cover story that checks out, no lights flash. He joined at a time when we were undermanned in the military, so some of the background checks were not 100% but we took him anyway."

"This is incredible, Mike! We train a guy, draft him into Special Forces where he learns ALL the secrets of our covert operations…and then he uses it against us. We should start advertising that we run courses for any walk of life no matter who or where they originate. I'm not having a go at you, Mike, but this just typifies the slackness of our security. Thanks for keeping me up to date."

Copeland left the CIA building and drove back towards his office in Washington, still seething as to how someone like that could infiltrate the US Special Forces.

*   *   *

Outside the official residence of the US Ambassador to Sierra Leone

"Morning, Mark," said Charles, as he climbed into the official car parked outside the front door of his residence. His wife, Sarah, looked on as the car traversed along the driveway.

"Morning, Sir," replied Mark Harris.

H. E. Charles Perez was the US Ambassadorial representative to Sierra Leone and was starting his second four year term under the new US Presidential Administration. Mark Harris was his bodyguard and had been with him some nine months. Twelve months was the maximum post for a security detail since any longer would lead to degradation of alertness allowing routines to set in.

"Straight to the office, sir?" asked Mark as he applied the central locking to the doors.

"Yes, please," confirmed Charles, as he sat back and opened his briefcase to start work on some documents before he arrived at the office.

Mark was armed with a sidearm that he had strapped in to his belt holster. Safety catch was on and the weapon was in condition one with a round already in the chamber. The driver, Idriss Adams, was recruited locally because of his local knowledge and had been a driver at the embassy for seven years. Idriss drove the Mercedes along Hennesy Street over the river and onto Kroo Town Road. As he turned left on to Banders Street, a stop sign at the road works was displayed. Idriss brought the car to a standstill. There was no other vehicle in the queue. Mark was trying to maintain all-around observation ready to react, as being stationary wasn't a healthy status.

Without warning, two pick-up trucks drove in both front and back of the Mercedes, blocking any escape route.

"Get down," shouted Mark to the Ambassador, as he climbed over the front seat and onto his principal, removing his weapon as he did so.

"Idriss, ram that front vehicle now on its back edge and let's get the fuck out of here," commanded Mark to the driver.

Idriss responded by flooring the accelerator and turning the steering wheel, so that the Mercedes would turn towards the rear of the front vehicle. Hopefully the weight of the truck engine would pivot the vehicle on its axis. Adrenaline was now pumping through Idriss' body, which meant his actions were not controlled and panic was starting to set in, a danger in itself.

"It won't budge, Mark. I've rammed it but it just won't move."

Mark was able to fire double tap rounds from the rear of the Mercedes through the side window at three of the targets that had jumped from the back of the pick-up trucks. They fell to the ground and didn't move again. The numbers were still overwhelming, and the odds were stacked against Mark.

"Idriss, move this piece of fucking shit will you!" Mark shouted.

There was no response, but the wheels of the car were still spinning. He was sure that Idriss had been hit since he didn't respond to his commands. The driver always seemed to be the first to get hit. Mark quickly glanced towards Idriss and saw he was slumped over the steering wheel.

"Shit!" shouted Mark, and soon realised that no amount of training could get him out of this situation. He was still laid on top of the Ambassador. He glanced up, but it wasn't what he wanted to see. The car was now surrounded and rounds were starting to enter the car from all sides. Mark turned around again to try and fire off some more rounds, but as he did so, a bullet caught him on the side of his neck which caused his body to twist violently. The Ambassador was splashed with his blood, and panicked thinking that he himself had been shot.

"I've been hit, I'm hit!" shouted the Ambassador in panic. He didn't feel any pain. That was a good sign. The car doors were opened, and Mark was dragged out and thrown to the floor. He lay there in a crumpled heap, not moving. One of the terrorists dragged Charles out and shoved him into one of the ambush vehicles. Charles managed to look around and see what damage Mark had done to the terrorists before an oily and stained Hessian bag was placed over his head. Three dead. Mark had done his duty. He'd taken the bullet that might otherwise have killed the ambassador.

The vehicles sped away, heading along Waterloo Street and in the direction of Pademba Road heading towards…he wasn't sure. He could only guess now. Charles's nightmare was just beginning, and he had no idea why he'd been singled out.

CHAPTER TWELVE

The White House, Pennsylvania Ave, Washington DC

Phil Scott, the National Security Advisor to the President of the United States, moved quickly along the corridors of the White House, heading for the Oval Office. So quick was his forward motion that occasionally he would bump into other members of staff causing them to lose balance. He wasn't concerned about them, focusing on the immediate news he had to relay to his boss, the President. The Secret Service Agent posted outside the President's office saw the urgency of the NSA and immediately opened the office doors. Phil brushed by the agent and was trying to speak whilst catching his breath.

"Mr President, we have some bad news. You've got to see this."

The NSA moved towards the television and switched it on.

"There is a news broadcast to be given by CNN just about now. I think we should watch it," Phil Scott continued.

The CNN programme came to life from the studios in New York fronted by Declan Andersen:

"...We are receiving reports that during the night a series of simultaneous explosions have occurred at a number of US embassies in the Middle East. We're crossing live now via telephone to Katherine Solomon in Tripoli. Katherine, what can you tell us?"

"Well, Declan, during the night two massive bombs, believed to be car bombs, have exploded outside the US embassies here in Tripoli and Casablanca, Morocco. Both buildings appear to have suffered extensive damage, but as luck would have it there appear to be no US casualties. There have been, however, a number of casualties amongst the local population. First indications suggest sixty-two people dead, most of them from the block of flats adjacent to the embassy here in Tripoli, which also suffered major structural damage. Information is still coming in regards to Morocco but it is reported that only a handful of people were injured. This is Katherine Solomon for CNN in Tripoli, Libya. Back to you, Declan."

"Thanks, Katherine. As more news comes in concerning these explosions we will of course bring you further updates."

The President continued to look at the television in disbelief.

"For Christ's sake, Phil, what the hell is happening?"

"Mr President, this is a serious breach of National Security. The destruction of US Government buildings is tantamount to aggressive action against our country."

"I know all that bullshit, Phil. What I want to know is why the hell didn't we know that something like this was going to happen? We're supposed to have the best intelligence service in the world, and they never even got a sniff of this one. What the hell are they playing at? They eat half the national budget, have more technology than Silicon Valley, and still don't know what's happening in the world."

"To be fair, Mr. President, Jack Copeland did have a hunch that this was going to happen and was looking at these regions. That has to be a plus." The CNN broadcast continued with Declan Andersen.

"I'm now hearing that a further two explosions have occurred at two other US embassies in the Middle East. We'll cross live to Patty Davis in Cairo, Egypt. Patty, what's happening where you are?"

"Declan, it's total confusion and chaos here in Cairo. The US embassy has been targeted and badly damaged by a car bomb early this morning. There don't appear to be any US casualties but a number of locals have been seriously injured. Additionally, a number of buildings adjacent to the embassy have suffered major damage and will have to be levelled. It has also been reported, but not yet confirmed, that the recently opened US embassy in Khartoum, Sudan has suffered the same frontal attack as the embassy in Cairo. As I say, this hasn't yet been confirmed. This is Patty Davis for CNN in Cairo, Egypt. Back to you Declan."

The President was now in a state of shock. "Jesus H Christ, Phil. This is going to cripple our foreign relations. Nobody will have any confidence in the US. We need to strike whilst the iron is hot. Get me the Joint Chiefs of Staff and Jack Copeland, and have them in my office in one hour for a crisis meeting. Also get me the FBI chief and CIA Director."

As Phil Scott was leaving the President's office, the CNN broadcast continued with further alarming news.

"News is just coming in of an attack against the US Ambassador in Sierra Leone. We'll cross live now to Elisabeth Young in Sierra Leone. Elisabeth, what are the latest developments there?"

"Well, Declan, it seems that an audacious attack was carried out on the official vehicle of the US Ambassador to Sierra Leone this morning as he was travelling to work. Ambassador Charles Perez was travelling in a single car with his bodyguard and driver. Eyewitnesses report that the car stopped at road works near the embassy, when two vehicles surrounded it, impeding its escape. A gun battle then ensued with shots being fired by the terrorists towards the Ambassador's vehicle, killing the locally employed driver instantly. The Ambassador's bodyguard managed to kill three terrorists before he himself was badly injured. It is believed that the Ambassador was taken from the vehicle alive, but his present whereabouts is not known. This is Elisabeth Young for CNN in Freetown, Sierra Leone. Back to you, Declan."

"Elisabeth, are there any early indications as to who may have carried out the kidnapping of the Ambassador?"

"None whatsoever, Declan. It is probably too early to speculate in any case. No communications have yet been received from the kidnappers either to the embassy or his family. There are however a number of small groups of former military personnel who used to be part of the Sierra Leone army. There is a possibility that it may be one of these groups. No one knows at the moment."

"This is worse than a nightmare, Phil. This will be the real test of my Presidency. We've had an easy ride up to now," said the President as Phil Scott left the room.

One Hour Later

"Right, gentlemen, the shit has really hit the fan and our global superiority is starting to crumble. We have to do something about it, and swiftly. Have you all been brought up to speed with the latest developments in the Middle East?"

Everybody in the room nodded and some murmured their reply.

"Good. That makes it easier because we can get right to the point. This is one hell of a mess we're in, gentlemen, and someone's head is going to roll for this. Mike, how come the agency never got a whiff of this one? You were caught with your pants down for the '98 bombings, I didn't think it could happen twice."

"Mr President, it was known that terrorist strikes would occur in the Middle East and preventative measures had been circulated to those likely targets. Everything had been co-ordinated with Jack at Scorpion. He had his finger right on the pulse. He seems to be the only one who has got anything right so far, but no one is willing to listen and take it seriously," replied Mike.

Copeland shuffled in his seat. "Mr President, gentlemen," began Copeland.

"Mike is right: it has been apparent for some time through our own intelligence sources that the Middle Eastern embassies were the main targets. It wasn't considered that as many as this would be hit. That is the surprise part." Copeland was glad that he *had* focused on the Middle East embassies although he couldn't have prevented what had happened.

"The events have already occurred so there's no point in labouring the point," said the President, who continued, "What we have to do is to reassure our diplomatic staff and our host countries that the United States is not yielding to the pressure of terrorist action. We must maintain our foreign relationships and policies. What I need from you, General Hubbard, is a military solution to stabilise those regions affected, and from you, Jack, some kind of cohesive strategy on how we can recover our captured Ambassador. We have an excellent reputation for recovering our downed pilots and personnel missing in action. Let's not fail on this one. I want your solutions pronto, gentlemen. Is that clear?"

Deliberations now began in earnest. The Joint Chiefs from the military were consulting each other, looking for the best possible plan. The problem with military chiefs is that they find it hard to agree on the simplest of plans. They all want the glory for themselves and their particular arm, whether it be Army, Navy, Marines or Air Force. It's as if they're in competition with each other to find the best of the best. Joint operations tended to have conflicting orders as each military commander wanted to command his own troops rather than take commands from an overall task force commander. This often created problems and confusion, which sometimes led to compromises being made. Such compromises weren't necessarily the best option, since they were often flawed, gaps and overlaps weakening the operation. The limits of responsibility were always an area of conflict and discussion between the Joint Chiefs. In this instance the Commander in Chief, the President, made certain decisions for them.

Copeland was the first to speak. "Mr President, Scorpion is on 2 hours' notice to move. What I suggest is that a covert unit be inserted in to Sierra Leone to gather intelligence on the ground, and, if at all possible, determine the whereabouts of the Ambassador. The remainder of Scorpion and their equipment will also be deployed to the region but will be supported by the US Navy off Sierra Leone. Once he's been located then aggressive action can be taken to extract him. This is a workable solution, Sir."

"Chances of success, Jack?"

"I would say on the scale of one to ten, sir, possibly an eight."

"That's pretty good odds, Jack. What support do you need from the Navy?"

"Air support by the provision of their MH 53's once the action plan is implemented, and the extraction phase is under way. We'll use our own Apaches as air support and the '53's for the insertion of ground troops to secure the area once it has been identified. A SEAL Unit will also be deployed should the need arise."

The President turned and looked at Admiral Donald B Stoutman, the US Navy's Chief of Staff.

"Don," began the President, encouraging him to carry on the operational details from Copeland.

"The second fleet is already in the area, Mr President, but were due to return home next week for a refit. That order can be rescinded."

"Do it," ordered the President, "However, remember I want them moved into the area to give us an option, not to force us in to a situation. Is that understood?"

Admiral Stoutman nodded before the President continued,

"They will stay in the area until this is resolved, and the CAG will provide air support for Jack as and when required from the flat top."

CAG was the Chief Air Group who were responsible for the day-to-day flight operations, and the flat top was military slang for an aircraft carrier. The President remained familiar with forces' terms though he had retired from the Marines some 14 years ago.

The President gave orders to the FBI Director, Richard Garcia, to commence his investigations into the bombings with support from the Marines that Admiral Stoutman had been ordered to provide.

"Okay, Jack, you have a Go. God speed and good luck, gentlemen," concluded the President.

Copeland left the White House and headed back to the Scorpion offices. He needed to make a number of calls. This was the team's first real test. It had to be effective and it had to be successful. There would be no second chance.

*　　*　　*

Charles Perez lay in the back of one of the ambush vehicles. He was blindfolded with an oily rag, which was starting to sting his eyes. His hands had been tied behind his back, and he could feel that the rope or cord was beginning to cut into his wrists as he bounced up and down on the floor of the truck. They were no longer on smooth tarmac: it was obvious they had left the main roads and were heading cross-country.

The engine note altered, giving him the impression that they were heading into the mountains. Gear changing to the lower ratios was also more frequent as if the vehicle was struggling with the incline. The temperature was also starting to drop. He began to shiver. *'Probably a combination of the shock and the change in air temperature,'* he thought to himself.

The vehicles stopped and he could hear shouting. Issuing instructions or attracting attention from someone a short distance away? He wasn't sure. The native language was one that he hadn't learnt. He didn't need to since interpreters were always on hand. He now wished he had, so he could at least have a heads up as to what their intentions were. Maybe he didn't want to know. Suddenly he was grabbed by his arms and dragged from the vehicle. To where, he didn't know. He might have an idea once the blindfold had been removed. He was hoping that would be soon. The men kept talking between themselves as Charles was hauled along a track. He heard a door open and was pushed forward. His blindfold was removed, but his wrist ties remained.

At first the light was blinding, and Charles had to squint against the glare. He looked around him, and saw that he was in a small room with little more than a bed in one corner. There was a small window in one wall. He was sure this would be locked. Several men guarded him.

"Why have you brought me here? I demand to know! What do you want from me? Talk to me, man. I'm a citizen of the United States, and we don't take kindly to this kind of thing." Charles wondered if there was any point in speaking to the guard as he was unlikely to speak English. But he persevered.

"I'm starting to get cold now. Have you got any blankets?"

"I no understand. You wait moment," came a reply from one of the men in pigeon English, who then left the room. Charles didn't recognise them as anyone he had seen before, but all were wearing some kind of military uniform with an interesting collection of headgear. Each carried a different weapon. There appeared to be no uniformity or discipline. Was he at the mercy of a group of rebels with no leader? No leader meant no proper plan, which in turn meant conflicts within the group. He hoped very strongly that there *was* a leader, but it didn't look like any of these men were leadership material. Were they part of the Sierra Leone Army or a splinter group? He thought he would probably find out once he discovered why he was kidnapped.

Moments later another person entered the room.

"I believe you have a problem?" asked the man in almost perfect English.

"Yes, I'm starting to get cold. Do you have any blankets?"

The man flicked his fingers and spoke to the original guard. He scurried away returning with two blankets. They were dropped on Charles's bed.

"Thank you. Tell me, why am I being held captive here? What do you want?"

"That will be revealed in due course."

"What is your name?" demanded Charles.

"Why do you ask so many questions?"

"Well, I am being held here against my will and there has to be a reason. If you don't volunteer information I have every right to ask. What do you hope to gain from my abduction?"

The man made no attempt to answer so Charles continued,

"Will you take these ties off my hands, please? They're digging in and beginning to hurt," he said a little more loudly. He was beginning to lose patience.

"Later," the man said, as he retreated from the room along with the guard who followed like a lap dog, the others trailing them. As the last man left and closed the door Charles distinctly heard the sound of a key being turned. Charles was sure that a guard had been stationed outside the door, and that he was trapped. He had no way of escape. He was too old for that anyway. His only hope would be to co-operate with his captors to ensure that his stay at the camp, however long that may be, would be as tolerable as possible. His skills as a diplomat would now be tested even if it were only to increase his own chances of survival.

*   *   *

USS George Washington – Somewhere in the North Atlantic

"Sir, message received from CINCLANTFLT," said the telegraphist, entering the bridge and handing over the message to Captain Ian Cartwright.

"Thanks," said Cartwright, scanning its contents. He continued,

"Oh, great, just what we needed."

"Problem, sir?" asked the XO.

"We've been ordered to stay in this region until further notice."

"Any particular reason?" the XO asked.

"None given, further information to follow. It's on the orders of the President himself."

Cartwright knew that his men had been looking forward to shore leave next week whilst their ship was in dry dock undergoing refit and upgrade. He had to make the call.

"Attention all hands, this is your Captain speaking. As of ten minutes ago, USS George Washington has been ordered to remain in the North Atlantic off the African coastline until further notice. This was an order directly from our Commander in Chief, the President. Our return home next week has therefore been postponed. That's all, gentlemen."

Cartwright knew that some of his men would moan. Moaning was a way of life in the military since nothing ever went the way you expected it. There would always be last minute adjustments. Thirty minutes later, the telegraphist returned to the bridge and handed over a second message.

"Another message, sir, from LANTFLT."

"Thanks," said Cartwright, as he put out his right hand to take the message.

"Follow up to the first message?" asked the XO.

"Yep. General Jack Copeland is due to arrive in Senegal tomorrow. We're to send him a welcoming committee and recover him back to the George Washington for a briefing. Must be important if Scorpion are involved." Cartwright turned in his seat to his CAG, Joe Kessler.

"Joe, put in your air timetable the deployment of a '53 to collect General Copeland tomorrow. Time to be confirmed."

"Aye aye, sir."

*   *   *

US Military Airbase – Somewhere in Southern United States

Copeland and Dinger Bell had joined up with Captain Dave Short and the remainder of the Scorpion team at the US Airbase. Prior to leaving Washington DC, Copeland had sought authority from Air Force Special Operations Command (AFSOC) in Florida to assign two C-17 Globemaster III transport aircraft to the operation. Eagle One contained Scorpion troops, and Eagle Two carried two dismantled Apache AH64A combat helicopters. Their respective ordnance was palletised on the same aircraft.

"Eagle One Heavy, this is clearance control. You are cleared for immediate take-off, runway zero eight right as filed. Climb and maintain runway heading until flight level 2000. Wind ten knots at two seven zero degrees. Contact tower on one one four decimal six at DME eight for additional vectors. Good day, sir."

The pilot read back the instructions and, once confirmed by clearance control, he applied 80% thrust (N1) to the four Pratt & Whitney F117 turbofan engines in order to spool the engines and initiate a controlled forward momentum. Once the aircraft began to roll along the runway, full power was applied to provide him with the maximum thrust needed to reach take off speed required through V1 and V2. The same instructions were given to Eagle Two, which took off shortly after Eagle One.

Twenty minutes into the flight, Copeland stood up. Behind him was a map of the West African region.

"Okay, listen up, people. This is our first real test as a combined unit under the umbrella of Scorpion. The situation is this. The United States Ambassador to Sierra Leone, Charles Perez, has been forcibly kidnapped from his vehicle whilst travelling to work. The ambassador was taken at gunpoint from here," Copeland pointed to a position on the map, and then continued,

"In the capital, Freetown, and it was reported that the vehicles transporting him travelled in this direction," again Copeland pointed to the map,

"Suggesting that the mountain regions may have been their final destination. The op will be in six phases: Phase One will be the deployment of a recon unit from the USS George Washington to locate the Ambassador's whereabouts using Imagery

Intelligence (IMINT) satellites, constellating with the military satellites (MILSAT). Once the recon team, via SATCOM, has given the green light that the target has been acquired, Phase Two of the op commences. This will be the movement of both C-17's leaving Senegal for Freetown's main airport, arriving there under the cover of darkness. Phase Three will be the rebuild of the Apaches. Phase Four will be the arrival of the '53s from the flat top, USS George Washington, to collect you bunch of ugly brutes. Phase Five will be the simultaneous deployment of both types of helicopters. The Apaches will go in and deliver a two-pronged attack, here and here," Copeland pointed on the map.

"At the same time, two '53s will transport us from Freetown to wherever the Ambassador is located and we will deploy on the ground. If the location of the rebel camp is near the river, the SEAL unit will deploy to the camp, and at the very last minute, once they hear the rotors of the inbound birds, they will secure the objective at all costs, protecting him until the opposing forces have been eliminated. Phase Six will be the exfiltration phase and recovery back to Liberty Base – USS George Washington. That is the game plan at the moment, gentlemen. As more intel comes in the likelihood of the goal posts changing increases. This is primarily a recovery operation though there is a kill order for any hostiles who are deemed a significant threat. Any questions?"

"Yes, sir, do we have any idea as to which group have kidnapped the Ambassador, and if so what kind of opposition and firepower we are up against?" asked Sergeant John Vickers.

"Good question, Vicks. The answer to both is no, not yet. Those answers should come from the recon team once the target has been spotted and acquired," replied Copeland.

"This will be a non-stop flight with two re-fuels in mid-air. It should take us about 20 hours, so get as much rest as you can."

All Copeland could do now was wait until they arrived in Senegal.

*   *   *

Rebel Camp, Sierra Leone – The next day

The door opened allowing light to shine into the eyes of Charles Perez as he lay on his bed. He squinted against the sudden brightness. He couldn't put his hands to his face to protect his eyes, since they were still tied behind him. His shoulders were becoming numb with lack of movement and his fingers had lost almost all feeling. He'd had no food since he had arrived at the camp and that was…he'd lost track of the days. Charles managed to focus his eyes, and only then saw the two men who had entered.

"On your feet," said the man who spoke English. Charles recognized him as the man he had seen on his first day, and was sure he was their leader. Charles did as he was ordered, though slowly, since he was weak with lack of food and exercise.

"Come," said the same man, who turned around and led the way. The second man, his lap dog, held Charles's arm and directed him in the same direction.

"Where are we going now?" asked Charles.

Maybe he was being released. No, they would have removed his wrist ties if that were the case. Perhaps he was being taken to meet somebody else? Or did the rebels have no further use for him? Charles began to have flashbacks of his childhood memories and the happy times with his wife Sarah. He snapped himself out of the melancholy mood. He had to be stronger; he needed the will to survive.

Charles was led to another hut, which held a table and two chairs. The man leading the way moved behind the table and sat on the chair facing towards Charles. The guard standing behind Charles forced him to sit on the remaining chair, facing towards the man who spoke English.

"What is your name?" asked the man.

Charles realised this was some kind of interrogation. He would be coerced into admitting to something that he hadn't done, and it would be broadcast across the world with him paraded as a battered pawn in a political game. There was just one thing missing – the camera.

"Charles Perez."

"Why are you in Sierra Leone?"

"You know who I am, and what I'm doing here."

"Just answer the questions!" shouted the interrogator.

"I am the United States Ambassador to Sierra Leone."

"How long have you been here?"

"This is ridiculous! Do you have a grudge against me or my country?"

Charles sensed the guard move from behind him to stand beside the table. Suddenly he was struck on the side of his face. He guessed it was a punch from the guard's fist. He hadn't expected it. He'd never been in a situation like this before. Violence was something he had never experienced. He could feel a trickle of something warm from the corner of his mouth. He checked it with his tongue and tasted what he had surmised. The warm thick taste of iron indicated that the skin in his mouth was lacerated. Another blow, this time to the other side. Was he going to be used as a punching bag?

"That's enough," said the man to the guard, then looked back at Charles and continued, "We are both powerful men and you know how these things work out."

"Five years."

"You know something about our country then?"

"Enough, yes."

"Good. You are a diplomat so you know how to negotiate with people."

This was the crunch point where their demands would be spelled out, Charles hoped to himself.

"What we need is some form of communications link, such as a SatPhone, with your embassy, so that we can negotiate our demands. We do not have this tech so we will have to ask for some. Do you have satellite communications in the embassy?"

"Yes, but it isn't portable," replied Charles, trying to be helpful. He then continued,

"There is a remote possibility, though, that one could be obtained through the embassy from another source."

"Excellent, Charles. Now you're starting to think like a negotiator," said the interrogator patronisingly before continuing,

"You will be given a sheet of paper on which you are to spell out our demand for this kind of communication from your embassy. Is that clear?"

"Yes. What do I call you? You know my name, what is yours?" asked a cautious Charles, hoping he wasn't provoking another punch.

"All that will become clear as soon as I have my means of communication."

The interrogator and the 'boxer' guard spoke in their native tongue. The guard scurried away, returning moments later with paper and a pen, and placed them on the table in front of Charles. A brief conversation took place between the two rebels. The guard moved towards Charles who grimaced in anticipation of another strike to his face. It never came. The rope tying his hands was cut.

"Now, write what I tell you."

Charles carefully moved his shoulders, painful as they had been locked in the same position for two days. He wouldn't be able to attack anyone since the pain would be excruciating. He would've had a go if he were younger. They knew what they were doing.

The interrogator spoke carefully, telling Charles the words that he wanted written on the piece of paper. The delivery, by whatever means, of this piece of paper would signify that negotiations had been opened with the rebels holding an ambassador from the United States. Charles was keen to co-operate. Help would be on hand to rescue him soon. He was sure of that. It would take time, but it would come. He just had to hang on for the sake of himself and his family. Once Charles had finished writing, he handed the paper back to his interrogator but hid the pen under his cuff in case he had the chance to use it later.

"Good," said the interrogator, scanning the letter before leaving the room. The guard stayed and Charles remained seated. The interrogator returned and continued,

"The letter has now been sent to your embassy. If they value your life, then I am sure they will respond positively. We shall wait and see."

*   *   *

US Embassy, Freetown, Sierra Leone

A white Toyota pickup van stopped outside the main entrance to the embassy. A black youth, dressed in camouflage trousers and a black singlet vest, jumped down from the back cargo area and walked the short distance to the Marine posted outside. Clutching a sheet of paper folded in two, the youth handed it over to the guard and pointed to the name on the front. The Marine read what was being pointed out to him. It read: 'To be handed to the Deputy Ambassador – URGENT'.

"Hey, buddy, who's this from?" shouted the Marine, but realised he wouldn't get a response. The youth had already retreated to the truck, which had started to pull away as the youth was clambering over the tailgate. The truck disappeared as quickly as it had arrived. Against protocol, the Marine opened the letter to scour the contents before handing it in to the receptionist. He was shocked by what it said, and immediately entered the embassy and asked the receptionist to get the Deputy Ambassador to come down to the reception area. John Fitzgerald, the Deputy Ambassador, arrived at reception.

"What's the problem, Marine?" asked the Deputy Ambassador.

"This letter has just been delivered by a youth who said it was to be given directly to you and no one else. It's pretty important, Sir."

"Thanks, Marine," said John Fitzgerald, who began to read as he walked through the receptionist's area.

"Christ. He's alive!" exclaimed John, rushing up the embassy stairs towards the communications room. "Get me a secure direct line to the NSA now," he said to the cryptographer.

"Secure line now, sir," said the cryptographer.

John relayed to Phil Scott the contents of the letter and the NSA was relieved to hear that Charles was still alive. In what condition, was anybody's guess. The main problem would be obtaining a SATCOM system. John had an idea. The NSA was glad to be offered a possible solution.

*   *   *

USS George Washington – Somewhere in the North Atlantic

"Sir, message from CINCLANT," said the telegraphist as he handed over the message to the XO. Captain Cartwright was in his cabin, and the XO required confirmation of what action to take.

"Bridge to Captain," he said over the tannoy.

"Captain, Aye. What is it, XO?"

"We've had another message from CINCLANT. I think you should see it."

"On my way."

Captain Cartwright arrived on the bridge moments later and was handed the message by his XO.

"That's a strange request, a portable SATCOM. Ask the Quartermaster if we have one?"

"Aye aye, Sir," responded the XO as he left the bridge.

Twenty minutes later the XO returned.

"Sir, we have four SATCOM's in total. That includes the one used by the SEAL unit."

"Get a message off to CINCLANT. Tell them we have two operational on board. Let's hold one in reserve."

"Aye aye, sir."

*   *   *

On board *Eagle One Heavy* – Somewhere over the North Atlantic

The loadmaster approached Jack and asked him to go forward to the flight deck. Jack responded.

As he climbed into the flight deck, the pilot handed him a set of headphones and invited him to plug them in. As he did so, the pilot said,

"There's a call coming in for you, General, from the Pentagon."

"Thanks," Copeland acknowledged.

"Jack, this is Mike Goddard. We've had a result. A message has been received from the Ambassador's captors this morning, and it appears he is still alive."

"Did they issue any demands in the message?" asked Copeland.

"Yep, they want a SATCOM link to be able to communicate with the outside world."

"We don't have any spare ones in our inventory, Mike." declared Copeland.

"That's okay, Jack. I've sent a message to the USS George Washington asking for one of theirs. As luck would have it, they have two operational ones on board."

"This could actually work in our favour. If we give them a SATCOM, we should be able to locate where the transmission is being relayed from. That would narrow the search area to one grid square. How is it to be handed over?" asked Copeland.

"The finer details are being worked on at the moment. Give me a call from the George Washington once you're on board. I should be able to update you then."

"Sure. Thanks for that info. That's good news."

"Thought you'd be pleased."

"Make sure, though, that the SATCOM isn't handed over until we arrive in the area, just in case they only transmit for short periods."

"You've got it. Anything else?"

"Not at present. Talk with you soon."

Copeland returned to the cargo bay of the C-17 and brought his men up to date with the latest developments. This was good news since he could get the rebels to play directly in to his hands. Their location, he was sure, would be known soon. All he then needed was their numbers and weaponry.

CHAPTER THIRTEEN

Leopold Sedar Senghor International Airport, Dakar, Senegal – the Next Day

"Eagle One Heavy, this is Dakar control tower. You are cleared for immediate landing on runway zero three. Wind is six knots, with a three hundred degree crosswind. Leave runway at taxi point six, and follow guide vehicle to holding area."

The pilot acknowledged his instructions and prepared his aircraft for landing. The two C-17's broke through the morning cloud at two thousand feet, and entered the final approach pattern into Senegal's International Airport. The two aircraft landed within sixty seconds of each other, and were guided to a remote area well away from the main terminal buildings. Copeland and Dinger left the aircraft by the tailgate door.

"General Copeland?" asked the man in US naval uniform. As he approached the aircraft he'd saluted.

"Yeah?" Copeland confirmed, and returned the salute.

"I'm Commander Steve Talbot, the XO on the USS George Washington, sir."

"Commander, this is my 2IC, Major Bell."

"Major," said the XO as he shook Dinger's hand. "I've been sent as your welcoming committee, and to recover you to the Washington. Your ride is this way, General," said the XO, as he pointed towards the helicopter, its blurred rotors showing full flight readiness.

The three men boarded the helo, and were swiftly airborne heading west across the Atlantic towards the George Washington, which was anchored two miles off the African coastline.

Ten Minutes Later

Once the helicopter had touched down on the flight deck, the XO led Copeland and Dinger to the bridge.

"This is General Copeland, sir," said the XO, as he introduced him to the ship's Captain.

"Jack, pleased to meet you. I'm Captain Ian Cartwright, the CO of this floating airport."

Copeland introduced Dinger to Cartwright and all three exchanged pleasantries and professional courtesies.

"Can I get you some coffee?" asked Cartwright of his guests.

Both accepted the offer and Cartwright ordered it to be brought to the wardroom.

"How was the flight, Jack?"

"One hell of a hop. Military aircraft were never designed with comfort in mind."

"What do you expect for a free ride? Let's go down to my quarters and you can fill me in."

Cartwright led the way down the many gangways and stairs, eventually arriving at the wardroom.

"What's the game plan then, Jack?"

"Firstly, did you have a request to provide a SATCOM module?"

"Yeah, that's a strange one. What's the reason?"

Copeland briefed Cartwright on what he already knew and the outline of the proposed plan. The plan required the assistance of some of his crew, so he was obliged to brief their CO. The aircrew would be used to fly the '53s into the designated areas, and drop off SCORPION's ground troops. The recon unit would be the eyes and ears on the ground, gaining valuable intelligence. The information that they fed back would dictate the way in which the mission evolved.

"Can I use a phone, Ian, to call the Pentagon?" asked Copeland.

"Sure, I'll get the comms op to transfer it to this number."

The call was put through a short while later.

"Admiral, this is General Jack Copeland."

"Are you on the George Washington yet?"

"Just arrived. What's the latest?"

"No further news. We need to make the arrangements for the transfer of the module to the rebels. How do you want to play this one?"

"Were there any instructions in the original letter sent to the embassy?"

"They gave the Deputy Ambassador forty-eight hours to provide the SATCOM. They would return at that time to collect."

"That's cutting it fine. We've only just got here so it'll be a bit of a scramble to organize within the time frame. It's important that we go along with their instructions: it gives them the feeling that they're calling the shots."

Copeland finished by suggesting that a helicopter be deployed to Freetown airport where they would hand the equipment to an embassy official, together with the operating instructions.

One hour later, the module was on its way to Freetown

*   *   *

US Embassy, Freetown, Sierra Leone 0530 hours (twenty-four hours later)

The handover went as arranged. The white pickup pulled up outside the embassy, and one of its occupants walked towards the front entrance. He was cautious, having no intention of becoming a hostage himself. The Marine guard stepped outside with the Deputy Ambassador. The module was handed over to the rebel. The instructions were handed over separately, so as to emphasise their importance.

"You must use these to operate the phone," said the Deputy Ambassador. The rebel simply shrugged his shoulders, denying any understanding of the English language. The Deputy Ambassador realised there was no point in attempting further conversation. The case, its instructions, and the contact phone numbers at the embassy were carried back to the waiting vehicle, which then sped off.

The module phone number had already been passed back to Langley for the monitoring of its activities. Their part of the agreement fulfilled, it was now up to the rebels to make the next move.

*   *   *

Rebel Camp – Somewhere in Sierra Leone

The vehicle zigzagged as it travelled along the mountainous tracks, partly to avoid the many potholes, but mostly as a result of the driver's inebriated condition.

"Give me some wine," the driver said to his passenger

"None left," the passenger had replied and up-ended the bottle to prove his point.

The driver turned on his radio to listen to the local station. He looked down and increased the volume, looking back up barely in time to see the camp gates. He braked harshly, skidding as he did so, and managed to stop short of the entrance. They spoke briefly with the sentry who opened the gates for them. Once through the gates, the vehicle was swiftly abandoned and they walked to their commander's hut.

"They have given us the telephone and this piece of paper," said one of the youths as he handed them over.

"Good," said the commander, as he looked over the instructions and phone numbers. He would make a call later.

*   *   *

USS George Washington – Anchored off the West African Coastline - Officers Mess

Copeland and Dinger enjoyed the hospitality of their host, having been invited to join Cartwright for lunch. While they were eating, the TV mounted high in one corner of the mess had announced a CNN Special African Report.

"Hey, guys, I need to hear this," said Copeland as he increased the volume using the remote control. The broadcast came to life after a short break.

"…Welcome back. I'm John Burbank. The news has been dominated over the last few days by the events in the Middle East, and the West African City of Freetown in Sierra Leone. We're gonna cross live first to Freetown for a Special Report from our African correspondent, Elisabeth Young."

"There seems to be an endless spiral of lawlessness here in Sierra Leone as rebel groups, corrupt officials, and renegade government soldiers struggle with a West African coalition of peacekeepers for control of the country's precious mineral resources. The citizens of Freetown are under virtual twenty-four hour curfew, many still without food, water or electricity, following large scale fighting at the beginning of this month. Outside the capital of Freetown, it has long been impossible to say who has control. Now, the same is true of the capital itself. It is estimated that, of a population of four million, some one hundred thousand people have been killed in Sierra Leone since 1991. The hope of finding Charles Perez, the US Ambassador to Sierra Leone, alive, diminishes as each day

passes with no news from his captors. With communications virtually non-existent it has to be wondered if and how the rebels intend to get their messages or demands through. This is Elisabeth Young for CNN in Freetown, Sierra Leone. Back to you, John.

"Thanks, Elisabeth. And now for some other stories that have been dominating the news…" said John, as he was faded away.

Copeland had listened intently to the report since they were often more up to date than his own briefings. CNN didn't know anything about the phone module. He was hoping that a partial news blackout could be imposed, primarily to protect Scorpion and, of course, the rescue mission. Copeland was becoming intrigued by Elisabeth. He wanted to know more about her. She was only two miles away and he hadn't yet seen her. There was time. The wait would be worthwhile, he was certain. Presently he had to remain focused on the mission.

Copeland and Dinger would remain on board the George Washington until the rebels had used the SATCOM phone. Only then would Phase One of the mission be actioned. In the meantime, all he could do was wait and enjoy the hospitality of his host.

*　　*　　*

Rebel Camp – Somewhere in Sierra Leone, 2100 Hours (CET)

"American Embassy, this is the commander of the group who are holding your Ambassador. Can you hear me?"

"Yes. What is your name?" said the comms operator who had been placed on duty to monitor such calls. There was also a duty officer on call to mediate with the rebels.

"My name is Brigadier Maxin Sankoah. I am the Commander of an elite group of soldiers. Our unit is called the Sierra Leone Freedom Fighters – the SLFF."

The comms operator quickly summoned the duty officer who was in a room nearby. Colonel Harris, the Military Liaison Officer, came through into the comms centre and picked up the conversation where the operator had left off.

"Brigadier Sankoah, my name is Colonel George Harris. The first question that I need to ask you is, what is the condition of our Ambassador?"

"He is alive for now, but for how long depends on you. On whose authority do you speak with me?"

"My Deputy Ambassador. What are your demands, Brigadier?"

"You get straight to the point, don't you? In exchange for your Ambassador, I demand the release from jail of one of my officers. His name is Colonel Paul Kabbah. Unless he is released on my terms, you will never see your Ambassador again."

"This may take time to negotiate with your government, especially at this time of night."

"We will resume our talks tomorrow. I will call in twelve hours' time. Have a reply for me then."

*   *   *

CIA Headquarters, Langley, VA – 1500 hours (SET)

The video screen came to life, and caught the duty analyst by surprise. He immediately hit the record button, and called his Director. Mike arrived minutes later.

"Get a fix on that transmission area," ordered Mike.

"Already onto it."

The analyst was using a series of satellites to cross-reference the location of where the broadcast was being made from.

"Bingo, sir," said the elated analyst. They prided themselves in the knowledge that no task was too great for them. The technology available would make it a breeze.

Mike continued to listen attentively to the broadcast for any hint or snippet of information that the agency could use to its advantage and that of Scorpion. Mike looked at the images of the Ambassador. He was gaunt, sallow-faced, with beard growth that aged him by ten years. He also had cuts to his face and bruising that cast shadows under his eyes. Mike needed to act quickly.

*   *   *

USS George Washington – two Miles off the West African Coastline

"Message from Langley, sir," said the telegraphist, as he handed the message sheet over to his captain. He waited in case there was a reply.

"Ask General Copeland to meet me in the Control Room in five minutes."

"Aye aye, sir."

*   *   *

The Control Room – Five Minutes Later

"What is it, Ian?"

"This message was received from Langley ten minutes ago." Cartwright handed the message over to Copeland.

"Take a look at this," Cartwright continued as he switched on the video down link monitor.

Copeland, Dinger and Cartwright looked at the monitor, and the effects the trauma were having on the Ambassador.

"He's taken a bit of a pasting. The politicians will sort out the release crap. Now we can get to work."

Copeland looked at the co-ordinates that had been transmitted from Langley.

"Ian, have you got a map of this region?" asked Copeland, only realising what he had said after his mouth shut again.

"We've got charts *and* maps of the whole wide world, Jack. Here you go," smiled Cartwright, as he pulled out a rolled map from under the electronic map board and handed it to Copeland.

"Dinger, plot these co-ordinates, will you?"

Copeland handed over the message, together with the map. Dinger busied himself using rulers and chinagraph pencils.

"There it is, right there," confirmed Dinger, as he pointed to the spot on the map where the first transmission had been broadcast from. Copeland looked at the map to ensure he had all the info he needed to start the operation.

"Okay, it's thirty miles east of Freetown along the Rokel Creek. Phase One is about to be launched." Copeland turned. "Ian, can you get me the Team Leader of your Recon outfit and have him meet me in your wardroom? That's if you don't mind?"

"Sure, no problem." Cartwright issued instructions to a subordinate to make the arrangements.

*   *   *

Captain's Wardroom – Ten Minutes later

Copeland was still looking over the map with Dinger and Cartwright when there was a knock on the bulkhead door.

"Yeah," said Copeland casually as he looked up. The door opened and in stepped a Marine in camouflage uniform.

"General Copeland, sir, I'm Captain Steve Mills. Commander of the Recon Platoon," said Mills, as he saluted.

"Thanks, Captain, stand easy. I have a mission for you and your team that may be a long and protracted one. However, I'm sure you guys are used to laying around waiting for something to happen."

Mills smiled and said, "It does have its moments. What's the mission, sir?"

Copeland asked Mills to step over to the map. He was given an overview as to the problem and the solution.

"You will have an eight man team, lightly equipped with minimal weapons systems. You are to avoid contact with the SLFF at all costs, because if your cover is blown, the life expectancy of the objective will be drastically reduced. You will have to be self-contained and may have to divide your team depending on what you find. You will infiltrate here." Copeland pointed to the map in the Geri Bena and Forodugu regions. "Your mission will be to monitor movements, and ascertain the strengths and morale of the rebel camp. You are also to identify the location of the objective and which hut he most frequently uses. This is the man you're looking for." Copeland pointed to the recent video still of the Ambassador. "The information that you provide will dictate when Phase Two of the mission commences. Any problems with that, Captain?"

"Will the team be involved with the rescue of the objective?"

"No. You will remain covert until the cavalry have come and gone. You are a vital and integral component of this op. Without your team, this couldn't get off the ground."

"When do you want us to move out, Sir?"

"0400 tomorrow."

"Anything else, General?"

"That's all, Captain. Good luck and good hunting."

"Thank you, Sir," said Mills, as he saluted and turned about.

Copeland turned back to Cartwright.

"Ian, can you arrange for their infiltration at 0400 by helo to this point here, two miles short of the site." Copeland indicated the designated DZ.

"Sure, no problem."

"It's down to them now. Let's hope they find him alive and then we can kick some arse."

*　　　*　　　*

0400 Hours – The Following Morning

The MH-53J Pave Low III helicopter had already commenced its start-up sequence with their huge seven blade main rotor and four bladed canted tail rotor in full rotation as Captain Steve Mills walked across the flight deck of the USS George Washington. His team followed. They were airborne within minutes. Flight time would be twenty minutes. His men knew the importance of their mission. No one talked; they just focused on what their individual responsibilities were. Captain Mills, who had plugged his headphones into the helicopter's comms system, heard some chatter from the flight deck.

"Captain Mills, five minutes to the DZ," said the navigator.

"Acknowledged," confirmed Mills.

Captain Mills put up his hand to signify five minutes to the drop zone. He knew their hearts would be pounding and adrenaline rushing as they commenced the mission proper.

Mills could sense the forward momentum begin to slow, so he opened the slide doors in front of him and pointed for the same to happen on the other side. The helo was able to land in a clearing. Eight men dismounted and assumed prone positions until the helicopter was well away.

They listened for twenty minutes in case their arrival had been observed. Nothing. Captain Mills flipped down his night vision goggles, and looked around him to see where the remainder of his troops were. They had taken up defensive positions looking outwards from their insertion point. Mills then checked his GPS against the map. Check. He knew his direction and bearings. He gave the gestured order to move out.

Two and a half hours later, they approached the rebel camp. Mills surveyed the area, mapping out what had to be done next. He'd briefed the team beforehand and was glad to see the plan needed no revision. They would take up positions so that they could observe the camp from differing perspectives, and Mills waved them into place. He noted that there was another camp three hundred meters away, across the river on the embankment of Forodugu. *'This must have been what General Copeland was on about,'* Mills said to himself. Although the second camp posed no immediate threat to their recon mission, it was an area that Mills would have to keep an eye on.

Captain Mills was equipped with the latest SATCOM equipment that allowed him to use a keyboard to send messages instead of voice. This was ideal for covert ops where stealth was vital. He sent a simple message: 'Now in place'. Mills knew that the

Pentagon and the President would also know of their status. His next transmission would be in six hours as pre-arranged.

*   *   *

The Rebel Camp at Geri Bena, Sierra Leone – 0900 Hours

Charles didn't hear the door open. He was getting progressively more tired and physically weaker as the days passed. Food was in short supply and his movements had been severely restricted, so he wasn't able to exercise. He felt something shaking his body, so he turned over and slowly opened his sunken and battered eyes.

He had difficulty in focusing at first, but eventually saw two people who appeared to be boys. One was dressed in jeans and the football shirt of an English football team, the other in combat trousers and a black singlet vest. They both carried rifles. They spoke in their native tongue, which meant nothing to Charles. The boys realised this and pointed to the door. Charles slowly rose from his bed and was pushed towards the door, with his hands still tied behind his back. He was motioned towards the hut behind his, where he had been punched several times over the course of his interrogations.

The brightness of the morning sun hit Charles square in the eyes. He was unable to move forward until he could open them and readjust to the brightness. He stood there for what seemed like forever, but was probably only a couple of minutes.

He then followed the boys. He was pushed into the hut and down onto the chair he had occupied before. Behind the table was their leader, Brigadier Maxin Sankoah, who was dressed in his cream military uniform.

"Do you know the whereabouts of one of my officers, Colonel Paul Kabbah?"

"No, I don't," replied Charles.

Again someone stepped around him and punched him in the face. The blow seemed harder this time. Probably because his face had lost some of its flesh and his cheekbones were now more prominent.

He grimaced at the pain. He was surprised that his jaw hadn't broken yet. Any more of this punishment and neither his wife – nor anyone else, for that matter – would recognise him.

"Don't lie to me. You get reports given to you on everything regarding both political and military matters here in my country. How can you sit there and tell me that you don't know?"

"That's one area I haven't been following."

Charles was punched in his stomach this time. He doubled over trying to ride the wave of pain. Was he going to be hit again?

"Unlikely. These soldiers of mine sometimes have a mind of their own and can be quite uncontrollable. Unless you tell me where he is, I will step outside and leave them here with you."

Charles looked at the youth. He didn't like the odds since he couldn't defend himself from any physical attacks. His only option would be to cooperate.

"He was transferred from Nairobi to Freetown jail. That's where he is at the moment."

"Thank you. Now, that wasn't so difficult, was it? I'm going to send another transmission, and you are going to use your diplomatic skills to obtain his release. Do you understand?"

"Mm," Charles mumbled, the pain in his jaw preventing him from speaking clearly.

"United States Embassy, this is Brigadier Sankoah. Can you hear me?"

"Yes, Brigadier. What do you require?"

"Have you obtained the release of my officer yet?"

"We are having problems in locating him. It will take us a little while longer."

"You don't have much time to carry out my very simple request. You say you do not know where my Colonel is, well I have a surprise for you…"

Sankoah turned the set around, so that it faced Charles. The built in camera showed the damage to his face and the strain he was under. Charles began to speak slowly through swollen lips.

"I have told them that Colonel Kabbah is in the jail in Freetown. You will have to act on that. I do understand it will take time to obtain the governmental authority to release him, but I don't expect you to give into these demands just for my sake."

Charles found it hard to say those last few words. He was choking with emotion. He might have signed his own death warrant, though, on the other hand, it might spur his own government in to doing something positive. He would like to have confidence in the latter course of action, but given the unpredictability of these boys – especially when under the influence of drugs and their local drink, Popsicle, he wasn't so sure. He had seen reports at the embassy that this same bunch of rebels was considered responsible for some of the worst atrocities in Sierra Leone's civil war. Amputating the limbs of children with machetes, murdering families, and torching houses. Additional reports had also been submitted stating that young girls had been assigned to each rebel to become his sexual property, and young boys fought alongside the men using firearms and hand grenades. He hadn't seen any girls in the camp, but there were certainly boys here mimicking the men's training. Sankoah swivelled the SATCOM back to his side of the table.

"I have another demand. I, the SLFF Commander, demand that the government of Sierra Leone step down and all detainees be set free. This is not up for discussion. I will contact you again in twelve hours."

Sankoah cut the transmission. He might not get both of his demands met, but at least one of them would be. Charles was pushed back to his hut, the door slamming closed behind him. The guard took up his usual position outside.

*   *   *

Recon Platoon – Geri Bana Four Hours later – 1300 Hours

Captain Mills had noted every detail of the comings and goings inside the rebel camps on both sides of the Creek. It was time he made his report. He uploaded all details 'as at 1300 hours'. In six hours he would update that report.

*   *   *

USS George Washington

There was a knock on the bulkhead door of the Captain's wardroom.

"Yeah," said Cartwright

"Message just in on the SATCOM teleprinter, sir."

"Thanks."

Cartwright read over the message and then headed towards Copeland's bunk. A knock on the door confirmed he was in.

"Come in." Cartwright could see that Dinger was still asleep on the top bunk.

"Jack, this has just been received from the recon platoon. It's exactly what we needed," said Cartwright, as he handed the report over to Copeland.

"Good. They know which hut Charles is being held in and how many rebels. Weapon systems, yep, nothing too testing here. I see we have another camp across the water. I thought as much. Not a problem. So that's info after six hours. Pretty damn good.

Their next report is due in six hours' time, isn't it? Let's see whether anything changes between now and then."

"When do you propose to deploy, Jack?"

"When the time is right, Ian. I can't go in half-baked because lack of adequate preparation is a recipe for disaster. I have to have all of the intel I possibly can in order to ensure the greatest possible chance of success. I owe it to the guys and to H.E. If I don't get it right, there's no second chance and, well, if we're compromised at any stage, the rebels may feel that they have no further use for Charles. All this would then have been for nothing."

"Are you getting much support from back home?"

"Limited. The Joint Chiefs are a real pain in the butt. They won't like it if it all goes well. Ian, I need to send a message to Langley. Can you arrange that for me?"

"Yeah, what is it?"

Copeland explained that he needed a MILSAT image of both camps blown up to maximum resolution. It would have to be downloadable to the control room on the Washington. The photos would be invaluable in fine-tuning the operation.

On a personal note, he also wanted to know how Joanne Wiley was doing.

*   *   *

Six Hours Later

"Sir, message from the Recon team," said the telegraphist, as he handed over the message to

Cartwright on the bridge. Ian scanned the report before handing command over to the XO and heading down to Copeland's cabin.

"Jack, another message," Cartwright said as he knocked and entered.

"Who from?" enquired Copeland.

"The Recon platoon."

Copeland began to read the message.

"There only ever seems to be about thirty people in the camp at any one time. They've observed more weapons, heavy ones this time, but on the other side of the river. It looks like their personal weapons are the old British Army 7.62 SLR, the usual Kalashnikovs, and hand grenades…oh, and here's an interesting twist, rocket propelled grenades. Let's hope they don't know which way to point them. Those camouflage uniforms appear to be old British Army ones too. As their equipment isn't as technologically advanced as ours I'm going to take them seriously, especially as they are a bunch of unpredictables with weapons. That's not an ideal combination and one, which presents its own risks. I think, Ian, we're moving closer to the 'off'. However, I want to wait at least two days before I move in. That gives the recon lads the chance to produce consistent reports. If there's no change, then we're okay. If there is a change, then we can either go with what we already know or put the change down to a one off circumstance."

"What about the rest of your guys?"

"They'll fly down from Senegal at the last minute. Bearing in mind the on-board '64's will have to be reassembled. When that happens, three of your

'53's will have to RV with us at Freetown's Lungi Airport, again at the last minute, so as not to arouse any suspicions."

∗   ∗   ∗

Rebel Camp Geri Bana, Sierra Leone two Hours Later – 2100 Hours

"US Embassy, this is Brigadier Sankoah. Can you hear me?"

"Yes, Brigadier," came the reply.

"Do you have any news for me?"

"The second demand that you made was passed to the Sierra Leone government, but was refused. The US Government has no influence on the actions of foreign governments. It is for the people of the country to show a vote of no confidence. As for your first demand, your government appears to be listening, and I hope to be able to give you some positive news on your next transmission."

"The clock is ticking. The longer you stall, the longer the suffering your Ambassador has to endure. I will call back in twelve hours' time."

Sankoah cut the connection. He pulled out a bottle of locally produced gin from the drawer beneath his desk. He took a swig and then put it back. Outside, he could hear the joviality of his troops. He stepped away from his desk and looked through the window. Some of them were stripped to their waists; their bodies were covered with sores. 'Juju', a potent mixture of raw cocaine and jungle roots, was being rubbed in to these sores and cuts. This produced an instant high.

Sankoah looked at his soldiers and remembered that only a few months ago, they were fighting alongside government and international armies against the rebels of the Revolutionary United Front. That relationship was short lived: he fell out with the government after a series of car-jackings, robberies, and rapes. He now commanded his own army, spurred on by his own ideals and claims that the Sierra Leone Government was not delivering what they had promised to their people.

*   *   *

On Board the USS George Washington – Four Hours Later 0100 Hrs

The duty telegraphist tore the sheet of paper from the teleprinter and recognised its source. He had instructions to wake his Captain on receipt of any information from Geri Bena. This was one such message.

He knocked on Cartwright's cabin door. No reply. He knocked again, and heard movement and stirring inside.

"Yeah," said Cartwright.

"Sir, message from Geri Bena," said the telegraphist as he opened the door.

Cartwright read the contents of the message then dismissed the sailor.

"No reply. That'll be all."

"Aye aye, Sir."

Cartwright knew that Copeland would want to see the message so he headed to his bunk. He knocked and entered.

"Jack, it's Ian."

"Uh. What time is it?"

Cartwright switched on the bunk light to illuminate Copeland's bed space. "We've had another report from the recon team," Cartwright said as he handed over the message.

"No change in numbers. That's good. They've identified the rebel's accommodation huts and their Commander. Even better. If we can capture him alive, that'll be a good result. Mills also reports that some of the rebels were seen to be in high spirits, possibly from drugs or alcohol. That's all we need, a drug-crazed soldier carrying a loaded weapon who's uncontrollable even by his own leader. These are loose cannons we could do without. I think, Ian, we are almost ready to launch tomorrow morning. We'll decide the final plans later today."

"Okay, Jack, goodnight."

Copeland would bring Dinger up to date first thing in the morning. What he needed now was rest. The military had a saying 'Rest when you can, because you never know when the next chance is going to be'. He intended to listen to this advice and grab some whilst he could.

*   *   *

Six Hours Later – 0700 Hours

The teleprinter in the ops room came to life. The telegraphist tore off the message and confirmed its origin. He quickly read the message, which stated simply 'NO CHANGE'. He would hand it to his Captain at the first opportunity.

*   *   *

SLFF Rebel Camp – Geri Bena, Sierra Leone Two Hours Later – 0900 Hours

Charles was getting used to the morning routine of being woken up and shepherded in to another hut for the purposes of being put on display for the captive audience that Sankoah now commanded.

His hands were still tied behind his back and he'd had no food for…probably two days. He'd been able to drink water with the help of his guards, who thought it a great joke to tease him knowing that he couldn't do anything about it in his present incapacitated state. Charles could feel his weight loss since he was having trouble keeping his trousers up. He reeked. Excrement, urine and body odours were his constant companions, making Charles feel unhealthy, dirty and vulnerable. He wasn't sure how much more of this he could take, but he had every confidence in his government, knowing they were actively working to secure his release. As a diplomat he knew the time frames of negotiating demands, but when put in such a position yourself, when you are the one being bargained over, human nature expects it to happen a lot quicker. As Charles entered what he now thought of as 'The Interrogation Chamber', Brigadier Sankoah was already sitting behind the desk with the portable SATCOM lit up and ready to transmit.

"Sit down, Charles," said a patronising Sankoah. "Sleep well I hope?"

"No, I didn't and I think your hospitality stinks. I've had no food now for two days. If I die of starvation how are you going to negotiate any deal? Your bargaining chip will have slipped through your fingers."

"You will be released soon, I am sure. I feel the time is getting closer where both sides will be satisfied. Let me find out how it is progressing. US Embassy this is Brigadier Sankoah, can you hear me?"

"Yes, we can," confirmed the embassy official.

"What news do you have for me?"

"Your government say they will consider releasing Kabbah tomorrow morning, but firstly we need to be satisfied that our Ambassador is still alive."

Sankoah turned the SATCOM module around to face Charles. His image was now being transmitted to the United States and the horrors of his torture were readily apparent to the people receiving the up-link. They would be shocked at how their Ambassador could have been reduced to this. At least Sankoah hoped that that would be their reaction. He knew how emotional the Americans were and on seeing one of their own in this condition, they would agitate for his demands to be met. He had no reason to believe anything else. No one knew where his camps were.

"We'll have you released soon, Ambassador," said the embassy official.

Sankoah turned the module back to face himself. "I will call in twenty-four hours to make the final arrangements. If at that time you continue to delay me, then you will leave me no alternative."

Sankoah cut the connection and closed the module, leaving his last statement as an ultimatum. The Americans would now be considering whether or not he was serious and whether they should call his bluff and wait it out. It was in the hands of the Americans now.

"So, Charles, how do you like my camp?"

"If you like festering in your own filth then its fine."

"No need to be like that. Your stay should hopefully only be a temporary one, provided your people do as I ask of them."

"You will not get away with holding someone against their will. At some point you will be brought to justice for your crimes."

Charles thought to himself that he might have said something that struck a chord with Sankoah. His reaction would go either way.

"Our government has no laws to speak of. The police are corrupt so people can get away with crimes. As a respectable member of our community, the police leave me well alone."

"Your whole society is crumbling around you, but you can't see that. All this in-fighting is fragmenting the country, and to rebuild any trust that you expect from other countries, you will have to get your own house in order first."

"We expect standards that are not being met by our government."

"Using the bullet and violence is not the answer. The ballot box is. Unless you stop all these killings then you won't have a country worth fighting for, nor anyone to put into government. That's the truth of the matter, but you won't realise that until it's too late. Just think what you are doing, Sankoah, before you cripple everything. This country could be a wealthy one given the output from your mines, but you need to capitalise on that and everyone needs to rally around and pull in the same direction, not opposing ones!"

"You are telling me there has to be a political solution, Charles?"

"Yes, Sankoah, that's sensible talk and how I see the future for this country. You asked me before how much I knew about your country, well, I know a lot, and unless you all work together, you will have no homeland to speak of or to be proud of. An honourable defeat is better than a dishonourable victory. The stark choice is yours."

Sankoah sat quietly, contemplating what Charles had said. Charles was thinking to himself, *'I hope that sounded convincing. Sankoah needs to understand that the violence must stop!'* Sankoah didn't reply. He just gestured to the guards to remove him. Charles was pushed and pulled back to his hut. The door was, as always, closed and locked.

Charles could hear loud voices outside which didn't seem to fit in with the camp routine, at least during the time he had been there. He struggled to get up from his bed, rolling over onto his side first. He moved across to the window. There appeared to be twelve more boys in the camp. He hadn't seen them before. Was this a guard change or reinforcements? He didn't know, nor did he care. He returned to his bed and lay down. His arms were almost dead numb now and the feeling of the ropes cutting in to his wrists had almost disappeared. That was a bad sign. He hoped gangrene hadn't set in. If they had to be amputated, he couldn't imagine himself without hands. He would feel useless, a burden on his wife and having to rely on others to do things for him. How would his wife manage? How was she? Was she coping with the situation?? Did she know where he was, and had she seen the pictures of him?

He had to snap out of this mental downward spiral and focus on positive things. He couldn't think of any at the moment, but he would keep searching his grey matter to keep his sanity. Once he lost that, then his will for survival would be compromised, and it would only be a matter of time before he…no, that wasn't going to happen, surely. He kept running over things in his mind and before long had drifted off into an uneasy sleep…again.

CHAPTER FOURTEEN

On Board the USS George Washington Five Hours Later – 1300 hours

As the countdown clock to mission launch continued ticking, Copeland wanted to be involved with all the prep activities. He was in the ops room when the scheduled report came through from the recon team. He had seen the previous report and had expected its comments. Now he was reading the latest report. He tore the sheet from the teleprinter and headed to the bridge. Dinger was trying out Cartwright's chair for size.

"Enjoy it while you can, Dinger."

"Any news, Jack?" asked Dinger, who seemed at ease in this position.

"Yeah, there was a visit this morning, which was added to Captain Mills' report. They seem to have come from the direction of the other camp across the river, roughly about another dozen or so boys. It seems to have been a replenishment party, and probably an excuse for a piss up. They only stayed for a short while, then returned."

Copeland turned to Cartwright. "Any news from Langley regarding those photographs?"

"I'll just check," said Cartwright, as he pressed the ops room intercom.

"They're on their way up as we speak," confirmed Cartwright.

A sailor entered the bridge carrying an envelope. "These are the items that you wanted, Sir," said the sailor.

"Thanks." Cartwright handed the envelope over to Copeland.

Copeland was keen to see the telex message concerning Joanne Wiley. He was relieved to read that she was conscious and able to walk, but was saddened by the injuries that had devastated her beauty. This would have dire consequences to her self-esteem and ability to interact with people. She would have to undergo a further four operations with skin grafting. What a mess. As a footnote to the message, Joanne thanked Copeland for his kind enquiry and wished him every success in his forthcoming operation. She also wanted him to say hi to Dinger. Copeland felt bitter, but knew that this could not affect his judgement or the mission.

Copeland glanced over the four large satellite photographs of the rebel camps. Two photos each of Geri Bana and Forodugu. He had one last thing to do before he settled his battle plans. He headed down to the ops room and asked the operator to connect him to a number he provided. He was connected almost at once. This was technology at its best and it never ceased to amaze him.

"May I speak with Elisabeth Young, please?"

"Who's calling?"

"Jack Copeland."

"Thank you, sir. I'll try and locate her for you. One moment, please."

247

Copeland was hoping that she wouldn't be out on an assignment, as he desperately wanted to speak with her.

"Jack, how are you?" asked Elisabeth.

He had longed to hear her voice again and when it came he was rendered speechless. This increased his heartbeat. He hadn't felt like this since he met his ex-wife all those years ago. It was good to feel this way again. The only drawback was that he hadn't yet met her. He took a deep breath.

"I'm OK, thanks. Listen, there is something urgent I need to discuss with you this afternoon."

"Okay. On the phone?"

"No, in Freetown."

"You're here now?"

"Five minutes away."

"I can't believe it. I'm free this afternoon. Give me a time?"

"Say 1500 at the airport?"

"Sure, I'll drive down and pick you up. What flight are you coming in on?"

"One courtesy of the US Government. A big helicopter."

"You certainly travel in style, Jack. Have they increased your budget?" she asked, chuckling.

"Ha, ha," Copeland said sarcastically. "I'll see you at 1500."

Copeland left the ops room and returned to the bridge.

"Ian, I need to get shore side for an appointment at 1500 this afternoon. If we are to launch the mission in the morning I need to put a lid on media reports that may jeopardise the mission status. I have a contact in Freetown who works with the CNN, and I'm hoping she will be able to help me."

"No problem, Jack. Be ready at 1450."

Copeland knew that Cartwright would arrange it for him. All he had to do was turn up.

*   *   *

Lungi International Airport, Freetown, Sierra Leone 1500 Hours

As Copeland stepped from the helicopter in his battlefield fatigues, he saw in the distance a white van with CNN emblazoned on its side in large black letters. A huge whip antenna bent from the front bumper to a fastening on the side of the vehicle. As he began to walk over the vehicle began to move towards him, and then stopped alongside.

"How does a guy hitch a lift around here?" asked Copeland.

"It depends who you are. You must be Jack Copeland? Spot the stranger in town."

"You must be Elisabeth Young. Full of wit as usual."

"Climb in. What's the urgency?" she asked, as she began to drive the vehicle away from the aircraft parking area.

"Is there somewhere that we can go to be private?" asked Copeland sheepishly, not knowing how that would be taken.

"Yeah, sure. We'll go to my place."

"You mean they give you accommodation as well as a company car? Wow, I'm in the wrong job."

"Don't act so surprised Jack. This is the twentieth century. Mobility and comfort are the name of the game."

Twenty-five minutes later, they were on the other side of the bay having taken the fifteen-minute hovercraft journey from Tagrin dock to Kissy. There wasn't a scheduled service, but it seemed to mesh with aircraft movements.

Elisabeth pulled up outside the front of her apartment block. Copeland was impressed by the view. The outside of the flat didn't look much, but if all you wanted was a place to put your head down after a day at the office, it didn't matter where it was or what it looked like. She led Copeland through the ground floor entrance, up one flight of stairs and into her flat. Copeland's first thoughts were *'It's small but cosy with a definite woman's touch'*.

"Would you like a coffee, Jack?"

"Yeah, that's fine, thanks. Milk no sugar."

"So what brings you to Sierra Leone?"

"The recent trouble here…"

Elisabeth nodded.

"Well, I've been sent as a trouble–shooter."

"Has it something to do with the Ambassador?"

"Don't you ever let up asking questions?" asked Copeland as he smiled.

"The curious and inquisitive nature of a reporter. The old adage of course is, unless you ask, no-body will ever tell you."

Elisabeth brought two coffee cups out from the kitchenette and handed one to Copeland. She sat on one of the soft chairs whilst Copeland occupied the sofa.

"I'm glad to have finally had the chance to meet you. You're as I expected, I mean I've seen your broadcasts, but you are much more beautiful in person than the TV portrays you."

"Thanks, Jack, that's a nice compliment. You're not as I expected. I thought, being a general, you would have a big belly, grey hair, double chin. I'm impressed."

"You don't pull your punches, do you? Straight to the point, which reminds me. Elisabeth…" Copeland looked in her eyes and paused, "…what I am about to tell you is eat-before-you-read secret. The National Security kind of secret."

"You're probably telling the wrong person, Jack. Media people can't keep secrets. Secrets make the best headlines whether right or wrong," she interrupted him.

"I want you to hear me out, Elisabeth, but first, I want you to give me your word that none of today's conversation will be disclosed until I say so. Agreed? It never happened unless I say otherwise."

"Sounds intriguing. As a reporter I find it hard to hold back on anything, but I've trusted you before, Jack, so go ahead. Agreed."

"Thanks. It'll all become clear in a minute. The reason why I am here is to do with the capture of the Ambassador, Charles Perez, as you quite rightly guessed."

"I reported on him just the other day."

"Yes, I saw it and a very good report it was. Scorpion has been deployed to provide a military solution and effect his release."

"You mean you're going in to rescue him?"

251

"Elisabeth, let me finish. This is the part where secrecy must be maintained, otherwise you will be putting lives at risk. Tomorrow morning, my team and I will launch a mission to rescue the Ambassador. I'm asking you as a friend to use your influence to impose a media blackout on anything to do with this mission. If anything is reported as being seen at the airport it will come with complete deniability, but would be reported as being part of the overall international effort to withdraw innocent civilians. Suffice to say though, once the mission has been concluded, you will have sole rights to broadcast the outcome. I will give you that personally."

"That's one hell of a daring mission, Jack!"

"Yep."

"Do you know where he is being held?"

"Yep. I wouldn't be launching tomorrow if I didn't."

"Do you know if he's alive or…?" Elisabeth didn't want to think the unthinkable.

"He's alive, barely. I'm counting on you, Elisabeth. There is no one else who can do this for us."

"Okay, Jack, it's difficult for a reporter to do what you're asking, but I'll make an exception in your case."

"Thanks, I owe you a big one."

"Your IOU's are stacking up, Jack. When do I cash them in?"

"Soon, I promise."

"I'll hold you to that."

"I need to head on back to the airport now. Can I trouble you for a lift in your company car?"

"No need to grovel, Jack. Where are you staying anyhow?"

"On board the aircraft carrier, George Washington."

"Is it far away?"

"If you swim, yes, but by helicopter, no."

"Stop teasing, you know what I mean."

"Two miles offshore."

"Okay, let's go then. I'd offer to drive you all the way, but the van's not amphibious," she quipped.

Both Copeland and Elisabeth burst into laughter at her comment.

As they drove towards the airport, Elisabeth pointed out various landmarks in the city, including the US Embassy and the point from where the Ambassador had been kidnapped. They soon arrived at the airport, and Elisabeth drove on to the aircraft parking area, using her CNN official status to drive through the gates. She stopped short of the aircraft. Copeland turned to her.

"Thanks, Elisabeth, both for your understanding and company today. It was a real pleasure to have had the chance to see you in person. I must say it was worth the wait."

"Likewise, Jack. Anytime you want a chat give me a call."

Copeland looked into her eyes and could feel his heart pounding against his ribcage. He sensed the feeling was mutual. Their eyes lingered, neither knowing what to say. He leant forward and kissed her on the left cheek. He then stepped from the vehicle and headed towards his ride back.

He turned and waved as she began to drive away. She reciprocated. *'That's one hell of a woman,'* he thought to himself. He felt comfortable with her and wore a broad smile as he approached the helicopter. Copeland was happier than he had been in a long time. Soon the aircraft was airborne and heading west.

*   *   *

On board the USS George Washington – 1630 Hours

The helicopter carrying Copeland touched down on the flight deck and began to refuel. Copeland made his way to the bridge.

"How did it go, Jack?"

"With what?" Copeland asked defensively.

"With the media, of course?"

"No problems. I said I would give them exclusive rights at the end. A personal brief is the just reward. That gives me the green light to start briefing to the rest of the guys. The helo that's refuelling at the moment, can that be tasked to take me to Senegal?"

"Sure, we're here to support your mission, Jack. Ask and if we have it, it's yours. What else do you want us to do before you go?"

"I'm gonna leave Dinger on board to brief your SEAL team Commander on their tasks for tomorrow. He'll then hitch a ride with the '53's in the morning and RV with us at Lungi. Which brings me to my next point. Ian, can you have three '53's on the ground at Lungi Airport by 0615? That's as it stands at the moment. If the next two reports by the recon team show no change, we're a Go. If I don't hear from you, Ian, I'll see you when we get back. Thanks for your help."

"Consider it done: all part of the service."

Copeland knew that Dinger would brief the SEAL Commander, Captain Martin 'Iceman' Hamilton on his mission with an overview of the whole plan. They would be expected to travel by their CRRC with the engine muffled along Rokel Creek and land near the camp perimeter. Their orders would be to stand fast until they heard the noise of the inbound helicopters approaching the camp, then to enter the camp and secure the objective. Hamilton was nicknamed 'Iceman' for his coolness under pressure. He always seemed to remain calm when others were in disarray.

"Control Room to Bridge," said the operator over the intercom.

"Bridge, aye" answered Cartwright.

"Sir, we have a scrambled message from Langley for General Copeland."

"Bring it up"

"Aye aye, sir."

Cartwright recalled Copeland to the bridge to receive the incoming message.

Moments later the message arrived on the bridge and was handed directly to Copeland. He left the bridge, returned to his cabin, and collected the satellite pictures of the rebel camps. He then headed to the flight deck and boarded the aircraft. Moments later the aircraft was airborne and heading in a north-easterly direction.

$$*\qquad*\qquad*$$

Leopold Sedar Airport, Dakar, Senegal – 2000 hours

As he stepped from the aircraft, Captain Dave Short met Copeland, and having given him a short status report on the team, he confirmed the team were one hundred percent combat ready. Copeland had expected nothing less. They were the crème de la crème. They would be hungry for action. All they needed now was a plan that would be convincing enough, and one that demonstrated it had been meticulously thought through. Copeland entered the hangar that had been the team's home for the last couple of days. It was organised, as you would expect from a military outfit. There was a place for everything and everything had a place.

"Hey, guys, how you all doing?" asked Copeland generally.

"Ready to go, sir. Just give the word," shouted a couple of Marines.

"You'll get your chance sooner than you think."

Copeland pinned the enlarged satellite images of the camps against the hangar wall. The team arranged themselves into positions where they could see the pictures whilst Copeland did the briefing.

"We now know where the Ambassador is being held captive. It's in this region, an area called Geri

Bana," said Copeland as he pointed to the location on the satellite pictures.

"There are approximately thirty men or boys in the camp, armed with a variety of weapons. Rifles mainly but it's known that some have RPG's. Their commander is 'Brigadier' Maxin Sankoah, and he heads the rebel group calling themselves the Sierra Leone Freedom Fighters. That's him there," and Copeland pointed at the mug shot.

"On the other side of the water is another camp called Forodugu. That side of the river holds the heavy weapons that pose a threat to our aircraft, mainly machine guns. This is how I see the operation going…"

Copeland briefed his men on every aspect of the operation from the deployment through the recovery phase and back to the George Washington. He also highlighted the dangers they knew about, and warned that, despite their detailed planning, an element of unpredictability remained. Although Copeland didn't want to admit it, he knew that he might lose some of his team during the op. The terrain was unfriendly, the enemy undisciplined and irresponsible, and the outcome uncertain. As Copeland wrapped up his briefing, he opened it up to the floor.

"Where are we staging from, Sir?" asked one of the Marines.

"Lungi airport in Freetown."

"Any more questions?"

Copeland looked around. No one moved or murmured.

"Six hours to go, gentlemen, before we move out. Synchronise watches, twenty-one thirty hours… now," confirmed Copeland.

*   *   *

Six Hours Later – 0330 Hours

The first C-17 began its roll along the runway and lifted gracefully into the black night sky, almost disappearing except for the internationally required navigational lights. The second C-17 followed shortly after. Both aircraft turned and headed south for the five hundred mile journey to Lungi Airport in Freetown, Sierra Leone. The mission to recover the US Ambassador was now underway.

CHAPTER FIFTEEN

08°37'N 13°12'W Lungi Airport, Freetown, Sierra Leone
0515 Hours (local)

Both C-17's landed and had been given instructions by tower control to park near the aircraft hangars away from the terminal buildings. The only information the airport authorities had been given was that the planes were part of a humanitarian mission to withdraw civilians from the troubled regions. This ensured a no-questions-asked landing approval.

Copeland knew that the crew of the second aircraft would now be unloading the Apache helicopters, and rebuilding and rearming the state-of-the-art gunships. Scorpion themselves would remain on board the aircraft until the '53's from Liberty Base – the USS George Washington – had arrived. Each Apache would be loaded with sixteen Air-to-Ground Hellfire missiles and 76 2.75inch rockets. There would be one turret mounted M230E1 30mm chain-gun for additional firepower. This was a massive quantity of ordnance, but Copeland intended to be prepared for every contingency. He couldn't leave anything to chance.

He considered what the '53's had to offer. He'd travelled in them many times and they were the largest and most powerful helicopters in the Air Force inventory. This model was also the most technologically advanced helicopter anywhere in the world. It boasted terrain following, terrain avoidance radar, and a forward looking infra-red sensor, along with projected displays enabling the crew to follow contours and avoid obstacles, making low level penetration possible. The 53's were also equipped with armour plating and a 7.62mm mini gun for self-defence but Copeland had no personal experience with the defence systems. Among the modifications the MH 53J had received were the addition of GPS, Doppler navigational systems, and an on-board computer and integrated avionics system enabling precise navigation to and from target areas.

Having double-checked his assets, Copeland knew that he had the best equipment available as well as the most effective fighting force. He just hoped it was enough.

*   *   *

One Hour Later – 0615 Hours

Right on cue, Copeland could hear the distinctive thud, thud, thud, of the inbound helicopters from the George Washington. They would land in extended formation a short distance from the C-17, and as they prepared to land, the Apaches would begin their start-up sequence.

Once the '53's had landed, Dinger waited for the hand signal from Copeland before he led the troops across the open area to the waiting transport. Each helicopter would carry thirty men, Copeland being in the lead chopper, and Dinger in the last. This way all eggs would not be in one basket and if Copeland's helicopter went down, Dinger could continue the mission as briefed.

Five minutes later all five helos were airborne and heading in a north-north-easterly direction. Before long they reached their cruising speed of one hundred and fifty knots, travelling at tree top height following the curves of the terrain.

This operation had to be swift, clean, and maximise the benefits of the element of surprise. Copeland looked at his watch: 06:25 hours. The flight time was fifteen minutes, tops. He looked out of a cabin window and saw one of the '64's sweep south to take up position targeting the camp across the water at Forodugu. The other '64 peeled off to the north to come into the camp through the back door. He also noticed that it had begun to rain. It was that fine mist that made everything wet; it also meant that the visibility of the pilots was diminished, but this was where the terrain-following radar would play a key role.

The '53's were now on their own with their minimal firepower. The door gunners were sweeping the machine guns across their arcs of fire, ready to unleash the heavy 7.62mm rounds at the first sign of a threat. The '53's were equipped with counter measures, carrying ALE-39 chaff and flare dispensers as well as the AAR-47 missile warning system.

Copeland found himself thinking that, this close to the ground and with such a heavy airframe the counter measures would be useless, since the automatic deployment of the chaff and flares needed time to assimilate the data being received from the missile warning system. This was not a comforting thought to go in to battle with. He hoped that they wouldn't be needed.

Listening in to the radio he heard that the southern '64 had fired its rockets into the heavy machine gun area, disabling the threat from that quarter. It would now remain in the region scanning for other threats.

Ten minutes into the flight, Copeland for some reason looked through the gap where the door gunner was standing. What he saw made his heart miss several beats.

The white plumes he could see were the tell-tale sign of a launched missile. Was it a ground to air or an RPG? More importantly, where was it heading? Behind Copeland's helicopter were two more. Were they aware of this immediate threat? Copeland quickly depressed his microphone.

"Helos two and three deploy your counter measures *now*. Missile at your four o'clock." Copeland hoped that he had been quick enough to warn them.

He broke out into a cold sweat and if it had been daylight, his face would have been ashen grey. He'd done what he could.

"Liberty Base, Helo three, MAYDAY, MAYDAY, tail rotor out. Am going..."

Transmission broke off and all Copeland could hear was static. The radio fell quiet, the crews of the remaining helos not quite understanding what had happened.

At one hundred and fifty knots, this height, and surrounded by trees, the crew and occupants would have little to no chance of survival. Dinger was on that aircraft. He had to do something.

"Liberty Base, this is mission leader, launch the standby helo to the last fix on helo three and recover casualties, over."

Liberty Base acknowledged the request and Copeland had to hold back tears as images of the incident flashed before him.

As Copeland was organising the recovery helo, the door gunner unleashed a burst of tracer rounds in the general direction of the smoke plume, not knowing whether they would hit the launch site. It was an instinctive reaction, attempting to ensure that no further launches would be initiated, and those on the ground would feel the impact of the tracers heading towards them.

The MH-53 had no substantial firepower with which to engage in a confrontational fire fight so it would have been pointless to re-route away from the objective. The launcher would probably have left the area by now anyhow. '*Damn it!*' Copeland exclaimed to himself. How did he miss that location? The Apaches would have had to pass over the area to sweep towards their targets. Their NVG's should have picked something up. They were obviously very well camouflaged.

Copeland had underestimated the rebels' willingness to defend. Were they part of the same group or a renegade outfit? He didn't have the answer to that and he would probably never know. The '53's continued towards their target. The downing of one of their own helicopters placed an even greater emphasis and urgency on this mission being successful.

He had to focus on what was still ahead. He looked at his watch: three minutes to the target area.

*   *   *

Naval SEAL Unit outside rebel camp at Geri Bana, Sierra Leone

Captain Hamilton pointed to his ear, then to the sky as he brought the sound of the inbound helicopters to the attention of the other three members of his team. It was their turn now. Using hand signals, he instructed them to move off as quickly and as quietly as possible to secure the objective. All four scaled the perimeter gate. They heard a door opening to their right. Two boys and what appeared to be a girl walked out of the hut. The nearest SEAL member fired two silenced rounds into each target. They dropped to the ground and didn't move again.

There wasn't a guard outside the objective's hut. Hamilton tested the door. It was locked. *'Damn it,'* he thought to himself. It wouldn't take much to knock it down, but it would have been easier if there had been a guard: at least they would have had the key. He shoulder charged the door, which gave way immediately. All four entered the hut, providing cover to each other as they moved in.

"Cap, over here," said Hutchinson. Hamilton quickly moved over to where Hutch was. He saw the figure of what he assumed to be the Ambassador. He was face down on the bed. Was he dead or asleep?

"Hutch, check him over," ordered Hamilton.

"He's alive, Cap, but only just. He's hanging in there."

"That's exactly what we need to do now. Once the rebels hear those inbound birds they'll probably realise what we're after and come charging into the hut. So be ready and focused, guys."

The door to the hut burst open. The light outside silhouetted the figures of two people. The SEAL unit fired four rounds; two in to each target. They dropped and didn't move again. The bodies were dragged into the room, and the door closed behind them.

The noise of the '53s was now deafening. The objective was secure, their mission almost complete. All they had to do now was hang on.

*   *   *

Onboard Helo One Assault Team, Geri Bana, Sierra Leone

The reports from the reconnaissance team had told Copeland exactly where the rebel commander, so-called Brigadier Sankoah was housed. He wanted him alive to face the consequences of his actions. As the remaining '53's dropped into the established DZ, Copeland quickly reorganised his troops, since he was now 30 short of his starting line-up.

The Apaches appeared overhead with their great rotor blades chopping through the air. They would be the eyes and ears for the ground troops, able to cut down any threats. The camp would now be alive, buzzing with activity. The rebels would be alert, disorganised and intent on taking on the invading army. The superior technology and the discipline of the rescuers should ensure a swift mission. Copeland physically directed troops to various tasks throughout the camp. Weapons were at the ready, and their grenade launchers had been loaded and primed. It just needed the squeeze of a trigger and anything near the site of the explosion would be toast.

It wasn't long before the Apaches launched their rockets into the camp area, setting huts ablaze, and then the noise of gunfire from both sides added to the racket of the helicopters. Battle had been joined. There could only be one winner.

Copeland led his troops towards the rebel camp and Captain Short took his. He was now the 2IC as Helo Three had been taken out. Movement would have to be quick and precise. Copeland gestured two of his men to enter the quarters of the rebel commander. They wanted him alive, but he would be spared the privations that he had visited upon the Ambassador. His troops played by the rules, much to the distaste of some.

Doors to different huts opened as the rebels began to engage the invading troops. Their efforts were fruitless. They were out-numbered and out-gunned. The door to the rebel commander's hut suddenly opened and there stood Brigadier Sankoah on the top step as if inspecting his troops from afar.

Copeland nodded to his men to bring Sankoah to him. Copeland could imagine what was going through Sankoah's mind right now. No commander likes to admit defeat, but against overwhelming odds and the need to keep some respect and dignity amongst what was left of his rebels, he would have no choice but to accept what Copeland was about to offer him.

Sankoah's side arm was removed from his holster, and the two commanders were now face to face.

"At last we meet, Brigadier. To avert any further bloodshed you are to surrender, and instruct your forces to lay down their arms and hand themselves over to my forces."

Sankoah looked around and saw for himself the devastation that his camp had endured and understandably, but reluctantly, accepted defeat. He capitulated and gave the order for surrender to his men by looking toward the centre of the camp and placing his hand on top of his head.

Moments later, all remaining rebels exited their huts and laid their weapons on to the ground.

"That was a sensible move, Brigadier. You must have realised you couldn't get away with this. You have one thing to be grateful for by surrendering to US forces, and that is that the treatment you will receive will be in accordance with humanitarian laws, and not the barbaric ones which you inflict on your captives."

Sankoah showed no remorse as he replied to Copeland's statement.

"To take on a powerful nation like the US was a challenge which tested the perseverance and loyalty of my army. They did well."

"Take him away," ordered Copeland.

Sankoah was led to one of the waiting '53's. He would be conveyed to Freetown and handed over to the local judicial system.

As the firefight subsided and the remaining rebel forces were captured, Copeland surveyed the battlefield. The door to the hut in front of him opened. Out came two Navy SEAL's followed by their objective, supported by the other two SEALs. He had no strength to stand. He almost had to be carried by Hamilton and Hutchinson down the steps of the hut.

Copeland could see the Ambassador looking towards the retreating figure of Sankoah. He was trying to smile though his pain, an expression which Copeland interpreted as one of relief, mixed with happiness and some anger. Copeland walked towards the Ambassador and saluted him.

"Mr Ambassador, my name is General Jack Copeland of the United States Special Forces. Your captivity has now ended. We're taking you home, sir."

Charles slowly and gingerly extended his right arm to say thank you to Copeland. He almost fainted from the pain. Copeland instructed the SEAL team to take the Ambassador over to the waiting helicopter. He instructed that the prisoners to be taken to the second one.

He stood in the centre of the camp looking around and wondering whether it was worth it. He began counting the cost of the mission in terms of lives lost. Ten rebels dead including two women; five escaped into the jungle to the north; and the catastrophic loss of Helo Three and her valuable cargo. He hadn't yet been given confirmation of the total number of casualties on board, but he didn't hold out much hope.

Copeland headed back to his helicopter and was soon heading west. The pilot flew over the crash site, which was still smouldering: wreckage was strewn over a wide area. Search and rescue troops were on the ground looking for survivors. The crew would have had little or no time to respond to a damaged tail rotor. If he needed confirmation of the mission cost this surely was it.

*   *   *

On Board the USS George Washington – 0900 hours

As Helo One and Two settled on to the flight deck, Copeland stepped out and breathed deeply of the fresh morning air, attempting to clear his mind. He looked back to see the Ambassador being loaded onto a stretcher bound for the sick bay where he would be treated and then rest. He'd be looked after now. Copeland walked up to the bridge.

"Good work, Jack," said Cartwright.

"Tell that to their families. It wasn't necessary. That was a complete waste of life. I missed something, Ian, that put their lives at risk."

"You can't hold yourself responsible, Jack. You did the best that any commander could have done. Casualties are a fact in any hostile situation. You're not the first and you certainly won't be the last commander to lose men on the battlefield."

"It's the fact that it happened on my shift and on my mission which makes me feel a personal responsibility for these guys. Any news on Helo Three?"

"Rescue crews are at the scene as we speak. Their initial report lists twelve survivors. The crew died and, I'm sorry, Jack, Dinger didn't make it."

Copeland moved over to the window looking out from the bridge. Losses were inevitable in any conflict but Copeland felt a responsibility in part for any which occurred on his watch even though he had no control over the situation. No matter how much planning he would put into the mission, there was always the unpredicatability of the enemy that would ultimately alter the profile of the mission. It had always been hard and he had never come to terms with loss. He always planned missions with the intention of bringing all of them back alive.

He'd lost his best and dearest friend, Dinger. They had risen through the military together and now Copeland was on his own. He would have to rethink his military career, and decide whether to 'soldier on' or resign his commission. He didn't want to be on the Bridge right now. He wanted to be somewhere else and in someone else's company. That was something to look forward to.

He conjured up images of Elisabeth that momentarily took his mind away from that morning's events. Copeland still had unfinished business. He turned back from the window and looked towards Cartwright.

"I need to send a secure message to Langley, Ian?"

"Sure. You know where the ops room is. Help yourself."

"Thanks."

Copeland left the bridge and headed down towards the ops room. He came alongside his bunk, but found it hard to walk past. He stepped inside, looked at the bed space that had been Dinger's and saw a visual of him laughing and joking. That was Dinger, 'Carefree'.

Copeland found himself saying out loud "I'll finish this business for you, Dinger. I'll get the bastards."

He left the cabin, entered the ops room and dictated a message to the telegraphist for transmission to the CIA Director. Copeland wanted an up to date report on the satellite crossing over Afghanistan. He also wanted the co-ordinates of the terrorist leader's hideout. He requested an update on the investigation into the bombings: both the '98 and the current ones. Copeland knew that it would take a little while for Mike to amass the information requested, so he decided to head down to the ships hospital and check up on the patient.

"How's he doing, Doc?"

"Remarkably well, considering. He's very weak through lack of nutrition, but it won't take long to fatten him up."

"I heard that, Doctor. I'm not a Thanksgiving turkey!"

Copeland headed over to Charles' bed. "You look younger now that you've had a shave," Jack touched Charles's shoulder in a friendly gesture.

"I don't think I could have held out much longer, Jack. They hardly fed me, my hands were constantly tied behind my back and being beaten black and blue was the final straw."

"Have you spoken with your wife yet, Charles?"

"Sarah, yes. I was able to make a quick call to her."

"How is she after these anxious few days?"

"Relieved, as we all are, I guess."

"When do you expect to be released?"

"Probably tomorrow. What about you, Jack? When are you leaving?"

"Don't know yet. I still have some things to sort out. I'll see you before I go, though."

Copeland left the sick bay, and headed back to the ops room. He dictated another message, this time to AFSOC. He was sure that his request for a B-52 bomber to be flown to Ramstein AFB in Germany would stir up a hornet's nest in the Pentagon, and probably surprise the President.

Now that things had calmed down Copeland would have to report to the President at the earliest opportunity. He would choose his words carefully. The President had got what he wanted, but at a price. The Joint Chiefs, although elated, would nevertheless be seething as to the way Scorpion carried out its missions with a total disregard of the usual chain of command. He would send an initial report now, but he needed to make a phone call.

He had a more important appointment to keep. It was a promise that he had made, one that he intended to honour.

CHAPTER SIXTEEN

Lungi International Airport, Freetown

E lisabeth collected Copeland from the airport as she had done previously. They hugged, and Copeland kissed her on the cheek. He didn't feel it was the right moment for anything else. He was here to give her the story that he had promised. Anything else would just have to go on the back boiler for now. They drove to her apartment where she made two coffees without asking Copeland whether he wanted one or not. She was getting to know him, so she was sure he would have said yes.

Elisabeth set up the tape recorder on the coffee table and recorded an introduction to lead Copeland into his part of the story. He was given the count of five to begin to recount the events that had unfolded that morning. He explained with clarity, leaving no detail out of any aspect of the mission. He mentioned the condition of the Ambassador, who his captives were, and the human price that had been paid to secure his release. He mentioned the downed helicopter, and the loss of his dear friend and other members of the Scorpion team.

Copeland had to stop at that point, fighting back tears before he was able to regain his composure. She sat next to him and placed her arm around his shoulder to comfort him. She realised that it must have been very hard for him to have to talk about something still so vivid in his mind. He had spoken for forty-five minutes, after which he seemed satisfied that Elisabeth had sufficient for broadcast.

"Was that okay?" he asked.

"You were great, Jack."

"When will it go out?"

"Tonight, around six pm local time. That'll give me time to edit it and select a backdrop, probably the airport. Before I forget, Jack, you asked me to try and find out any information on the Islamic Group terrorist organisation, but I haven't been able to find anything current."

"Thanks for trying, anyhow. I knew it was a long shot."

"I did find something about the man behind the group..."

"You little beauty," said Copeland with a broad smile. "What did you come up with?"

"He's linked in one way or another with Islamic militants all over the world."

"Yeah, we had an idea he was up to something like that. Did you find any names?"

"I'm one step ahead of you, Jack"

"Marvellous! You've not only got the beauty, but you've got the brains to complete the package."

"Flattery will get you everywhere. Anyway, where was I?" she asked, as she looked towards Copeland, momentarily distracted by his admiring gaze.

"About to give me some names," he reminded her.

"Oh, yes. The first name is Ayman al-Zawahiri. He is the leader of the Egyptian Islamic Jihad, and often speaks for Bin Laden in public. He is a middle-aged physician and a gifted organiser, and he supplies the core of Bin Laden's Al Quaeda – The Base. Another one is Sheikh Mir Hamzah who is purported to be the secretary of a militant Islamic Group in Pakistan. The information on file suggests that he is both an ideologue and an operative, and a vital link to Bin Laden's allies and bases in Afghanistan."

"Wow, you *have* been busy. I'm impressed."

"I haven't finished yet. There's another three to go."

"Okay, great."

"The next one is Imad Mugniyah who is reported as being the security chief of Hezbollah in Lebanon, and it is thought that he planned the bombing of the Marine barracks in Beirut in 1983. The last two are a bit of a stretch, but Juma Namangani is the military commander of the fundamentalist Islamic Movement of Uzbekistan and he threatens the stability of former Soviet republics in Central Asia. The last one is Raed Hijazi who is an American citizen, apparently a former taxi driver out of Boston, and is suspected of being a courier for Bin Laden. That's all I could find out in the short time."

"How the hell do you pronounce that last one?" said Copeland with a hint of sarcasm. "Anyhow, you've done a great job! I don't know how to thank you."

"Don't mention it, but don't make a habit of it either. I seemed to go through the third degree, people asking me why I needed to know."

"I'm sorry to have had to put you through that, but the media seem to be able to easily gather that kind of information. It seems to be more difficult for the Intelligence services."

"Probably because terrorist groups want global media coverage and we're able to provide them with that forum. Does this help in any way?"

"It expands what we already know, but you have added names which give an interesting angle."

"How long are you staying over this side for?" she asked.

"Another hour if that's okay?"

"You can stay for as long as you want, Jack," she said with a shy smile.

"Elisabeth, there is something else I need to discuss with you."

"I thought you'd never get round to it," she said teasingly.

"What. No, no not that," Copeland replied as he realised what Elisabeth was implying. It was a lovely suggestion but this was not the right time.

"Okay, what else am I putting my career on the line for?"

"This is a personal favour for me and something that Dinger would have wanted to happen."

"Sounds intriguing. Okay, I'm listening. Go for it."

"You'll probably think I'm stark raving mad when I tell you what my plan is. I hope you'll understand why I'm doing it. I know where the terrorist leader Bin Laden is hiding out. He's in the area near the Hindu Kush mountain range. The problem here is that it is in an inhospitable and a difficult area to penetrate using normal means, in other words with ground forces. It's just too big; over six hundred miles long and almost one hundred and forty nine miles wide. My option is the only viable one given the terrain. If we want to finish this we have to act now. I've got the co-ordinates and I'm about to launch a B-52 bomber from Germany to fly towards Afghanistan. It will then drop several air to ground cruise missiles, which will obliterate that area."

"Jack, that's murder. Surely the President wouldn't sanction such a plan?"

"He doesn't know yet."

"You've got to tell him, or you'll be arrested and end up in jail! Your career would be finished and I'll never see you again! Don't do it, Jack, please, for me," she pleaded.

"Elisabeth, don't judge me yet. I've put together a response to the Joint Chiefs' arguments against such a strike that I think is a solid option, and one that will raise the popularity of the President."

"More like offer an open invitation to other terrorist groups to retaliate against the US."

"The thing is, though, the financial muscle for a number of terrorist groups is provided by this Saudi guy, Bin Laden. If he was to be eliminated, it is hoped that there will be a cessation – or at the very least, a drastic reduction – of hostile acts against certain US assets which are perceived to be easy targets."

"Where do I come in to this?" she asked, realising that this plan might have some credibility after all.

"I intend to convince the President that this is the way to rid the Middle East of one of the world's principal terrorists. In fact it may be the only way. He will no doubt ask how we intend to get away with it. This may be seen as a single act if it goes wrong rather than an orchestrated global and cohesive response that the world would rather have but time is running out. How well do you know the bureau chief in Kabul?"

"I've never had any dealings with them so to answer your question, I don't. Why?"

"Over the next twenty-four hours they are going to hear something with a lot of chatter and I would rather give the viewers the real story rather than some cock and bull report that others would like you to hear. What I'm asking of you Elisabeth is for you to give the story to Kabul outlining the events as I've explained to you. Nothing must be held back if the impact and outcome of this is to be as devastating as I hope it will be. Folks back home will support this if it means eliminating the target and our main threat. Once the missiles are launched and have hit their designated target, CNN will report that a unprecedented missile strike had been launched including all the other bits leading up to this."

"Will the President agree to this scheme?"

"Yes, I'm sure he will."

"I'm not the Middle-Eastern correspondent, Jack, I'm the bureau chief in Sierra Leone but I'll certainly give it my best shot. All the offices work independent of each other but I'm sure I'll be able to convince them enough of the validity of the report and source."

"I fully understand that and I wouldn't ask if I didn't think it wasn't important enough but unless we do something like this we will always be looking over our shoulders wondering not if, but when."

"When do you intend to speak with the President?"

"Tomorrow morning, why?"

"Once you've spoken to him then give me a call and let me know what he has or hasn't agreed to. Then I'll think about what I'm going to do. You don't make things easy, do you, Jack? I'll help you as much as I can. Is that enough?"

"More than enough. Thanks. Right now I need to get back to the ship before your broadcast this evening. I'll have to brief the President on what he will be seeing later on. It's best he hears it from me rather than see it on TV!"

"Sure, I understand."

Copeland looked at Elisabeth and was momentarily transfixed. He held out his hands, reaching for hers. She didn't pull away. *'That's a good sign,'* thought Copeland to himself.

"Elisabeth, do you believe in fate?"

"In certain things, yes. Why, what are you getting at, Jack?"

"I feel as though our meeting like this was more than just chance."

"Yeah, I feel the same way. It's as if I have known you for ages, and yet it's only been a couple of days. I've been dragged into something completely new, and it feels like a roller coaster ride. It's never boring when you're around, Jack!"

Copeland smiled and said, "Can you keep your schedule free tomorrow evening?"

"Why?"

"My mission here is almost complete, after which I'll have to return to DC. I'd like to spend these last few hours here with you – and I still owe you dinner..."

"I'd be honoured, Jack. Give me a call when you want picking up from the airport."

"I will, and thanks. Listen, I'm going to have to shoot back and get everything squared away before tomorrow. Make sure there are no loose ends and all that. Thanks for the coffee. I really enjoyed being here."

Copeland and Elisabeth drove back to the airport. Again not wishing to overstep the mark, Copeland kissed her on her cheek. She looked disappointed, but Copeland didn't notice. He left the vehicle and headed back towards his lift. He turned and waved. She reciprocated with a more positive wave than the last one. He was sure tomorrow would be special, for more than one reason.

*   *   *

The White House, Washington DC, 1200 Hours (SET)

Phil Scott had already handed the initial report from Copeland to the President which warned that a media report would be broadcast at 1800 hours CET, and that the broadcast contained a full account of the mission. The President, NSA and the Joint Chiefs of Staff were assembled. The broadcast came to life:

"…an audacious airborne dawn strike, spearheaded by the Special Forces assigned to Scorpion, has this morning freed US Ambassador, Charles Perez, who was being held hostage in the sweltering Sierra Leone jungle. A gun battle erupted after sixty Scorpion troops leapt from helicopters and launched a two-pronged attack on the ramshackle camp of the Sierra Leone Freedom Fighters rebel group, who had seized the Ambassador several days ago. The mission in the mangrove swamps of Rokel Creek took just ninety minutes. The firefight left ten of the rebel group members dead including two women, with fifteen arrested. It is believed a further five escaped to the north. The rebel leader, the so-called Brigadier Maxin Sankoah was captured. The mission was marred by the loss of a military helicopter similar to the one behind me, and eighteen Scorpion personnel were killed in the crash. Twelve survived. It is thought an RPG rocket smashed the tail rotor and because the aircraft was very close to the ground, the flight crew had insufficient time to react. The Ambassador is presently on board the aircraft carrier, USS George Washington, receiving medical attention, and it is expected that he will be released in the next day or so. On a day of joy and sadness, this is Elisabeth Young for CNN in Freetown, Sierra Leone."

The Chairman of the Joint Chiefs was the first to speak.

"I told you, Mr President, that Jack was a liability."

"You authorised his appointment along with the rest of you gutless morons. On the face of it he's done a damned good job. I just have to convince the House that it was justified."

*   *   *

On board the USS George Washington – The Next Day

"Jack, your B-52 has been approved and is airborne as we speak. It's a bit of an elaborate way to get home. You like to do things in style. So what you gonna do with it?" asked Cartwright

"It'll all become clear soon, Ian. Be patient."

The internal intercom whistle sounded. "Control Room to Bridge."

"Bridge, aye."

"Sir, message from Langley for General Copeland."

"Bring it up to the bridge."

"Aye aye, sir."

Moments later the message was brought to the bridge and handed directly to Copeland.

"What's it say, Jack?" enquired Cartwright.

"I know we've been tied up with events here in Sierra Leone, but do you remember the recent bombings of US Embassies in the Middle East?"

"Yep, how could we forget with all that paper traffic passing backwards and forwards?"

"The one in Khartoum wasn't hit, also one of the terrorists in the '98 bombings has been arrested in the UK. He's an Arab businessman working in London going by the name Abdul bin Aziz and is said to be a supporter of Bin Laden. The US has applied for extradition so that he can be tried for his crimes in the US. Here's some more good news, three alleged terrorists, believed to have been involved in the recent spate of bombings, have also been arrested. One is from Iraq, one from Egypt, and the other from Saudi Arabia. A right mixed bag."

"So the investigations are almost complete then?"

"Not quite. There's a twist which links the Israeli Intelligence Service with the bombings."

"Why would they want to do that?" exclaimed Cartwright.

"To ruin US – Arab relations, at a guess."

"That's a bit steep, Jack."

"It might look that way but it's a possibility that cannot be overlooked. Intelligence services have been involved in similar hostile attacks in the past in an effort to change world opinion. It will always be denied, of course, but those who are astute enough to be suspicious often do not believe denials. Anyhow, Ian, I have a plane to catch, see you when I get back."

The intercom whistle sounded again. "Control Room to Bridge."

"Bridge, aye."

"The Pentagon is on the scrambler wishing to speak with General Copeland, sir."

"Tell them he's on his way," said Cartwright.

"Aye aye, sir."

"My, you are popular today, Jack."

"Yeah, not necessarily a good thing to be."

Copeland left the bridge and headed down to the Control Room.

"Copeland here."

"Jack, it's Walter Zieglar. What the hell are you doing? Bob Studeman over at AFSOC tells me you've ordered a B-52 to Ramstein, and put it on standby for a future op. This wasn't part of your brief, Jack. We need to know what your intentions are. You've been given a lot of slack at Scorpion, but this has the makings of a one-man crusade. There is still the requirement for proper authorisation to requisition additional government assets. You don't own that plane, the American people do. The Joint Chiefs will not support any renegade or maverick mission that you wish to pursue for personal gains. This could jeopardise all the hard work you've put in over the years, not to mention your present career!"

Copeland had guessed right: the Joint Chiefs were really wound up and pissed off.

"You really haven't got a clue as to what's happening in the real world. All you pencil pushers sit on your shiny fat arses all day wondering how you can cut the budget for the next fiscal year. You're out of touch with your own people. You're a military man, General; you've read the briefs and know what's been happening in the Middle East. If you don't agree to this then you will be guilty of condoning the atrocities of this insane terrorist. You may as well have the blood the terrorists have spilled on your own hands," snapped Copeland.

Copeland realised that he had probably overstepped the mark, and the support he wanted from the Joint Chiefs had almost certainly been withdrawn. He needed that additional asset and he would stop at nothing until its authorised deployment for what Copeland had in mind had been agreed. The UN Resolutions during the Gulf campaign in '91 stopped short of authorising the capture of Saddam Hussein. He didn't wish to repeat that red-tape-strangled bureaucracy.

"Your aggressive action, Jack, goes beyond the core business with which you and Scorpion were initially tasked. The mission objective, as you may recall, was to rescue the US Ambassador. There can be no other operation or deployment, or your actions will be misinterpreted and you will be held accountable. Is that understood, General?"

"Is this your own viewpoint or have you discussed your opinions with the President?"

"It is the opinion of the Joint Chiefs, based on proper military protocol, which is something you seem to have forgotten."

"I'll take the matter up with the President myself," snapped Copeland.

Jack knew that the Chairman of the Joint Chiefs would rush to brief the President on his actions. The President would either agree or disagree, but Copeland would need a convincing argument, conclusive enough so as to not cause embarrassment or damage to the US, or go against its Constitution. He'd already spoken to the one person he could turn to, to provide that assurance: all he had to do now was to convince the President.

Copeland next requested a link to the White House.

"Mr President, Sir, its Copeland."

"Goddammit, Jack, what the hell are you playing at? I've got the Joint Chiefs breathing down my neck, giving me some bullshit story about you ordering a

B-52 to Germany. You're in Africa, so why a '52 in Germany? Tell me it's not true!"

"I'm afraid it is, Sir."

"Your mission parameters were the Sierra Leone extraction. Step outside of that and you'll be facing a Court-Martial. You have secured the release of the Ambassador and that is the end of your assignment. Is that clear?"

Copeland realised that he might be putting the President into a situation which could endanger his continuing occupancy of the White House. Something he would *not* be willing to hazard.

"Mr President, please hear me out and then if you don't see this as a feasible option, I will recall the B-52."

"That's big of you, Jack. *I* can pick up the phone right now and recall it. You haven't forgotten that I'm the Commander in Chief of all the Armed Forces?"

"No, Sir, but you wouldn't want to recall the aircraft without understanding why it's needed in the first place. You would have recalled it not knowing what might have happened. It could be the solution to many of our problems. You don't want to be in one of those 'what if' scenarios that we all love to hate."

"Okay, but it had better be good. The Joint Chiefs are telling me that you're on some kind of personal mission. A crusade"

"It's all to do with the bombings of the US Embassies in the Middle East. The mastermind and the tactician behind these atrocities has been identified and located in Afghanistan at a remote area to the north of Kabul. Confirmation has been obtained using our own MILSATs over a period of time. I feel that the rescue of the Ambassador gets us no closer to the end of our problems. That was almost like a distraction. To rid the Middle East of this megalomaniac terrorist, there is one more thing that has to be done."

"I don't like the sound of this, Jack."

"Mr President, I would like you to give the order to launch the B-52 from Ramstein.

"What is it carrying, Jack?"

"ALCM's. The latest, the best and the safest."

"How many do you intend to off-load?"

"At least four. The centre of the explosion would be at ground zero within the grid square which Langley have identified."

"Sounds like all-out war, Copeland, surely we would be inviting repercussions from such an attack? It'll be like handing out invitations to the world's terrorist groups," asked the President rhetorically.

"Sir, unless we do something drastic we will always be wondering when, not if, the next attack against a US asset will take place. Your Presidency is on the line, Sir."

"Don't threaten me, Jack. Convincing the House puts my presidency on the line, what you're suggesting brings the removal vans much sooner than expected. I'll probably be finished. I'm not convinced that this is the best solution. How would we get away with it?"

Copeland realised that the President was now starting to ask questions that might well bring him on-side.

"I have a contact with CNN in Freetown who will pass on the full story to her bureau chief in Kabul. I have given her full access and exposure to the operation so that no detail is left unturned. The fact that this warlord is about to be vapourised will raise your position ten fold amongst the world stage. The rest of the world talks a good talk with diplomatic solutions but it's down to the US to act. We are seen to be the enforcer and you can only fight these people with fire. They don't understand anything else."

"How did you manage to get CNN on side?" said the President before continuing, "You realise we are breaching national security here by revealing our actions and basically putting our cards on the table?"

"I agree Sir, but we need to be transparent. Reporters can smell a cover up at anytime. Our actions here are nothing new. It's twentieth century warfare, fire and forget strategy. Its simple, he plays by the sword and must die by the sword."

"What are you suggesting, Jack?"

"In the interests of openeness this will give your presidency credibility and people will judge you on this act alone. This will be key since there is an election coming up soon and will be seen as a major legacy of yours if you wish to succeed for another term. The demise of the man who troubles the free world will certainly be a vote winner. If you do nothing you will stand accused of being an irresponsible and weak President, and your position will quickly become untenable. You will have wolves at the door asking for your resignation."

"If this doesn't work, Jack, it will only increase the mystique of this man, our most elusive and dangerous enemy."

"Trust me on this, Mr President."

"I only wish I had your confidence, Jack. I've got everything to lose."

"You've also got a lot to gain; stability, mutual support, and peace. Shall I go on? Remember the words of President F Roosevelt in 1933 when he said '*The only thing we have to fear is fear itself*', well that's how everyone will be living unless this is resolved and military action is the only thing he understands. John F Kennedy summed it up, saying '*Mankind must put an end to war, or war will put an end to mankind*'. So what will you go down as saying, Mr President?"

The President hesitated before giving his answer, "Okay, okay."

"What's that, Sir?"

"Do it. Your head is on the block, General, if this backfires. Do you understand?"

"Fully, Sir."

Copeland immediately made the call to Ramstein AFB, Germany, and gave the order to launch, citing the President as his authority. He made another call to the offices of CNN in Freetown.

*   *   *

Ramstein AFB, Germany 1400 Hours CET

It moved like a giant albatross, but at the pace of a snail. Its cigar shaped body moved graciously from the northeast side of the runway. Its wings, heavily laden and bouncing from the uneven surface were stabilized at each tip by a retractable wheel. The final checks were completed and as the centre line came into view, the distinctive thunderous roar of the eight Pratt & Whitney TF33-P-3 engines surged the B-52 Stratofortress along runway twenty-seven.

The aircraft was loaded with eight internal rotary-launched air to ground AGM-129 Advanced Cruise Missiles, each with a W80 5-kiloton warhead designed to evade air and ground-based radar and to strike against heavily defended, hardened targets.

Once the aircraft reached its launch position, the co-ordinates would be programmed in to the missiles using the coded switch system. The aircraft climbed to its cruising height of forty three thousand feet, and forged ahead at a speed of five hundred and sixteen knots. At the appropriate time they would drop to thirty eight thousand feet.

*   *   *

Freetown, Sierra Leone 1930 Hours (CET)

Elisabeth collected Copeland from the airport as planned, and drove straight to her flat, parking in a vacant slot opposite.

"It's such a beautiful evening, Jack, let's take a walk along the promenade?"

"Yeah, I'd like that."

An occasional light zephyr blew across the bay, disturbing the warm evening air. The breeze did little to change the ambient temperature, but gave the psychological feeling that it was cooler.

The water in the bay was like a mill pond. It reminded Copeland of the times when, as a boy, he used to throw flat stones to see how far he could skim them across the water and in how many bounces. His father would always be able to throw his the farthest. That was the past; he had to consider the present and instead of his father being next to him, he was in the company of a very beautiful woman.

They both stopped and leant on the waist high railings, looking out over the bay. She stared up at the sky. It was a clear night and she was able to see millions of twinkling stars. Copeland joined her in her gaze.

"Did you see that shooting star?" Elisabeth asked as she pointed.

"Yeah. Blink and you could actually miss them. You can often see satellites moving across the sky on a night like this. Red flashing lights visible to the naked eye."

They both continued to look out over the bay.

"So, Elisabeth, tell me about yourself. How old are you?"

"You don't ask a lady her age. But if you must know I'm forty-five."

"Never. I wouldn't have put you in that bracket," said Copeland teasing.

"Careful, Jack, you may be walking on thin ice," she said with a coy smile.

"How about marriage?"

"Yep, tried it once. I was married at an early age. Not really sure why, but I was probably naive and it's every woman's dream to walk down the aisle. We had a short engagement before we married."

"Are you still married?" Copeland asked hoping that she wasn't.

"No. We lived apart for two years, and we're now divorced."

"Any children?"

"Yeah. Two beautiful girls."

"I take it they have flown the nest?"

"Both are married and have children of their own now."

"You're too young to be a grandma"

"I've never liked that word, it makes you feel old. We have a saying in Sweden called Mormor, which means the same and I much prefer that."

"What happened in your marriage breakdown? Only if you want to talk about it."

"Sure, I don't mind. He was abusive towards me. Not physically but verbally. He was out chasing anyone in a skirt all the time. It's as simple as that. I found it hard to bear, though, and couldn't understand for a while. I gave everything I could to the marriage, but obviously it wasn't enough. He had his own agenda, which didn't include the children or me. I accepted it for a while and I made the decision to leave in the end but hoped in a away that it could be salvaged. I knew something was happening and he openly admitted it but I was committed to raising our family, and that was the last thing on my mind so it wasn't a workable option."

"Was he military?"

"Yeah. Army, why?"

"I sensed a military connection somewhere along the line from the first time we spoke on the phone."

"I was hurt, Jack. I gave him all my love, but all he wanted to do was be a single guy with no responsibilities. After that I felt that I couldn't trust anyone else in the military, or to love again. I decided that I would just think of myself, and my life would be mine without complications and a career that I would be proud of."

"I'm military."

Copeland turned towards Elisabeth and held both her hands. He wanted to comfort her, hold her and reassure her that not everyone should be tarred with the same brush or cut from the same cloth.

"Yes, but I see something different in you, Jack. I see commitment, honesty, trust and love. These are qualities that are hard to find in a man these days."

"Tell me about your family: parents, sisters or brothers?" enquired Copeland.

"My father died a few years ago. I was very close to him as I think most daughters are. It devastated my mom, but she has the support of both my brother and I, and that has helped her through those traumatic times. I just have the one brother who I rarely talk to. He's a few years older. I have two lovely daughters who were both born in England and I hold them dear to my heart."

"You miss home, don't you?"

"Yes, I do.

"Where's home for you?"

"I'm originally from Stockholm in Sweden. I left home some thirty-odd years ago to come to England.

I married an Englishman, but life took us our separate ways and I only wish I had left him sooner as I mentioned before. It was our children that kept me from walking away. It's nice to be able to make new friends wherever your work takes you, but there isn't anything better than being with your own family or with someone that you love. Enough about my life, what about yours?"

"Just like you, I was married once, for twenty-one years."

"What happened?"

"She just couldn't understand my job. In the end, she became hostile, even threatened me with a knife, at which point the relationship was irretrievable. I had to do something, so I sued for divorce on the grounds of unreasonable behaviour."

"Any children?"

"Yep, one. He's eighteen now, hoping to go into the aviation industry once he finishes College."

"Any brothers or sisters?"

"One sister. She's three years older than me. She's got a good job as a teacher."

"Any regrets about getting divorced, Jack?"

"After that length of time it comes as a shock, however, I've never been happier. What about you?"

"I'm happy in my work, which takes up a lot of my time. I value true friends, and I see them as my pillars of strength, able to support me in any time of crisis. My social calendar has never been as full.

"What's you maiden name?" asked Jack

"Bergstrom"

"Very Swedish."

"So how did you become involved with Scorpion, Jack?"

"I spent time in the British Special Forces and was head-hunted to take over at TWaID in the States. The '98 bombings in Nairobi and Tanzania that you so superbly reported on prompted the US Government to act, and the President initiated a new unit, Scorpion. The President had already decided that he wanted me for the job. I couldn't very well refuse, could I? It's a high profile position, often very uncomfortable for a military commander, since we prefer to remain covert, lurking under the umbrella of National Security. Scorpion is very much in the public eye. What are your plans, Elisabeth?"

She paused before answering,

"I've still a lot of assignments that I'm working on, which I want to finish…After that, who knows? I may be whisked off to some far-flung paradise with the man of my dreams. What about you?" she tested.

"I have to return back to Washington very soon, possibly tomorrow. I've got debriefings to attend, and give, which seem to go on forever after an op. Everything gets scrutinised, a fine toothcomb pulling the whole thing apart, and it often makes you wonder if you're being put under a microscope. Other than that I don't know at the moment, but I may have found what I haven't actually been looking for."

Copeland looked at Elisabeth who realised what he had just said.

"You've walked in to my life, Elisabeth, for which I shall be eternally grateful. It might sound soft of me to say, but I don't want to let you go."

"You men and this macho image. You have feelings just as we woman do. Come on, let's go back to the flat," she said, taking him by the hand.

They kissed as soon as the door closed behind them. Copeland put his hands on her hips and pulled her close. She kissed his neck before moulding herself warmly against him. Taking his other hand, she placed it on her breast and he felt the nipple harden beneath his caressing fingers.

"Mmmm!" she murmured.

They were both laughing, but their movements were urgent now. They kissed passionately – a long kiss, but one that swiftly proved to be less than either of them wanted or needed. She led him to the bedroom confidently walking backwards as she knew where every piece of furniture and doorway was, somehow managing to unbelt him and to remove her white cotton blouse as she went. An old double bed draped with a light blue eiderdown offered itself, and by then she was unzipping and stepping out of her skirt, dropping it to the floor. His hand moved to the damp triangle between her legs, hers to the zip of his trousers. She twisted Copeland around, throwing him to the bed. She lowered herself gratefully onto him, gasping as she felt him thrust hard inside her. Her back arched and her long blonde hair fell away from the tanned oval face. She gasped and drove herself against him, hot and wet, clenching and releasing her hands, rising and falling.

*　　　*　　　*

The White House, Washington DC, 1800 (SET)

The President watched every news broadcast that came on in the hope of finding the one that would save his career. When it came, he didn't know what to expect. He just hoped that it had gone the way Copeland had convinced him it would. He listened, but didn't take in what was being said by the reporter.

"An unprecedented missile strike in the region of the Hindu Kush mountain range north of Kabul was unleashed by the US Air Force this evening. At least four cruise missiles were launched from a B-52 bomber that hit with pinpoint accuracy a designated target that had been identified earlier by the CIA. It is believed that the world's most wanted terrorist leader and mastermind of many Middle-Eastern atrocities may have been in the area at the time..."

CHAPTER SEVENTEEN

The early morning sun was beginning to rise above Kroo Bay. Its rays were already reflecting across the rippling clear blue water and through the open curtains into the apartment. The sudden brightness disturbed Copeland. It was a beautiful morning, but for all the wrong reasons. He looked at his watch on the bedside cabinet; it showed 6 am. He slipped from the sheets, sat on the edge of the bed and looked behind him. Elisabeth was still asleep. She looked more beautiful, sexy and radiant than he had ever seen her before. She also looked vulnerable. She was curled in the foetal position as if defending herself against a threat. The cotton sheets were pulled across her tanned, slim, naked body. Her breasts were silhouetted through the thin sheets, and her long blonde hair, glistening from the sun's rays, was spread across her pillow giving her a goddess-like appearance. Copeland knew that he was in love with her.

He didn't want to leave her in this god-forsaken place. He was hoping last night that she would change her mind and travel back with him to New York for them to start a new life together, but he respected her decision to continue reporting for CNN as she felt as though she hadn't yet completed her assignments. He was inwardly hurting, but she knew that he would always be there for her. Rather than clean up in the flat and disturb her, Copeland decided to don his combats and walk to the embassy. He was sure the Ambassador would let him have a shower there. After all, he *was* the hero. It would also give him time to think. He would ring her from the embassy before he left for the airport.

He collected his grip, looked back at her one last time, and quietly slipped from the flat, closing the door behind him. He went down the single flight of stairs, through the entrance, and stepped out into the morning air breezing in across the promenade. It was surreal, almost eerie. After the events of the previous twenty-four hours, everything was so quietly calm and peaceful. He took the short route to the embassy along the sea front then left into Walpole Street. At the entrance to the embassy he was met by a Marine guard in full dress uniform. The Marine stood to attention and saluted.

"Good morning, General Copeland, sir," said the Marine as he opened the outer door.

Copeland replied, "Morning." He returned the salute. "I see we have another scorching day to contend with."

Copeland walked through the open door into the sizeable reception area where he was confronted by a large bulletproof glass screen. Behind the screen was the receptionist, Jessica Vincent, who immediately recognised Copeland and pressed the buzzer under her desk, which released the access door to the rest of the embassy. Copeland held the handle and pulled the door towards him.

Passing Jessica's desk, he said: "Morning, Jessica. Is he in?" referring to the Ambassador.

"Morning, General Copeland. Yes. He's been in since five am."

Copeland felt like he needed the exercise, so he walked up the stairs to the fourth floor where the Ambassador had his office. He walked the short distance along the corridor passing the two Diplomatic Protection Agents posted outside, through the secretary's office and finally entered the Ambassador's office, where he found the Ambassador sitting behind his desk. He noted how eerily quiet the embassy was at that time of morning.

"Morning, Charles. I didn't expect to see you in this morning. You're supposed to be convalescing. What's the occasion, anyway?" asked Copeland.

"Don't tell my wife, but I find it a little boring at home. I'd rather be doing something to occupy my mind."

In the harsh light of day, Copeland could clearly see the extent of the injuries Charles had received at the hands of his captors. The bruising to his face was evident, though it was starting to fade to yellow, and his facial cuts had already scabbed over. His wrists were heavily bandaged to protect the deep lacerations created by the ropes used to tie his hands together. His days in captivity had taken their toll on Charles, but Copeland was sure he was a survivor and would come out of this experience cherishing the true values of humanity where, in times of crisis, no one is forgotten. He knew the extent of the operation to rescue him, and the many lives that were lost along the way. He could never repay that debt, but undoubtedly would talk about his situation for many months and years to come with great admiration for those people whom he would label heroes. That would be some comfort, knowing that those who had sacrificed their lives had not been forgotten.

"I have a lot of catching up to do, bureaucratic paper work and all that, before I hand over to my deputy. I will then take a well-earned vacation. I'm being recalled and have been ordered to rest and so aid my recuperation."

"Excellent advice, Charles. Doctor's orders, I take it?"

"No, Sarah's actually. Have you heard the news this morning, Jack?"

"No, I haven't. Anything of importance?"

"There was a major military assault in Afghanistan late yesterday afternoon. Several cruise missiles were launched by a single B-52. Not much hope for those in the area, I would imagine."

"Did the news say whereabouts in Afghanistan?"

"Somewhere to the north of Kabul."

"There isn't much there except mountains," said Copeland, playing the incident down. Charles would never know that it had been Copeland who had orchestrated this '*Unprecedented attack*'.

"Yeah, you're probably right. Jack, we had a telex from Washington this morning, and they want you back ASAP. You'll be choppered to Conakry, and then board a civilian airline back to New York. Civilian clothes and cabin baggage is the order of the day."

"I didn't bring...' began Copeland.

"One of our attachés has been instructed to pick something up for you from one of the markets. Should be back any minute."

"I've got my hand luggage packed already. Could do with a shower though," he said.

The Ambassador nodded as if he knew what he was thinking.

"Everything's in there, Jack. The beauty of having a self-contained safe room. Have you eaten yet?"

"I haven't had time."

"Okay, I'll have a traditional African breakfast brought up for us before you go."

"Thanks."

Copeland reappeared twenty minutes later, dressed in a flowery bright coloured bush shirt, tightly fitting beige chino's that seemed a little short on leg material, and blue plastic sandals that only just fitted. According to the attaché, the selection was pretty limited – apparently.

Copeland wasn't convinced and he sensed this was a practical joke, so that he could go out in style and take a piece of Africa with him, and hopefully see the funny side later. Breakfast had arrived while he was in the shower.

"So what's this traditional breakfast then, Charles?"

"Mandazi."

The Ambassador noticed a frown on Copeland's forehead.

"It's a semi-sweet doughnut. Tastes rather nice." He explained as he poured out the coffee.

"I was sorry to hear about Major Bell, Jack. You two were close."

"Yeah. It'll take a bit to get used to. Combat is almost as unpredictable as the weather."

"Any family?"

"He was divorced. You could say I was his family." Copeland shifted topic as he had one more urgent thing to do.

"Charles, can I use your phone?"

"Sure, Elisabeth?" asked the Ambassador with a smile.

Copeland nodded his head, and Charles left the office. Jack dialled her mobile number, but was connected to her voice mailbox. He hated talking to machines so he cut the call. He was disappointed to be unable to speak with her.

After a short while, Copeland made his farewells to the Ambassador and boarded the waiting Blackhawk that was in the grounds of the embassy.

Moments later, he saw the curve of Kroo Bay and Elisabeth's apartment block disappear beneath him for the last time. A fine spray of rain, almost continuous in this part of the country, continued unabated and saturated everything. The wipers were moving to and fro, trying to clear the forward screen. It wasn't cold; in fact it was quite humid as was evident from the pilot's khaki t-shirt: it was dark with sweat beneath his arms and down his back.

"Another hot day, eh, sir?" said the pilot over the intercom. It sounded as if he wanted a conversation with his passenger.

"Yep, sure is," Jack replied, but wasn't in the mood to continue the conversation. His thoughts were with Elisabeth, back in Freetown. He settled himself back into the seat, as he knew they had the best part of thirty-five minutes flying time.

In about ten minutes they would be over the border and into Guinea. Like any other military pilot, they followed the obvious features to aid navigation, so they followed the coastline to Guinea. If all went well they should be touching down at Conakry at ten thirty am.

He kept looking at his watch: the closer he got to Conakry the further he would be from Elisabeth. He looked out through the air gunner's sliding door window determined to enjoy the view.

At Conakry, he found the Delta Airlines desk mixed in with Air France and was informed that he was the last passenger to board the aircraft, and that it had been delayed awaiting his arrival. He'd never been in that position before, especially on a civilian flight. He quite liked the feeling of being somewhat important.

"You must be *very* important, Sir," remarked the stewardess who met him impatiently at the door of the aircraft.

"We've been held up for twenty-five minutes!" she continued, looking him up and down, and at his footwear with a hint of a wry smile.

"Are you ready to walk the gauntlet?"

As the passengers realised he was the reason for their late departure they began a slow handclap. Passengers stared in his direction and he sensed hostility. Cynical and sarcastic comments came his way as he walked for what seemed like ten minutes to his seat at the back of the aircraft.

'How big is this thing? How many people have I annoyed???' he wondered.

Washington had certainly pulled out the stops for this one. His seat was, needless to say, towards the back of the aircraft. The stewardess had walked the aisle with him, but all eyes were on him, not her. She directed him to a window seat next to a well-proportioned woman. He guessed her to be in the region of fifty, and she seemed to smell heavily of body odour and coconut oil. He felt uncomfortable in the clothes he was wearing, which wouldn't have warranted a second look anywhere in Africa, but on a western aircraft were certainly out of place.

His fellow passenger looked him up and down with a smile of satisfaction,

"Well," she murmured suggestively, noticing the tightness of his trousers around his groin,

"Aren't I the lucky one!"

Copeland would have been amused under different circumstances, especially if she had been more attractive with a smaller frame, but he had a girlfriend and he wasn't that kinda guy. '*Christ, how long do I have to spend on this flight – fifteen hours?*'

"Are you travelling alone?"

"No, there are thirty-four of us." Gesticulating with her hands to the forward seats. 'But we're all here for much the same reason, really."

"What might that be?" he asked, realising he'd started a conversation he didn't particularly want.

"To meet the local boys, of course! I still have a bit of the old romantic in me." she replied, with a wink.

"Ah, I follow you."

"I find Africans are much more appreciative of woman with a fuller figure, you see, and they sure know how to press the right buttons with me, sugar. And without a single mention of sport or their prowess at DIY."

"Or their work?" added Copeland.

"Yep, exactly right. I'm Annabel by the way."

"Copeland, Jack Copeland," he reciprocated.

"So what brought you to this part of the world, then, Jack?"

He sensed that she was on a roll now and given half a chance she would talk all the way back.

"Well, I won't talk about my work because it's boring, really."

"Did you come here for work or for pleasure, then?" she said with another wink.

"Bit of both, really," he responded, realising that was, in fact, the truth.

"So, what do you do then?" she enquired further.

"Oh, um..." he hesitated, but luckily the conversation was interrupted as the stewardess offered boiled sweets. He chose a lemon one.

He felt the aircraft turn into the wind and began to power down the runway. He watched out of the window as the ground hurtled past.

"Jack, tell me, do you like big girls?"

'Bloody hell,' he thought. That was straight to the point. She's not one for wasting time or making small talk.

"How successful was your holiday then, Annabel?" he replied, hoping to bypass her last question, and trying to make it sound as if he wasn't remotely interested.

"Well, I'm glad you asked, Jack" she said, fishing out a colour photograph of a local boy wearing nothing more than a smile and a reversed baseball cap. His manhood stood firm with his obvious enthusiasm for this woman.

"You did ask, Jack!"

"Did you…um," he enquired.

"Jack!" her smile was the answer, "Now, answer the question, do you like big girls?"

He could see she was pleased with her conquests, and he tried to choose the right words so as not to squash her enthusiasm. She had hopeful eyes, which were yellow at the edges. Her hair was jet black, long and had been plaited. It also looked as if it hadn't been washed for a while.

"Annabel," he started, "Don't get me wrong, but I'm not one of those guys who likes big women, and I have a girl waiting for me back home."

A look of disappointment on her face said this wasn't what she'd wanted to hear.

An hour or so into the flight, breakfast was served. Copeland was hungry, so he ate the lot. Like sleep, the military held that you'd better eat any time you can, sleep and meals being unreliable when operational. He was hoping he might get served lunch too, if he was lucky.

As he reclined his seat and began to relax, images of the rescue began to flash before his eyes. The smouldering wreckage of the helicopter, the mortars hitting their target, and the gun fire that had seemed sporadic from the RUF soldiers. These visions would arise in the nightmares that he knew were to come. When he would stop seeing them, he couldn't answer. It could be weeks or even months. He fervently hoped he would be over them by the time he saw Elisabeth next.

$*$ $*$ $*$

Sleepily, he turned over and reached for her. With his eyes closed, he allowed his fingers a lazy exploration of her body. He felt the desire for her stir inside him once more. Something was different. Elisabeth had changed. Her breasts for a start were that much bigger and heavier than he remembered. They were being supported in a nylon bra against several warm rolls of flesh. The smells weren't those of 'La Perla' either, but that of stale air-conditioning.

His eyes opened cautiously and one at a time, not quite knowing what to expect. The face which lay inches from his, and the ample breast he was fondling, belonged to his fellow passenger, Annabel. In response her hand had grabbed his groin.

"I knew you liked big girls," she said lustfully. "In fact you're quite a big boy yourself, honey!" she said as her grip tightened in delight.

Copeland looked at her. Her teeth were yellow and he could see grey hair showing at the roots of her plaits. He glanced around, only to catch the eye of another female passenger who winked at him in a seductive and suggestive manner.

"A little bird tells me that you were about to join me in the mile high club," she whispered with a hint of excitement.

"That little bird is singing the wrong music."

"But I thought..."

"I was dreaming of my girl back home."

He pulled himself upright and used an in-flight magazine to cover his dignity. He could see she was disappointed, but would be surprised if she wasn't used to rejection. He looked at his watch: three hours to go. This was a long haul. He felt dirty even though he'd showered that morning. He wasn't sure what was waiting for him at the other end, but it had to be an improvement on this.

*   *   *

As he cleared through the arrivals lounge, he noticed two men in dark suits. They had to be his reception committee. They both had CIA written all over them. As he approached, he stopped and pulled out his cell phone, scrolling through the numbers stored in its memory. After a moment's hesitation, he selected one and, to his relief, made the connection.

"Elisabeth Young," she said, answering the phone sleepily.

"It's Jack. I'm in New York, sweetheart."

"I'll join you as soon as I can. Love You!"

That was all he wanted to hear.

OTHER BOOKS BY THE AUTHOR

Fire Storm
(ISBN 9781912505326)

The inauguration of the Joint Space programme between the US and the Russian Federation heralded a landmark in the advancement of space exploration. The sixty billion-dollar ISS was to be the platform in which to seek out and discover new worlds. Being self-contained, with its own laser guided defence systems and advanced life support facilities, it was designed to sustain life for long periods, but something more sinister outside the mission profile, was about to unfold…

This is the second book in the Jack Copeland series

Executive Protection – The Next Level
(ISBN 9781911090847)

Close Protection (CP) is renowned for its excellence in providing top level protection to many levels of society. The fact that CP is being used in the first place means that there is a real risk to the person being protected.

Providing the right calibre of individual or team is necessary to ensure that the correct concentric level(s) of security is measurable to the threat.

This book is aimed at those who aspire to be managers, team leaders or supervisors with the responsibility of recruitment and selection of a team.

Having a CP licence is merely the first step...

ISBN 978-1-912505-09-8

BV - #0035 - 010720 - C0 - 197/127/16 - PB - 9781912505098